G. K. CHESTERTON (1874–1936). A man of many literary talents, among his works are novels, short stories, poems, essays and biographies. He is also remembered for his skills as an orator and wit and for his mastery of the paradox and the pun.

Gilbert Keith Chesterton was born in London in 1874. He was slow and awkward at school and was described as having a possible future as either an idiot or a genius. After attending the Slade School of Art, he left without a degree and went into publishing, claiming that he had read more than ten thousand novels in six years. At the same time, he was gradually gaining a reputation as a journalist with so many articles appearing under his signature of G.K.C. that he was thought by some to be a committee. He often teamed up with Hilaire Belloc (author of *A Bad Child's Book of Beasts*, *Cautionary Tales*), to write controversial and anti-imperial articles for *The Speaker*, regularly satirizing stuffy Edwardian attitudes. Their long and fruitful friendship earned them the twin nickname of 'Chesterbelloc' from contemporary George Bernard Shaw. Chesterton's first publication was the privately printed collection of nonsense poems, *Graybeards at Play* (1900), which he illustrated himself; it was to be followed by eighty-four other and varied volumes. Among his best remembered works are the poems 'Lepanto' and 'The Donkey' and the novels *The Napoleon of Notting Hill* (1904) and *The Man Who was Thursday* (1908), but it was the Father Brown stories that were to bring him lasting fame.

Chesterton was an unmistakable figure in his large hat and cape, carrying his swordstick; he was also noted for his absence of mind, once sending his wife the telegram 'Am at Market Harborough. Where ought I to be?' He died in 1936, comforted by the rites of the Catholic Church which he had entered in 1922.

Father Brown first appeared in 'The Blue Cross' printed in the *Storyteller* in 1910 and reprinted the next year in *The Innocence of Father Brown*. This collection of stories was followed by several others, all featuring the inconspicuous priest whose subtle understanding of good and evil was to make him Chesterton's most popular creation.

PENGUIN POPULAR CLASSICS

FATHER BROWN STORIES

G. K. CHESTERTON

PENGUIN BOOKS

PENGUIN BOOKS

Published by the Penguin Group
Penguin Books Ltd, 80 Strand, London WC2R ORL, England
Penguin Putnam Inc., 375 Hudson Street, New York, New York 10014, USA
Penguin Books Australia Ltd, Ringwood, Victoria, Australia
Penguin Books Canada Ltd, 10 Alcorn Avenue, Toronto, Ontario, Canada M4V 3B2
Penguin Books India (P) Ltd, 11 Community Centre, Panchsheel Park,
New Delhi – 110 017, India
Penguin Books (NZ) Ltd, Cnr Rosedale and Airborne Roads, Albany, Auckland,
New Zealand
Penguin Books (South Africa) (Pty) Ltd, 24 Sturdee Avenue, Rosebank 2196, South Africa

Penguin Books Ltd, Registered Offices: 80 Strand, London WC2R ORL, England

www.penguin.com

Published in Penguin Popular Classics 1994
This edition published in Penguin Popular Classics 1994
9

Printed in England by Cox & Wyman Ltd, Reading, Berkshire

Contents

▼

THE INNOCENCE OF
FATHER BROWN

The Blue Cross

BETWEEN the silver ribbon of morning and the green glittering ribbon of sea, the boat touched Harwich and let loose a swarm of folk like flies, among whom the man we must follow was by no means conspicuous—nor wished to be. There was nothing notable about him, except a slight contrast between the holiday gaiety of his clothes and the official gravity of his face. His clothes included a slight, pale grey jacket, a white waistcoat, and a silver straw hat with a grey-blue ribbon. His lean face was dark by contrast, and ended in a curt black beard that looked Spanish and suggested an Elizabethan ruff. He was smoking a cigarette with the seriousness of an idler. There was nothing about him to indicate the fact that the grey jacket covered a loaded revolver, that the white waistcoat covered a police card, or that the straw hat covered one of the most powerful intellects in Europe. For this was Valentin himself, the head of the Paris police and the most famous investigator of the world; and he was coming from Brussels to London to make the greatest arrest of the century.

Flambeau was in England. The police of three countries had tracked the great criminal at last from Ghent to Brussels, from Brussels to the Hook of Holland; and it was conjectured that he would take some advantage of the unfamiliarity and confusion of the Eucharistic Congress, then taking place in London. Probably he would travel as some minor clerk or secretary connected with it; but, of course, Valentin could not be certain; nobody could be certain about Flambeau.

It is many years now since this colossus of crime

suddenly ceased keeping the world in a turmoil; and when he ceased, as they said after the death of Roland, there was a great quiet upon the earth. But in his best days (I mean, of course, his worst) Flambeau was a figure as statuesque and international as the Kaiser. Almost every morning the daily paper announced that he had escaped the consequences of one extraordinary crime by committing another. He was a Gascon of gigantic stature and bodily daring; and the wildest tales were told of his outbursts of athletic humour; how he turned the *juge d'instruction* upside down and stood him on his head, 'to clear his mind'; how he ran down the Rue de Rivoli with a policeman under each arm. It is due to him to say that his fantastic physical strength was generally employed in such bloodless though undignified scenes; his real crimes were chiefly those of ingenious and wholesale robbery. But each of his thefts was almost a new sin, and would make a story by itself. It was he who ran the great Tyrolean Dairy Company in London, with no dairies, no cows, no carts, no milk, but with some thousand subscribers. These he served by the simple operation of moving the little milk-cans outside people's doors to the doors of his own customers. It was he who had kept up an unaccountable and close correspondence with a young lady whose whole letter-bag was intercepted, by the extraordinary trick of photographing his messages infinitesimally small upon the slides of a microscope. A sweeping simplicity, however, marked many of his experiments. It is said he once repainted all the numbers in a street in the dead of night merely to divert one traveller into a trap. It is quite certain that he invented a portable pillar-box, which he put up at corners in quiet suburbs on the chance of strangers dropping postal orders into it. Lastly he was known to be a startling acrobat; despite his huge figure, he could leap like a grasshopper and melt into the tree-tops like a monkey. Hence the great Valentin, when he set out to find Flambeau, was perfectly well aware that his adventures would not end when he had found him.

But how was he to find him? On this the great Valentin's ideas were still in process of settlement.

There was one thing which Flambeau, with all his dexterity of disguise, could not cover, and that was his singular height. If Valentin's quick eye had caught a tall apple-woman, a tall grenadier, or even a tolerably tall duchess, he might have arrested them on the spot. But all along his train there was nobody that could be a disguised Flambeau, any more than a cat could be a disguised giraffe. About the people on the boat he had already satisfied himself; and the people picked up at Harwich or on the journey limited themselves with certainty to six. There was a short railway official travelling up to the terminus, three fairly short market-gardeners picked up two stations afterwards, one very short widow lady going up from a small Essex town, and a very short Roman Catholic priest going up from a small Essex village. When it came to the last case, Valentin gave it up and almost laughed. The little priest was so much the essence of those Eastern flats: he had a face as round and dull as a Norfolk dumpling; he had eyes as empty as the North Sea; he had several brown-paper parcels which he was quite incapable of collecting. The Eucharistic Congress had doubtless sucked out of their local stagnation many such creatures, blind and helpless, like moles disinterred. Valentin was a sceptic in the severe style of France, and could have no love for priests. But he could have pity for them, and this one might have provoked pity in anybody. He had a large, shabby umbrella, which constantly fell on the floor. He did not seem to know which was the right end of his return ticket. He explained with a moon-calf simplicity to everybody in the carriage that he had to be careful, because he had something made of real silver 'with blue stones' in one of his brown-paper parcels. His quaint blending of Essex flatness with saintly simplicity continuously amused the Frenchman till the priest arrived (somehow) at Stratford with all his parcels, and came back for his umbrella. When he did the last, Valentin even had the good nature to warn him not to take care of the silver by telling everybody about it. But to whomever he talked, Valentin kept his eye open for someone else; he looked out steadily for anyone, rich or poor, male or female, who was well up to six feet; for Flambeau was four inches above it.

He alighted at Liverpool Street, however, quite conscientiously secure that he had not missed the criminal so far. He then went to Scotland Yard to regularize his position and arrange for help in case of need; he then lit another cigarette and went for a long stroll in the streets of London. As he was walking in the streets and squares beyond Victoria, he paused suddenly and stood. It was a quaint, quiet square, very typical of London, full of an accidental stillness. The tall, flat houses round looked at once prosperous and uninhabited; the square of shrubbery in the centre looked as deserted as a green Pacific islet. One of the four sides was much higher than the rest, like a dais; and the line of this side was broken by one of London's admirable accidents—a restaurant that looked as if it had strayed from Soho. It was an unreasonably attractive object, with dwarf plants in pots and long, striped blinds of lemon yellow and white. It stood specially high above the street, and in the usual patchwork way of London, a flight of steps from the street ran up to meet the front door almost as a fire-escape might run up to a first-floor window. Valentin stood and smoked in front of the yellow-white blinds and considered them long.

The most incredible thing about miracles is that they happen. A few clouds in heaven do come together into the staring shape of one human eye. A tree does stand up in the landscape of a doubtful journey in the exact and elaborate shape of a note of interrogation. I have seen both these things myself within the last few days. Nelson does die in the instant of victory; and a man named Williams does quite accidentally murder a man named Williamson; it sounds like a sort of infanticide. In short, there is in life an element of elfin coincidence which people reckoning on the prosaic may perpetually miss. As it has been well expressed in the paradox of Poe, wisdom should reckon on the unforeseen.

Aristide Valentin was unfathomably French; and the French intelligence is intelligence specially and solely. He was not 'a thinking machine'; for that is a brainless phrase of modern fatalism and materialism. A machine only *is* a machine because it cannot think. But he was a thinking man, and a plain man at the same time. All his wonderful successes, that looked like conjuring, had been gained by plodding logic, by clear and commonplace French thought. The French electrify the world not by starting any paradox, they electrify it by carrying out a truism. They carry a truism so far—as in the French Revolution. But exactly because Valentin understood reason, he understood the limits of reason. Only a man who knows nothing of motors talks of motoring without petrol; only a man who knows nothing of reason talks of reasoning without strong, undisputed first principles. Here he had no strong first principles. Flambeau had been missed at Harwich; and if he was in London at all, he might be anything from a tall tramp on Wimbledon Common to a tall toastmaster at the Hôtel Métropole.

In such a naked state of nescience, Valentin had a view and a method of his own.

In such cases he reckoned on the unforeseen. In such cases, when he could not follow the train of the reasonable, he coldly and carefully followed the train of the unreasonable. Instead of going to the right places—banks, police-stations, rendezvous—he systematically went to the wrong places; knocked at every empty house, turned down every *cul de sac*, went up every lane blocked with rubbish, went round every crescent that led him uselessly out of the way. He defended this crazy course quite logically. He said that if one had a clue this was the worst way; but if one had no clue at all it was the best, because there was just the chance that any oddity that caught the eye of the pursuer might be the same that had caught the eye of the pursued. Somewhere a man must begin, and it had better be just where another man might stop. Something about that flight of steps up to the shop, something about the quietude and quaintness of the restaurant, roused all the detective's rare romantic fancy and made him resolve to strike at random. He went up the steps, and sitting down by the window, asked for a cup of black coffee.

It was half-way through the morning, and he had not breakfasted; the slight litter of other breakfasts stood about on the table to remind him of his hunger; and adding a poached egg to his order, he proceeded musingly to shake some white sugar into his coffee, thinking all the time about Flambeau. He remembered how Flambeau had escaped, once by a pair of nail scissors, and once by a house on fire; once by having to pay for an unstamped letter, and once by getting people to look through a telescope at a comet that might destroy the world. He thought his detective brain as good as the criminal's, which was true. But he fully realized the disadvantage.

'The criminal is the creative artist; the detective only the critic,' he said with a sour smile, and lifted his coffee cup to his lips slowly, and put it down very quickly. He had put salt in it.

He looked at the vessel from which the silvery powder had come; it was certainly a sugar-basin; as unmistakably meant for sugar as a champagne-bottle for champagne. He wondered why they should keep salt in it. He looked to see if there were any more orthodox vessels. Yes, there were two salt-cellars quite full. Perhaps there was some speciality in the condiment in the salt-cellars. He tasted it; it was sugar. Then he looked round at the restaurant with a refreshed air of interest, to see if there were any other traces of that singular artistic taste which puts the sugar in the salt-cellars and the salt in the sugar-basin. Except for an odd splash of some dark fluid on one of the white-papered walls, the whole place appeared neat, cheerful and ordinary. He rang the bell for the waiter.

When that official hurried up, fuzzy-haired and somewhat blear-eyed at that early hour, the detective (who was not without an appreciation of the simpler forms of humour) asked him to taste the sugar and see if it was up to the high reputation of the hotel. The result was that the waiter yawned suddenly and woke up.

'Do you play this delicate joke on your customers every morning?' inquired Valentin. 'Does changing the salt and sugar never pall on you as a jest?'

The waiter, when this irony grew clearer, stammeringly assured him that the establishment had certainly no such intention; it must be a most curious mistake. He picked up the sugar-basin and looked at it; he picked up the salt-cellar and looked at that, his face growing more and more bewildered. At last he abruptly excused himself, and hurrying away, returned in a few seconds with the proprietor. The proprietor also examined the sugar-basin and then the salt-cellar; the proprietor also looked bewildered.

Suddenly the waiter seemed to grow inarticulate with a rush of words.

'I zink,' he stuttered eagerly, 'I zink it is those two clergymen.'

'What two clergymen?'

'The two clergymen,' said the waiter, 'that threw soup at the wall.'

'Threw soup at the wall?' repeated Valentin, feeling sure this must be some Italian metaphor.

'Yes, yes,' said the attendant excitedly, and pointing at the dark splash on the white paper; 'threw it over there on the wall.'

Valentin looked his query at the proprietor, who came to his rescue with fuller reports.

'Yes, sir,' he said, 'it's quite true, though I don't suppose it has anything to do with the sugar and salt. Two clergymen came in and drank soup here very early, as soon as the shutters were taken down. They were both very quiet, respectable people; one of them paid the bill and went out; the other, who seemed a slower coach altogether, was some minutes longer getting his things together. But he went at last. Only, the instant before he stepped into the street he deliberately picked up his cup, which he had only half emptied, and threw the soup slap on the wall. I was in the back room myself, and so was the waiter; so I could only rush out in time to find the wall splashed and the shop empty. It didn't do any particular damage, but it was confounded cheek; and I tried to catch the men in the street. They were too far off though; I only noticed they went round the corner into Carstairs Street.'

The detective was on his feet, hat settled and stick in hand. He had already decided that in the universal darkness of his mind he could only follow the first odd finger that pointed; and this finger was odd enough. Paying his bill and clashing the glass doors behind him, he was soon swinging round into the other street.

It was fortunate that even in such fevered moments his eye was cool and quick. Something in a shop-front went by him like a mere flash; yet he went back to look at it. The shop was a popular greengrocer and fruiterer's, an array of goods set out in the open air and plainly ticketed with their names and prices. In the two most prominent compartments were two heaps, of oranges and of nuts respectively. On the heap of nuts lay a scrap of cardboard, on which was written in bold, blue chalk, 'Best tangerine oranges, two a penny.' On the oranges was the equally clear and exact description, 'Finest Brazil nuts, 4d. a lb.' M. Valentin looked at these two placards and fancied he had met this highly subtle form of humour before, and that somewhat recently. He drew the attention of the red-faced fruiterer, who was looking rather sullenly up and down the street, to this inaccuracy in his advertisements. The fruiterer said nothing, but sharply put each card into its proper place. The detective, leaning elegantly on his walking-cane, continued to scrutinize the shop. At last he said: 'Pray excuse my apparent irrelevance, my good sir, but I should like to ask you a question in experimental psychology and the association of ideas.'

The red-faced shopman regarded him with an eye of menace; but he continued gaily, swinging his cane. 'Why,' he pursued, 'why are two tickets wrongly placed in a greengrocer's shop like a shovel hat that has come to London for a holiday? Or, in case I do not make myself clear, what is the mystical association which connects the idea of nuts marked as oranges with the idea of two clergymen, one tall and the other short?'

The eyes of the tradesman stood out of his head like a snail's; he really seemed for an instant likely to fling himself upon the stranger. At last he stammered angrily: 'I don't know what you 'ave to do with it, but if you're one of their friends, you can tell 'em from me that I'll knock their silly 'eads off, parsons or no parsons, if they upset my apples again.'

'Indeed?' asked the detective, with great sympathy. 'Did they upset your apples?'

'One of 'em did,' said the heated shopman; 'rolled 'em all over the street. I'd 'ave caught the fool but for havin' to pick 'em up.'

'Which way did these parsons go?' asked Valentin.

'Up that second road on the left-hand side, and then across the square,' said the other promptly.

'Thanks,' said Valentin, and vanished like a fairy. On the other side of the second square he found a police-man, and said: 'This is urgent, constable; have you seen two clergymen in shovel hats?'

The policeman began to chuckle heavily. 'I 'ave, sir; and if you arst me, one of 'em was drunk. He stood in the middle of the road that bewildered that——'

'Which way did they go?' snapped Valentin.

'They took one of them yellow buses over there,' an-swered the man; 'them that go to Hampstead.'

Valentin produced his official card and said very rapidly: 'Call up two of your men to come with me in pursuit,' and crossed the road with such contagious energy that the ponderous policeman was moved to almost agile obedience. In a minute and a half the French detective was joined on the opposite pavement by an inspector and a man in plain clothes.

'Well, sir,' began the former, with smiling importance, 'and what may——?'

Valentin pointed suddenly with his cane. 'I'll tell you on the top of that omnibus,' he said, and was darting and dodging across the tangle of the traffic. When all three sank panting on the top seats of the yellow vehicle, the inspector said: 'We could go four times as quick in a taxi.'

'Quite true,' replied their leader placidly, 'if we only had an idea of where we were going.'

'Well, where *are* you going?' asked the other, staring.

Valentin smoked frowningly for a few seconds; then, removing his cigarette, he said: 'If you *know* what a man's doing, get in front of him; but if you want to guess what he's doing, keep behind him. Stray when he strays; stop when he stops; travel as slowly as he. Then you may see what he saw and may act as he acted. All we can do is to keep our eyes skinned for a queer thing.'

'What sort of a queer thing do you mean?' asked the inspector.

'Any sort of queer thing,' answered Valentin, and relapsed into obstinate silence.

The yellow omnibus crawled up the northern roads for what seemed like hours on end; the great detective would not explain further, and perhaps his assistants felt a silent and growing doubt of his errand. Perhaps, also, they felt a silent and growing desire for lunch, for the hours crept long past the normal luncheon hour, and the long roads of the North London suburbs seemed to shoot out into length after length like an infernal telescope. It was one of those journeys on which a man perpetually feels that now at last he must have come to the end of the universe, and then finds he has only come to the beginning of Tufnell Park. London died away in draggled taverns and dreary scrubs, and then was unaccountably born again in blazing high streets and blatant hotels. It was like passing through thirteen separate vulgar cities all just touching each other. But though the winter twilight was already threatening the road ahead of them, the Parisian detective still sat silent and watchful, eyeing the frontage of the streets that slid by on either side. By the time they had left Camden Town behind, the policemen were nearly asleep; at least, they gave something like a jump as Valentin leapt erect, struck a hand on each man's shoulder, and shouted to the driver to stop.

They tumbled down the steps into the road without realizing why they had been dislodged; when they looked round for enlightenment they found Valentin triumphantly pointing his finger towards a window on the left side of the road. It was a large window, forming part of the long façade of a gilt and palatial public-house; it was the part reserved for respectable dining, and labelled 'Restaurant.' This window, like all the rest along the frontage of the hotel, was of frosted and figured glass, but in the middle of it was a big, black smash, like a star in the ice.

'Our cue at last,' cried Valentin, waving his stick; 'the place with the broken window.'

'What window? What cue?' asked his principal assistant. 'Why, what proof is there that this has anything to do with them?'

Valentin almost broke his bamboo stick with rage.

'Proof!' he cried. 'Good God! the man is looking for proof! Why, of course, the chances are twenty to one that it has *nothing* to do with them. But what else can we do? Don't you see we must either follow one wild possibility or else go home to bed?' He banged his way into the restaurant, followed by his companions, and they were soon seated at a late luncheon at a little table, and looking at the star of smashed glass from the inside. Not that it was very informative to them even then.

'Got your window broken, I see,' said Valentin to the waiter, as he paid his bill.

'Yes, sir,' answered the attendant, bending busily over the change, to which Valentin silently added an enormous tip. The waiter straightened himself with mild but unmistakable animation.

'Ah, yes, sir,' he said. 'Very odd thing, that, sir.'

'Indeed? Tell us about it,' said the detective with careless curiosity.

'Well, two gents in black came in,' said the waiter; 'two of those foreign parsons that are running about. They had a cheap and quiet little lunch, and one of them paid for it and went out. The other was just going out to join him when I looked at my change again and found he'd paid me more than three times too much. "Here," I says to the chap who was nearly out of the door, "you've paid too much." "Oh," he says, very cool, "have we?" "Yes," I says, and picks up the bill to show him. Well, that was a knock-out.'

'What do you mean?' asked his interlocutor.

'Well, I'd have sworn on seven Bibles that I'd put 4s. on that bill. But now I saw I'd put 14s., as plain as paint.'

'Well?' cried Valentin, moving slowly, but with burning eyes, 'and then?'

'The parson at the door he says, all serene, "Sorry to confuse your accounts, but it'll pay for the window." "What window?" I says. "The one I'm going to break," he says, and smashed that blessed pane with his umbrella.'

All the inquirers made an exclamation; and the inspector said under his breath: 'Are we after escaped lunatics?' The waiter went on with some relish for the ridiculous story:

'I was so knocked silly for a second, I couldn't do anything. The man marched out of the place and joined his friend just round the corner. Then they went so quick up Bullock Street that I couldn't catch them, though I ran round the bars to do it.'

'Bullock Street,' said the detective, and shot up that thoroughfare as quickly as the strange couple he pursued.

Their journey now took them through bare brick ways like tunnels; streets with few lights and even with few windows; streets that seemed built out of the blank backs of everything and everywhere. Dusk was deepening, and it was not easy even for the London policemen to guess in what exact direction they were treading. The inspector, however, was pretty certain that they would eventually strike some part of Hampstead Heath. Abruptly one bulging and gas-lit window broke the blue twilight like a bull's-eye lantern; and Valentin stopped an instant before a little garish sweetstuff shop. After an instant's hesitation he went in; he stood amid the gaudy colours of the confectionery with entire gravity and bought thirteen chocolate cigars with a certain care. He was clearly preparing an opening; but he did not need one.

An angular, elderly young woman in the shop had regarded his elegant appearance with a merely automatic inquiry; but when she saw the door behind him blocked with the blue uniform of the inspector, her eyes seemed to wake up.

'Oh,' she said, 'if you've come about that parcel, I've sent it off already.'

'Parcel!' repeated Valentin; and it was his turn to look inquiring.

'I mean the parcel the gentleman left—the clergyman gentleman.'

'For goodness' sake,' said Valentin, leaning forward

with his first real confession of eagerness, 'for Heaven's sake tell us what happened exactly.'

'Well,' said the woman, a little doubtfully, 'the clergymen came in about half an hour ago and bought some peppermints and talked a bit, and then went off towards the Heath. But a second after, one of them runs back into the shop and says, "Have I left a parcel?" Well, I looked everywhere and couldn't see one; so he says, "Never mind; but if it should turn up, please post it to this address," and he left me the address and a shilling for my trouble. And sure enough, though I thought I'd looked everywhere, I found he'd left a brown-paper parcel, so I posted it to the place he said. I can't remember the address now; it was somewhere in Westminster. But as the thing seemed so important, I thought perhaps the police had come about it.'

'So they have,' said Valentin shortly. 'Is Hampstead Heath near here?'

'Straight on for fifteen minutes,' said the woman, 'and you'll come right out on the open.' Valentin sprang out of the shop and began to run. The other detectives followed him at a reluctant trot.

The street they threaded was so narrow and shut in by shadows that when they came out unexpectedly into the void common and vast sky they were startled to find the evening still so light and clear. A perfect dome of peacock-green sank into gold amid the blackening trees and the dark violet distances. The glowing green tint was just deep enough to pick out in points of crystal one or two stars. All that was left of the daylight lay in a golden glitter across the edge of Hampstead and that popular hollow which is called the Vale of Health. The holiday makers who roam this region had not wholly dispersed: a few couples sat shapelessly on benches; and here and there a distant girl still shrieked in one of the swings.

The glory of heaven deepened and darkened around the sublime vulgarity of man; and standing on the slope and looking across the valley, Valentin beheld the thing which he sought.

Among the black and breaking groups in that distance was one especially black which did not break—a group of two figures clerically clad. Though they seemed as small as insects, Valentin could see that one of them was much smaller than the other. Though the other had a student's stoop and an inconspicuous manner, he could see that the man was well over six feet high. He shut his teeth and went forward, whirling his stick impatiently. By the time he had substantially diminished the distance and magnified the two black figures as in a vast microscope, he had perceived something else; something which startled him, and yet which he had somehow expected. Whoever was the tall priest, there could be no doubt about the identity of the short one. It was his friend of the Harwich train, the stumpy little *curé* of Essex whom he had warned about his brown-paper parcels.

Now, so far as this went, everything fitted in finally and rationally enough. Valentin had learned by his inquiries that morning that a Father Brown from Essex was bringing up a silver cross with sapphires, a relic of considerable value, to show some of the foreign priests at the congress. This undoubtedly was the 'silver with blue stones'; and Father Brown undoubtedly was the little greenhorn in the train. Now there was nothing wonderful about the fact that what Valentin had found out Flambeau had also found out; Flambeau found out everything. Also there was nothing wonderful in the fact that when Flambeau heard of a sapphire cross he should try to steal it; that was the most natural thing in all natural history. And most certainly there was nothing wonderful about the fact that Flambeau should have it all his own way with such a silly sheep as the man with the umbrella and the parcels. He was the sort of man whom anybody could lead on a string to the North Pole; it was not surprising that an actor like Flambeau, dressed as another priest, could lead him to Hampstead Heath. So far the crime seemed clear enough: and while the detective pitied the priest for his helplessness, he almost despised Flambeau for condescending to so gullible a victim. But when Valentin thought of all that had happened in between, of all that had led him to his triumph, he racked his brains for the smallest rhyme or reason in it. What had the stealing of a blue-and-silver cross from a priest from Essex to do with chucking soup at wall-paper? What had it to do with calling nuts oranges, or with paying for windows first and breaking them afterwards? He had come to the end of his chase; yet somehow he had missed the middle of it. When he failed (which was seldom), he had usually grasped the clue, but nevertheless missed the criminal. Here he had grasped the criminal, but still he could not grasp the clue.

The two figures that they followed were crawling like black flies across the huge green contour of a hill. They were evidently sunk in conversation, and perhaps did not notice where they were going; but they were certainly going to the wilder and more silent heights of the Heath. As their pursuers gained on them, the latter had to use the undignified attitudes of the deer-stalker, to crouch behind clumps of trees and even to crawl prostrate in deep grass. By these ungainly ingenuities the hunters even came close enough to the quarry to hear the murmur of the discussion, but no word could be distinguished except the word 'reason' recurring frequently in a high and almost childish voice. Once, over an abrupt dip of land and a dense tangle of thickets, the detectives actually lost the two figures they were following. They did not find the trail again for an agonizing ten minutes, and then it led round the brow of a great dome of hill overlooking an amphitheatre of rich and desolate sunset scenery. Under a tree in this commanding yet neglected spot was an old ramshackle wooden seat. On this seat sat the two priests still in serious speech together. The gorgeous green and gold still clung to the darkening horizon; but the dome above was turning slowly from peacock-green to peacock-blue, and the stars detached themselves more and more like solid jewels. Mutely motioning to his followers, Valentin contrived to creep up behind the big branching tree, and, standing there in deathly silence, heard the words of the strange priests for the first time.

After he had listened for a minute and a half, he was gripped by a devilish doubt. Perhaps he had dragged the two English policemen to the wastes of a nocturnal heath on an errand no saner than seeking figs on thistles. For the two priests were talking exactly like priests, piously, with learning and leisure, about the most aerial enigmas of theology. The little Essex priest spoke the more simply, with his round face turned to the strengthening stars; the other talked with his head bowed, as if he were not even worthy to look at them. But no more innocently clerical conversation could have been heard in any white Italian cloister or black Spanish cathedral.

The first he heard was the tail of one of Father Brown's sentences, which ended: '. . . what they really meant in the Middle Ages by the heavens being incorruptible.'

The taller priest nodded his bowed head and said:

'Ah, yes, these modern infidels appeal to their reason; but who can look at those millions of worlds and not feel that there may well be wonderful universes above us where reason is utterly unreasonable?'

'No.' said the other priest; 'reason is always reasonable,

even in the last limbo, in the lost borderland of things. I know that people charge the Church with lowering reason, but it is just the other way. Alone on earth, the Church makes reason really supreme. Alone on earth, the Church affirms that God Himself is bound by reason.'

The other priest raised his austere face to the spangled sky and said:

'Yet who knows if in that infinite universe——?'

'Only infinite physically,' said the little priest, turning sharply in his seat, 'not infinite in the sense of escaping from the laws of truth.'

Valentin behind his tree was tearing his finger-nails with silent fury. He seemed almost to hear the sniggers of the English detectives whom he had brought so far on a fantastic guess only to listen to the metaphysical gossip of two mild old parsons. In his impatience he lost the equally elaborate answer of the tall cleric, and when he listened again it was again Father Brown who was speaking:

'Reason and justice grip the remotest and the loneliest star. Look at those stars. Don't they look as if they were single diamonds and sapphires? Well, you can imagine any mad botany or geology you please. Think of forests of adamant with leaves of brilliants. Think the moon is a blue moon, a single elephantine sapphire. But don't fancy that all that frantic astronomy would make the smallest difference to the reason and justice of conduct. On plains of opal, under cliffs cut out of pearl, you would still find a notice-board, "Thou shalt not steal."'

Valentin was just in the act of rising from his rigid and crouching attitude and creeping away as softly as might be, felled by the one great folly of his life. But something in the very silence of the tall priest made him stop until the latter spoke. When at last he did speak, he said simply, his head bowed and his hands on his knees:

'Well, I still think that other worlds may perhaps rise higher than our reason. The mystery of heaven is unfathomable, and I for one can only bow my head.'

Then, with brow yet bent and without changing by the faintest shade his attitude or voice, he added:

'Just hand over that sapphire cross of yours, will you? We're all alone here, and I could pull you to pieces like a straw doll.'

The utterly unaltered voice and attitude added a strange violence to that shocking change of speech. But the guarder of the relic only seemed to turn his head by the smallest section of the compass. He seemed still to have a somewhat foolish face turned to the stars. Perhaps he had not understood. Or, perhaps, he had understood and sat rigid with terror.

'Yes,' said the tall priest, in the same low voice and in the same still posture, 'yes, I am Flambeau.'

Then, after a pause, he said:

'Come, will you give me that cross?'

'No,' said the other, and the monosyllable had an odd sound.

Flambeau suddenly flung off all his pontifical pretensions. The great robber leaned back in his seat and laughed low but long.

'No,' he cried; 'you won't give it me, you proud prelate. You won't give it me, you little celibate simpleton. Shall I tell you why you won't give it me? Because I've got it already in my own breast-pocket.'

The small man from Essex turned what seemed to be a dazed face in the dusk, and said, with the timid eagerness of 'The Private Secretary':

'Are—are you sure?'

Flambeau yelled with delight.

'Really, you're as good as a three-act farce,' he cried. 'Yes, you turnip, I am quite sure. I had the sense to make a duplicate of the right parcel, and now, my friend, you've got the duplicate, and I've got the jewels. An old dodge, Father Brown—a very old dodge.'

'Yes,' said Father Brown, and passed his hand through his hair with the same strange vagueness of manner. 'Yes, I've heard of it before.'

The colossus of crime leaned over to the little rustic priest with a sort of sudden interest.

'*You* have heard of it?' he asked. 'Where have *you* heard of it?'

'Well, I mustn't tell you his name, of course,' said the little man simply. 'He was a penitent, you know. He had lived prosperously for about twenty years entirely on duplicate brown-paper parcels. And so, you see, when I began to suspect you, I thought of this poor chap's way of doing it at once.'

'Began to suspect me?' repeated the outlaw with increased intensity. 'Did you really have the gumption to suspect me just because I brought you up to this bare part of the heath?'

'No, no,' said Brown with an air of apology. 'You see, I suspected you when we first met. It's that little bulge up the sleeve where you people have the spiked bracelet.'

'How in Tartarus,' cried Flambeau, 'did you ever hear of the spiked bracelet?'

'Oh, one's little flock, you know!' said Father Brown, arching his eyebrows rather blankly. 'When I was a curate in Hartlepool, there were three of them with spiked bracelets. So, as I suspected you from the first, don't you see, I made sure that the cross should go safe, anyhow. I'm afraid I watched you, you know. So at last I saw you change the parcels. Then, don't you see, I changed them back again. And then I left the right one behind.'

'Left it behind?' repeated Flambeau, and for the first

time there was another note in his voice beside his triumph.

'Well, it was like this,' said the little priest, speaking in the same unaffected way. 'I went back to that sweet-shop and asked if I'd left a parcel, and gave them a particular address if it turned up. Well, I knew I hadn't; but when I went away again I did. So, instead of running after me with that valuable parcel, they have sent it flying to a friend of mine in Westminster.' Then he added rather sadly: 'I learnt that, too, from a poor fellow in Hartlepool. He used to do it with handbags he stole at railway stations, but he's in a monastery now. Oh, one gets to know, you know,' he added, rubbing his head again with the same sort of desperate apology. 'We can't help being priests. People come and tell us these things.'

Flambeau tore a brown-paper parcel out of his inner pocket and rent it in pieces. There was nothing but paper and sticks of lead inside it. He sprang to his feet with a gigantic gesture, and cried:

'I don't believe you. I don't believe a bumpkin like you could manage all that. I believe you've still got the stuff on you, and if you don't give it up—why, we're all alone, and I'll take it by force!'

'No,' said Father Brown simply, and stood up also; 'you won't take it by force. First, because I really haven't still got it. And, second, because we are not alone.'

Flambeau stopped in his stride forward.

'Behind that tree,' said Father Brown, pointing, 'are two strong policemen and the greatest detective alive. How did they come here, do you ask? Why, I brought them, of course! How did I do it? Why, I'll tell you if you like! Lord bless you, we have to know twenty such things when we work among the criminal classes! Well, I wasn't sure you were a thief, and it would never do to make a scandal against one of our own clergy. So I just tested you to see if anything would make you show yourself. A man generally makes a small scene if he finds salt in his coffee; if he doesn't, he has some reason for keeping quiet. I changed the salt and sugar, and *you* kept quiet. A man generally objects if his bill is three times too big. If he pays it, he has some motive for passing unnoticed. I altered your bill, and *you* paid it.'

The world seemed waiting for Flambeau to leap like a tiger. But he was held back as by a spell; he was stunned with the utmost curiosity.

'Well,' went on Father Brown, with lumbering lucidity, 'as you wouldn't leave any tracks for the police, of course somebody had to. At every place we went to, I took care to do something that would get us talked about for the rest of the day. I didn't do much harm——a splashed wall, spilt apples, a broken window; but I saved the cross, as the cross will always be saved. It is at Westminster by now. I rather wonder you didn't stop it with the Donkey's Whistle.'

'With the what?' asked Flambeau.

'I'm glad you've never heard of it,' said the priest, making a face. 'It's a foul thing. I'm sure you're too good a man for a Whistler. I couldn't have countered it even with the Spots myself; I'm not strong enough in the legs.'

'What on earth are you talking about?' asked the other.

'Well, I did think you'd know the Spots,' said Father Brown, agreeably surprised. 'Oh, you can't have gone so very wrong yet!'

'How in blazes do you know all these horrors?' cried Flambeau.

The shadow of a smile crossed the round, simple face of his clerical opponent.

'Oh, by being a celibate simpleton, I suppose,' he said. 'Has it never struck you that a man who does next to nothing but hear men's real sins is not likely to be wholly unaware of human evil? But, as a matter of fact, another part of my trade, too, made me sure you weren't a priest.'

'What?' asked the thief, almost gaping.

'You attacked reason,' said Father Brown. 'It's bad theology.'

And even as he turned away to collect his property, the three policemen came out from under the twilight trees. Flambeau was an artist and a sportsman. He stepped back and swept Valentin a great bow.

'Do not bow to me, *mon ami*,' said Valentin, with silver clearness. 'Let us both bow to our master.'

And they both stood an instant uncovered, while the little Essex priest blinked about for his umbrella.

The Secret Garden

ARISTIDE VALENTIN, Chief of the Paris Police, was late for his dinner, and some of his guests began to arrive before him. These were, however, reassured by his confidential servant, Ivan, the old man with a scar and a face almost as grey as his moustaches, who always sat at a table in the entrance hall—a hall hung with weapons. Valentin's house was perhaps as peculiar and celebrated as its master. It was an old house, with high walls and tall poplars almost overhanging the Seine; but the odd-ity—and perhaps the police value—of its architecture was this: that there was no ultimate exit at all except through this front door, which was guarded by Ivan and the armoury. The garden was large and elaborate, and there were many exits from the house into the garden. But there was no exit from the garden into the world outside; all round it ran a tall, smooth unscalable wall with special spikes at the top; no bad garden, perhaps, for a man to reflect in whom some hundred criminals had sworn to kill.

As Ivan explained to the guests, their host had telephoned that he was detained for ten minutes. He was, in truth, making some last arrangements about executions and such ugly things; and though these duties were rootedly repulsive to him, he always performed them with precision. Ruthless in the pursuit of criminals, he was very mild about their punishment. Since he had been supreme over French—and largely over European —police methods, his great influence had been honourably used for the mitigation of sentences and the purification of prisons. He was one of the great humanitarian French freethinkers; and the only thing wrong with them is that they make mercy even colder than justice.

When Valentin arrived he was already dressed in black clothes and the red rosette—an elegant figure, his dark beard already streaked with grey. He went straight through his house to his study, which opened on the grounds behind. The garden door of it was open, and after he had carefully locked his box in its official place, he stood for a few seconds at the open door looking out upon the garden. A sharp moon was fighting with the flying rags and tatters of a storm, and Valentin regarded it with a wistfulness unusual in such scientific natures as his. Perhaps such scientific natures have some psychic prevision of the most tremendous problem of their lives. From any such occult mood, at least, he quickly recovered, for he knew he was late and that his guests had already begun to arrive. A glance at his drawing-room when he entered it was enough to make certain that his principal guest was not there, at any rate. He saw all the other pillars of the little party: he saw Lord Galloway, the English Ambassador—a choleric old man with a russet face like an apple, wearing the blue ribbon of the Garter. He saw Lady Galloway, slim and thread-like, with silver hair and a face sensitive and superior. He saw her daughter, Lady Margaret Graham, a pale and pretty girl with an elfish face and copper-coloured hair. He saw the Duchess of Mont St. Michel, black-eyed and opulent, and with her her two daughters, black-eyed and opulent also. He saw Dr. Simon, a typical French scientist, with glasses, a pointed brown beard, and a forehead barred with those parallel wrinkles which are the penalty of superciliousness, since they come through constantly elevating the eyebrows. He saw Father Brown of Cobhole, in Essex, whom he had recently met in England. He saw—perhaps with more interest than any of those —a tall man in uniform, who had bowed to the Galloways without receiving any very hearty acknowledgment, and who now advanced alone to pay his respects to his host. This was Commandant O'Brien, of the French Foreign Legion. He was a slim yet somewhat swaggering figure, clean-shaven, dark-haired, and blueeyed, and as seemed natural in an officer of that famous regiment of victorious failures and successful suicides, he had an air at once dashing and melancholy. He was by birth an Irish gentleman, and in boyhood had known the Galloways—especially Margaret Graham. He had left his country after some crash of debts, and now expressed his complete freedom from British etiquette by swinging about in uniform, sabre and spurs. When he bowed to the Ambassador's family, Lord and Lady Galloway bent stiffly, and Lady Margaret looked away.

But for whatever old causes such people might be interested in each other, their distinguished host was not specially interested in them. No one of them at least was in his eyes the guest of the evening. Valentin was expecting, for spécial reasons, a man of world-wide fame, whose friendship he had secured during some of his great detective tours and triumphs in the United States. He was expecting Julius K. Brayne, that multi-million-aire whose colossal and even crushing endowments of small religions have occasioned so much easy sport and easier solemnity for the American and English papers. Nobody could quite make out whether Mr. Brayne was an atheist or a Mormon, or a Christian Scientist; but he was ready to pour money into any intellectual vessel, so long as it was an untried vessel. One of his hobbies was to wait for the American Shakespeare—a hobby more patient than angling. He admired Walt Whitman, but thought that Luke P. Tanner, of Paris, Pa., was more 'progressive' than Whitman any day. He liked anything that he thought 'progressive.' He thought Valentin 'progressive,' thereby doing him a grave injustice.

The solid appearance of Julius K. Brayne in the room was as decisive as a dinner bell. He had this great quality, which very few of us can claim, that his presence was as big as his absence. He was a huge fellow, as fat as he was tall, clad in complete evening black, without so much relief as a watch-chain or a ring. His hair was white and well brushed back like a German's; his face was red, fierce and cherubic, with one dark tuft under the lower lip that threw up that otherwise infantile visage with an effect theatrical and even Mephistophelean. Not long, however, did that *salon* merely stare at the celebrated American; his lateness had already become a domestic problem, and he was sent with all speed into the dining-room with Lady Galloway upon his arm.

Except on one point the Galloways were genial and casual enough. So long as Lady Margaret did not take the arm of that adventurer O'Brien her father was quite satisfied; and she had not done so; she had decorously

gone in with Dr. Simon. Nevertheless, old Lord Galloway was restless and almost rude. He was diplomatic
enough during dinner, but when, over the cigars, three
of the younger men—Simon the doctor, Brown the priest,
and the detrimental O'Brien, the exile in a foreign uniform—all melted away to mix with the ladies or smoke
in the conservatory, then the English diplomatist grew
very undiplomatic indeed. He was stung every sixty
seconds with the thought that the scamp O'Brien might
be signalling to Margaret somehow; he did not attempt
to imagine how. He was left over the coffee with Brayne,
the hoary Yankee who believed in all religions, and
Valentin, the grizzled Frenchman who believed in none.
They could argue with each other, but neither could
appeal to him. After a time this 'progressive' logomachy
had reached a crisis of tedium; Lord Galloway got up
also and sought the drawing-room. He lost his way in
long passages for some six or eight minutes: till he heard
the high-pitched, didactic voice of the doctor, and then
the dull voice of the priest, followed by general laughter.
They also, he thought with a curse, were probably argu-
ing about 'science and religion.' But the instant he
opened the *salon* door he saw only one thing—he saw
what was not there. He saw that Commandant O'Brien
was absent, and that Lady Margaret was absent, too.

Rising impatiently from the drawing-room, as he had
from the dining-room, he stamped along the passage
once more. His notion of protecting his daughter from
the Irish-Algerian ne'er-do-well had become something
·central and even mad in his mind. As he went towards
the back of the house, where was Valentin's study, he
was surprised to meet his daughter, who swept past with
a white, scornful face, which was a second enigma. If she
had been with O'Brien, where was O'Brien? If she had
not been with O'Brien, where had she been? With a sort

of senile and passionate suspicion he groped his way to
the dark back parts of the mansion, and eventually found
a servants' entrance that opened on to the garden. The
moon with her scimitar had now ripped up and rolled
away all the storm-wrack. The argent light lit up all four
corners of the garden. A tall figure in blue was striding
across the lawn towards the study door; a glint of moonlit silver on his facings picked him out as Commandant
O'Brien.

He vanished through the french windows into the
house, leaving Lord Galloway in an indescribable temper, at once virulent and vague. The blue-and-silver
garden, like a scene in a theatre, seemed to taunt him
with all that tyrannic tenderness against which his
worldly authority was at war. The length and grace of
the Irishman's stride enraged him as if he were a rival
instead of a father; the moonlight maddened him. He
was trapped as if by magic into a garden of troubadours,
a Watteau fairyland; and, willing to shake off such
amorous imbecilities by speech, he stepped briskly after
his enemy. As he did so he tripped over some tree or
stone in the grass; looked down at it first with irritation
and then a second time with curiosity. The next instant
the moon and the tall poplars looked at an unusual sight
—an elderly English diplomatist running hard and crying or bellowing as he ran.

His hoarse shouts brought a pale face to the study
door, the beaming glasses and worried brow of Dr.
Simon, who heard the nobleman's first clear words. Lord
Galloway was crying: 'A corpse in the grass—a blood-
stained corpse.' O'Brien at least had gone utterly from
his mind.

'We must tell Valentin at once,' said the doctor, when
the other had brokenly described all that he had dared
to examine. 'It is fortunate that he is here'; and even as

31

he spoke the great detective entered the study, attracted by the cry. It was almost amusing to note his typical transformation; he had come with the common concern of a host and a gentleman, fearing that some guest or servant was ill. When he was told the gory fact, he turned with all his gravity instantly bright and business-like; for this, however abrupt and awful, was his business.

'Strange, gentlemen,' he said, as they hurried out into the garden, 'that I should have hunted mysteries all over the earth, and now one comes and settles in my own backyard. But where is the place?' They crossed the lawn less easily, as a slight mist had begun to rise from the river; but under the guidance of the shaken Galloway they found the body sunken in deep grass—the body of a very tall and broad-shouldered man. He lay face downwards, so they could only see that his big shoulders were clad in black cloth, and that his big head was bald, except for a wisp or two of brown hair that clung to his skull like wet seaweed. A scarlet serpent of blood crawled from under his fallen face.

'At least,' said Simon, with a deep and singular intonation, 'he is none of our party.'

'Examine him, doctor,' cried Valentin rather sharply. 'He may not be dead.'

The doctor bent down. 'He is not quite cold, but I am afraid he is dead enough,' he answered. 'Just help me to lift him up.'

They lifted him carefully an inch from the ground, and all doubts as to his being really dead were settled at once and frightfully. The head fell away. It had been entirely sundered from the body; whoever had cut his throat had managed to sever the neck as well. Even Valentin was slightly shocked. 'He must have been as strong as a gorilla,' he muttered.

Not without a shiver, though he was used to anatomical abortions, Dr. Simon lifted the head. It was slightly slashed about the neck and jaw, but the face was substantially unhurt. It was a ponderous, yellow face, at once sunken and swollen, with a hawk-like nose and heavy lids—the face of a wicked Roman emperor, with, perhaps, a distant touch of a Chinese emperor. All present seemed to look at it with the coldest eye of ignorance. Nothing else could be noted about the man except that, as they had lifted his body, they had seen underneath it the white gleam of a shirtfront defaced with a red gleam of blood. As Dr. Simon said, the man had never been of their party. But he might very well have been trying to join it, for he had come dressed for such an occasion.

Valentin went down on his hands and knees and examined with his closest professional attention the grass and ground for some twenty yards round the body, in which he was assisted less skilfully by the doctor, and quite vaguely by the English lord. Nothing rewarded their grovellings except a few twigs, snapped or chopped into very small lengths, which Valentin lifted for an instant's examination, and then tossed away.

'Twigs,' he said gravely; 'twigs, and a total stranger with his head cut off; that is all there is on this lawn.'

There was an almost creepy stillness, and then the unnerved Galloway called out sharply:

'Who's that? Who's that over there by the garden wall?'

A small figure with a foolishly large head drew waveringly near them in the moonlit haze; looked for an instant like a goblin, but turned out to be the harmless little priest whom they had left in the drawing-room.

'I say,' he said meekly, 'there are no gates to this garden, do you know.'

Valentin's black brows had come together somewhat

crossly, as they did on principle at the sight of the cassock. But he was far too just a man to deny the relevance of the remark. 'You are right,' he said. 'Before we find out how he came to be killed, we may have to find out how he came to be here. Now listen to me, gentlemen. If it can be done without prejudice to my position and duty, we shall all agree that certain distinguished names might well be kept out of this. There are ladies, gentlemen, and there is a foreign ambassador. If we must mark it down as a crime, then it must be followed up as a crime. But till then I can use my own discretion. I am the head of the police; I am so public that I can afford to be private. Please Heaven, I will clear every one of my own guests before I call in my men to look for anybody else. Gentlemen, upon your honour, you will none of you leave the house till to-morrow at noon; there are bedrooms for all. Simon, I think you know where to find my man, Ivan, in the front hall; he is a confidential man. Tell him to leave another servant on guard and come to me at once. Lord Galloway, you are certainly the best person to tell the ladies what has happened, and prevent a panic. They also must stay. Father Brown and I will remain with the body.'

When this spirit of the captain spoke in Valentin he was obeyed like a bugle. Dr. Simon went through to the armoury and routed out Ivan, the public detective's private detective. Galloway went to the drawing-room and told the terrible news tactfully enough, so that by the time the company assembled there the ladies were already startled and already soothed. Meanwhile the good priest and the good atheist stood at the head and foot of the dead man motionless in the moonlight, like symbolic statues of their two philosophies of death.

Ivan, the confidential man with the scar and the moustaches, came out of the house like a cannon ball, and came racing across the lawn to Valentin like a dog to his master. His livid face was quite lively with the glow of this domestic detective story, and it was with almost unpleasant eagerness that he asked his master's permission to examine the remains.

'Yes; look, if you like, Ivan,' said Valentin, 'but don't be long. We must go in and thrash this out in the house.'

Ivan lifted his head, and then almost let it drop.

'Why,' he gasped, 'it's—no, it isn't; it can't be. Do you know this man, sir?'

'No,' said Valentin indifferently; 'we had better go inside.'

Between them they carried the corpse to a sofa in the study, and then all made their way to the drawing-room.

The detective sat down at a desk quietly, and even with hesitation; but his eye was the iron eye of a judge at assize. He made a few rapid notes upon paper in front of him, and then said shortly: 'Is everybody here?'

'Not Mr. Brayne,' said the Duchess of Mont St. Michel, looking round.

'No,' said Lord Galloway, in a hoarse, harsh voice. 'And not Mr. Neil O'Brien I fancy. I saw that gentleman walking in the garden when the corpse was still warm.'

'Ivan,' said the detective, 'go and fetch Commandant O'Brien and Mr. Brayne. Mr. Brayne, I know, is finishing a cigar in the dining-room; Commandant O'Brien, I think, is walking up and down the conservatory. I am not sure.'

The faithful attendant flashed from the room, and before anyone could stir or speak Valentin went on with the same soldierly swiftness of exposition.

'Everyone here knows that a dead man has been found in the garden, his head cut clean from his body. Dr. Simon, you have examined it. Do you think that to cut a man's throat like that would need great force? Or, perhaps, only a very sharp knife?'

'I should say that it could not be done with a knife at all,' said the pale doctor.

'Have you any thought,' resumed Valentin, 'of a tool with which it could be done?'

'Speaking within modern probabilities, I really haven't,' said the doctor, arching his painful brows. 'It's not easy to hack a neck through even clumsily, and this was a very clean cut. It could be done with a battle-axe or an old headsman's axe, or an old two-handed sword.'

'But, good heavens!' cried the Duchess, almost in hysterics; 'there aren't any two-handed swords and battle-axes round here.'

Valentin was still busy with the paper in front of him. 'Tell me,' he said, still writing rapidly, 'could it have been done with a long French cavalry sabre?'

A low knocking came at the door, which for some unreasonable reason, curdled everyone's blood like the knocking in *Macbeth*. Amid that frozen silence Dr. Simon managed to say: 'A sabre—yes, I suppose it could.'

'Thank you,' said Valentin, 'Come in, Ivan.'

The confidential Ivan opened the door and ushered in Commandant Neil O'Brien, whom he had found at last pacing the garden again.

The Irish officer stood disordered and defiant on the threshold. 'What do you want with me?' he cried.

'Please sit down,' said Valentin in pleasant, level tones. 'Why, you aren't wearing your sword! Where is it?'

'I left it on the library table,' said O'Brien, his brogue deepening in his disturbed mood. 'It was a nuisance, it was getting——'

'Ivan,' said Valentin: 'please go and get the Commandant's sword from the library.' Then, as the servant vanished: 'Lord Galloway says he saw you leaving the garden just before he found the corpse. **What** were you doing in the garden?'

The Commandant flung himself recklessly into a chair. 'Oh,' he cried in pure Irish; 'admirin' the moon. Communing with Nature, me boy.'

A heavy silence sank and endured, and at the end of it came again that trivial and terrible knocking. Ivan reappeared, carrying an empty steel scabbard. 'This is all I can find,' he said.

'Put it on the table,' said Valentin, without looking up.

There was an inhuman silence in the room, like that sea of inhuman silence round the dock of the condemned murderer. The Duchess's weak exclamations had long ago died away. Lord Galloway's swollen hatred was satisfied and even sobered. The voice that came was quite unexpected.

'I think I can tell you,' cried Lady Margaret, in that clear, quivering voice with which a courageous woman speaks publicly. 'I can tell you what Mr. O'Brien was doing in the garden, since he is bound to silence. He was asking me to marry him. I refused; I said in my family circumstances I could give him nothing but my respect. He was a little angry at that; he did not seem to think much of my respect. I wonder,' she added, with rather a wan smile, 'if he will care at all for it now. For I offer it him now. I will swear anywhere that he never did a thing like this.'

Lord Galloway had edged up to his daughter, and was intimidating her in what he imagined to be an undertone. 'Hold your tongue, Maggie,' he said in a thunderous whisper. 'Why should you shield the fellow? Where's his sword? Where's his confounded cavalry——'

He stopped because of the singular stare with which his daughter was regarding him, a look that was indeed a lurid magnet for the whole group.

'You old fool!' she said, in a low voice without pretence of piety; 'what do you suppose you are trying to prove? I tell you this man was innocent while with me. But if he wasn't innocent, he was still with me. If he murdered a man in the garden, who was it who must have seen—who must at least have known? Do you hate Neil so much as to put your own daughter——'

Lady Galloway screamed. Everyone else sat tingling at the touch of those satanic tragedies that have been between lovers before now. They saw the proud, white face of the Scotch aristocrat and her lover, the Irish adventurer, like old portraits in a dark house. The long silence was full of formless historical memories of murdered husbands and poisonous paramours.

In the centre of this morbid silence an innocent voice said: 'Was it a very long cigar?'

The change of thought was so sharp that they had to look round to see who had spoken.

'I mean,' said little Father Brown, from the corner of the room. 'I mean that cigar Mr. Brayne is finishing. It seems nearly as long as a walking-stick.'

Despite the irrelevance there was assent as well as irritation in Valentin's face as he lifted his head.

'Quite right,' he remarked sharply. 'Ivan, go and see about Mr. Brayne again, and bring him here at once.'

The instant the factotum had closed the door, Valentin addressed the girl with an entirely new earnestness.

'Lady Margaret,' he said, 'we all feel, I am sure, both gratitude and admiration for your act in rising above your lower dignity and explaining the Commandant's conduct. But there is a hiatus still. Lord Galloway, I understand, met you passing from the study to the drawing-room, and it was only some minutes afterwards that he found the garden and the Commandant still walking there.'

'You have to remember,' replied Margaret, with a faint irony in her voice, 'that I had just refused him, so we should scarcely have come back arm in arm. He is a gentleman, anyhow; and he loitered behind—and so got charged with murder.'

'In those few moments,' said Valentin gravely, 'he might really——'

The knock came again, and Ivan put in his scarred face.

'Beg pardon, sir,' he said, 'but Mr. Brayne has left the house.'

'Left!' cried Valentin, and rose for the first time to his feet.

'Gone. Scooted. Evaporated,' replied Ivan, in humorous French. 'His hat and coat are gone, too; and I'll tell you something to cap it all. I ran outside the house to find any traces of him, and I found one, and a big trace, too.'

'What do you mean?' asked Valentin.

'I'll show you,' said his servant, and reappeared with a flashing naked cavalry sabre, streaked with blood about the point and edge. Everyone in the room eyed it as if it were a thunderbolt; but the experienced Ivan went on quite quietly:

'I found this,' he said, 'flung among the bushes fifty yards up the road to Paris. In other words, I found it just where your respectable Mr. Brayne threw it when he ran away.'

There was again a silence, but of a new sort. Valentin took the sabre, examined it, reflected with unaffected concentration of thought, and then turned a respectful face to O'Brien. 'Commandant,' he said, 'we trust you will always produce this weapon if it is wanted for police examination. Meanwhile,' he added, slapping the steel back in the ringing scabbard, 'let me return you your sword.'

At the military symbolism of the action the audience could hardly refrain from applause.

For Neil O'Brien, indeed, that gesture was the turning-point of existence. By the time he was wandering in the mysterious garden again in the colours of the morning the tragic futility of his ordinary mien had fallen from him; he was a man with many reasons for happiness. Lord Galloway was a gentleman, and had offered him an apology. Lady Margaret was something better than a lady, a woman at least, and had perhaps given him something better than an apology, as they drifted among the old flower-beds before breakfast. The whole company was more light-hearted and humane, for though the riddle of the death remained, the load of suspicion was lifted off them all, and sent flying off to Paris with the strange millionaire—a man they hardly knew. The devil was cast out of the house—he had cast himself out.

Still, the riddle remained; and when O'Brien threw himself on a garden seat beside Dr. Simon, that keenly scientific person at once resumed it. He did not get much talk out of O'Brien, whose thoughts were on pleasanter things.

'I can't say it interests me much,' said the Irishman frankly, 'especially as it seems pretty plain now. Apparently Brayne hated this stranger for some reason; lured him into the garden, and killed him with my sword. Then he fled to the city, tossing the sword away as he went. By the way, Ivan tells me the dead man had a Yankee dollar in his pocket. So he was a countryman of Brayne's, and that seems to clinch it. I don't see any difficulties about the business.'

'There are five colossal difficulties,' said the doctor quietly; 'like high walls within walls. Don't mistake me. I don't doubt that Brayne did it; his flight, I fancy, proves that. But as to how he did it. First difficulty: Why should a man kill another man with a great hulking sabre, when he can almost kill him with a pocket knife and put it back in his pocket? Second difficulty: Why was there no noise or outcry? Does a man commonly see another come up waving a scimitar and offer no remarks? Third difficulty: A servant watched the front door all the evening; and a rat cannot get into Valentin's garden anywhere. How did the dead man get into the garden? Fourth difficulty: Given the same conditions, how did Brayne get out of the garden?'

'And the fifth,' said Neil, with eyes fixed on the English priest, who was coming slowly up the path.

'Is a trifle, I suppose,' said the doctor, 'but I think an odd one. When I first saw how the head had been slashed, I supposed the assassin had struck more than once. But on examination I found many cuts across the truncated section; in other words, they were struck *after* the head was off. Did Brayne hate his foe so fiendishly that he stood sabring his body in the moonlight?'

'Horrible!' said O'Brien, and shuddered.

The little priest, Brown, had arrived while they were talking, and had waited, with characteristic shyness, till they had finished. Then he said awkwardly:

'I say, I'm sorry to interrupt. But I was sent to tell you the news!'

'News?' repeated Simon, and stared at him rather painfully through his glasses.

'Yes, I'm sorry,' said Father Brown mildly. 'There's been another murder, you know.'

Both men on the seat sprang up, leaving it rocking.

'And, what's stranger still,' continued the priest, with his dull eyes on the rhododendrons, 'it's the same disgusting sort; it's another beheading. They found the second head actually bleeding in the river, a few yards along Brayne's road to Paris; so they suppose that he——'

'Great Heaven!' cried O'Brien. 'Is Brayne a mono-maniac?'

'There are American vendettas,' said the priest impassively. Then he added: 'They want you to come to the library and see it.'

Commandant O'Brien followed the others towards the inquest, feeling decidedly sick. As a soldier, he loathed all this secretive carnage; where were these extravagant amputations going to stop? First one head was hacked off, and then another; in this case (he told himself bitterly) it was not true that two heads were better than one. As he crossed the study he almost staggered at a shocking coincidence. Upon Valentin's table lay the coloured picture of yet a third bleeding head; and it was the head of Valentin himself. A second glance showed him it was only a Nationalist paper, called *The Guillotine*, which every week showed one of its political opponents with rolling eyes and writhing features just after execution; for Valentin was an anti-clerical of some note. But O'Brien was an Irishman, with a kind of chastity even in his sins; and his gorge rose against that great brutality of the intellect which belongs only to France. He felt Paris as a whole, from the grotesques on the Gothic churches to the gross caricatures in the newspapers. He remembered the gigantic jests of the Revolution. He saw the whole city as one ugly energy, from the sanguinary sketch lying on Valentin's table up to where, above a mountain and forest of gargoyles, the great devil grins on Notre Dame.

The library was long, low, and dark; what light entered it shot from under low blinds and had still some of the ruddy tinge of morning. Valentin and his servant Ivan were waiting for them at the upper end of a long, slightly-sloping desk, on which lay the mortal remains, looking enormous in the twilight. The big black figure and yellow face of the man found in the garden confronted them essentially unchanged. The second head, which had been fished from among the river reeds that morning, lay streaming and dripping beside it; Valentin's men were still seeking to recover the rest of this second corpse, which was supposed to be afloat. Father Brown, who did not seem to share O'Brien's sensibilities in the least, went up to the second head and examined it with his blinking care. It was little more than a mop of wet, white hair, fringed with silver fire in the red and level morning light; the face, which seemed of an ugly, empurpled and perhaps criminal type, had been much battered against trees or stones as it tossed in the water.

'Good morning, Commandant O'Brien,' said Valentin, with quiet cordiality. 'You have heard of Brayne's last experiment in butchery, I suppose?'

Father Brown was still bending over the head with white hair, and he said, without looking up:

'I suppose it is quite certain that Brayne cut off this head, too.'

'Well, it seems common sense,' said Valentin, with his hands in his pockets. 'Killed in the same way as the other. Found within a few yards of the other. And sliced by the same weapon which we know he carried away.'

'Yes, yes; I know,' replied Father Brown, submissively. 'Yet, you know, I doubt whether Brayne could have cut off this head.'

'Why not?' inquired Dr. Simon, with a rational stare.

'Well, doctor,' said the priest, looking up blinking, 'can a man cut off his own head? I don't know.'

O'Brien felt an insane universe crashing about his ears; but the doctor sprang forward with impetuous practicality and pushed back the wet, white hair.

'Oh, there's no doubt it's Brayne,' said the priest quietly. 'He had exactly that chip in the left ear.'

The detective, who had been regarding the priest with steady and glittering eyes, opened his clenched mouth and said sharply: 'You seem to know a lot about him, Father Brown.'

'I do,' said the little man simply. 'I've been about with him for some weeks. He was thinking of joining our church.'

The star of the fanatic sprang into Valentin's eyes; he strode towards the priest with clenched hands. 'And, perhaps,' he cried, with a blasting sneer: 'perhaps he was also thinking of leaving all his money to your church.'

'Perhaps he was,' said Brown stolidly; 'it is possible.'

'In that case,' cried Valentin, with a dreadful smile: 'you may indeed know a great deal about him. About his life and about his——'

Commandant O'Brien laid a hand on Valentin's arm. 'Drop that slanderous rubbish, Valentin,' he said: 'or there may be more swords yet.'

But Valentin (under the steady, humble gaze of the priest) had already recovered himself. 'Well,' he said shortly: 'people's private opinions can wait. You gentlemen are still bound by your promise to stay; you must enforce it on yourselves—and on each other. Ivan here will tell you anything more you want to know; I must get to business and write to the authorities. We can't keep this quiet any longer. I shall be writing in my study if there is any more news.'

'Is there any more news, Ivan?' asked Dr. Simon, as the chief of police strode out of the room.

'Only one more thing, I think, sir,' said Ivan, wrinkling up his grey old face; 'but that's important, too, in its way. There's that old buffer you found on the lawn,' and he pointed without pretence of reverence at the big black body with the yellow head. 'We've found out who he is, anyhow.'

'Indeed!' cried the astonished doctor; 'and who is he?'

'His name was Arnold Becker,' said the under-detective, 'though he went by many aliases. He was a wandering sort of scamp, and is known to have been in America; so that was where Brayne got his knife into him. We didn't have much to do with him ourselves, for he worked mostly in Germany. We've communicated, of course, with the German police. But, oddly enough, there was a twin brother of his, named Louis Becker, whom we had a great deal to do with. In fact, we found it necessary to guillotine him only yesterday. Well, it's a rum thing, gentlemen, but when I saw that fellow flat on the lawn I had the greatest jump of my life. If I hadn't seen Louis Becker guillotined with my own eyes, I'd have sworn it was Louis Becker lying there in the grass. Then, of course, I remembered his twin brother in Germany, and following up the clue——'

The explanatory Ivan stopped, for the excellent reason that nobody was listening to him. The Commandant and the doctor were both staring at Father Brown, who had sprung stiffly to his feet, and was holding his temples tight like a man in sudden and violent pain.

'Stop, stop, stop!' he cried; 'stop talking a minute, for I see half. Will God give me strength? Will my brain make the one jump and see all? Heaven help me! I used to be fairly good at thinking. I could paraphrase any page in Aquinas once. Will my head split—or will it see? I see half—I only see half.'

He buried his head in his hands, and stood in a sort of rigid torture of thought or prayer, while the other three could only go on staring at this last prodigy of their wild twelve hours.

When Father Brown's hands fell they showed a face quite fresh and serious, like a child's. He heaved a huge sigh, and said: 'Let us get this said and done with as quickly as possible. Look here, this will be the quickest way to convince you all of the truth.' He turned to the doctor. 'Dr. Simon,' he said, 'you have a strong headpiece, and I heard you this morning asking the five hardest questions about this business. Well, if you will now ask them again, I will answer them.'

Simon's pince-nez dropped from his nose in his doubt and wonder, but he answered at once. 'Well, the first question, you know, is why a man should kill another with a clumsy sabre at all when a man can kill with a bodkin?'

'A man cannot behead with a bodkin,' said Brown, calmly, 'and for *this* murder beheading was absolutely necessary.'

'Why?' asked O'Brien, with interest.

'And the next question?' asked Father Brown.

'Well, why didn't the man cry out or anything?' asked the doctor; 'sabres in gardens are certainly unusual.'

'Twigs,' said the priest gloomily, and turned to the window which looked on the scene of death. 'No one saw the point of the twigs. Why should they lie on that lawn (look at it) so far from any tree? They were not snapped off; they were chopped off. The murderer occupied his enemy with some tricks with the sabre, showing how he could cut a branch in mid-air, or what not. Then, while his enemy bent down to see the result, a silent slash, and the head fell.'

'Well,' said the doctor slowly, 'that seems plausible enough. But my next two questions will stump anyone.'

The priest still stood looking critically out of the window and waited.

'You know how all the garden was sealed up like an air-tight chamber,' went on the doctor. 'Well, how did the strange man get into the garden?'

Without turning round, the little priest answered: 'There never was any strange man in the garden.'

There was a silence, and then a sudden cackle of almost childish laughter relieved the strain. The absurdity of Brown's remark moved Ivan to open taunts.

'Oh!' he cried; 'then we didn't lug a great fat corpse on to a sofa last night? He hadn't got into the garden, I suppose?'

'Got into the garden?' repeated Brown reflectively. 'No, not entirely.'

'Hang it all,' cried Simon, 'a man gets into a garden, or he doesn't.'

'Not necessarily,' said the priest, with a faint smile. 'What is the next question, doctor?'

'I fancy you're ill,' exclaimed Dr. Simon sharply; 'but I'll ask the next question if you like. How did Brayne get out of the garden?'

'He didn't get out of the garden,' said the priest, still looking out of the window.

'Didn't get out of the garden?' exploded Simon.

'Not completely,' said Father Brown.

Simon shook his fists in a frenzy of French logic. 'A man gets out of a garden, or he doesn't,' he cried.

'Not always,' said Father Brown.

Dr. Simon sprang to his feet impatiently. 'I have no time to spare on such senseless talk,' he cried angrily. 'If you can't understand a man being on one side of the wall or the other, I won't trouble you further.'

'Doctor,' said the cleric very gently 'we have always got on very pleasantly together. If only for the sake of old friendship, stop and tell me your fifth question.'

The impatient Simon sank into a chair by the door and said briefly: 'The head and shoulders were cut about in a queer way. It seemed to be done after death.'

'Yes,' said the motionless priest, 'it was done so as to

47

make you assume exactly the one simple falsehood that you did assume. It was done to make you take for granted that the head belonged to the body.'

The borderland of the brain, where all the monsters are made, moved horribly in the Gaelic O'Brien. He felt the chaotic presence of all the horse-men and fish-women that man's unnatural fancy has begotten. A voice older than his first fathers seemed saying in his ear: 'Keep out of the monstrous garden where grows the tree with double fruit. Avoid the evil garden where died the man with two heads.' Yet, while these shameful symbolic shapes passed across the ancient mirror of his Irish soul, his Frenchified intellect was quite alert, and was watching the odd priest as closely and incredulously as all the rest.

Father Brown had turned round at last, and stood against the window with his face in dense shadow; but even in that shadow they could see it was pale as ashes. Nevertheless, he spoke quite sensibly, as if there were no Gaelic souls on earth.

'Gentlemen,' he said; 'you did not find the strange body of Becker in the garden. You did not find any strange body in the garden. In face of Dr. Simon's rationalism, I still affirm that Becker was only partly present. Look here!' (pointing to the black bulk of the mysterious corpse); 'you never saw that man in your lives. Did you ever see this man?'

He rapidly rolled away the bald-yellow head of the unknown, and put in its place the white-maned head beside it. And there, complete, unified, unmistakable, lay Julius K. Brayne.

'The murderer,' went on Brown quietly, 'hacked off his enemy's head and flung the sword far over the wall. But he was too clever to fling the sword only. He flung the *head* over the wall also. Then he had only to clap on another head to the corpse, and (as he insisted on a private inquest) you all imagined a totally new man.'

'Clap on another head!' said O'Brien, staring. 'What other head? Heads don't grow on garden bushes, do they?'

'No,' said Father Brown huskily, and looking at his boots; 'there is only one place where they grow. They grow in the basket of the guillotine, beside which the Chief of Police, Aristide Valentin, was standing not an hour before the murder. Oh, my friends, hear me a minute more before you tear me in pieces. Valentin is an honest man, if being mad for an arguable cause is honesty. But did you ever see in that cold, grey eye of his that he is mad? He would do anything, *anything*, to break what he calls the superstition of the Cross. He has fought for it and starved for it, and now he has murdered for it. Brayne's crazy millions had hitherto been scattered among so many sects that they did little to alter the balance of things. But Valentin heard a whisper that Brayne, like so many scatter-brained sceptics, was drifting to us; and that was quite a different thing. Brayne would pour supplies into the impoverished and pugnacious Church of France; he would support six Nationalist newspapers like *The Guillotine*. The battle was already balanced on a point, and the fanatic took flame at the risk. He resolved to destroy the millionaire, and he did it as one would expect the greatest of detectives to commit his only crime. He abstracted the severed head of Becker on some criminological excuse, and took it home in his official box. He had that last argument with Brayne, that Lord Galloway did not hear the end of; that failing, he led him out into the sealed garden, talked about swordsmanship, used twigs and a sabre for illustration, and——'

Ivan of the Scar sprang up. 'You lunatic,' he yelled; 'you'll go to my master now, if I take you by——'

'Why, I was going there,' said Brown heavily; 'I must ask him to confess, and all that.'

Driving the unhappy Brown before them like a hostage or sacrifice, they rushed together into the sudden stillness of Valentin's study.

The great detective sat at his desk apparently too occupied to hear their turbulent entrance. They paused a moment, and then something in the look of that upright and elegant back made the doctor run forward suddenly. A touch and a glance showed him that there was a small box of pills at Valentin's elbow, and that Valentin was dead in his chair; and on the blind face of the suicide was more than the pride of Cato.

The Queer Feet

IF you meet a member of that select club, 'The Twelve True Fishermen,' entering the Vernon Hotel for the annual club dinner, you will observe, as he takes off his overcoat, that his evening coat is green and not black. If (supposing that you have the star-defying audacity to address such a being) you ask him why, he will probably answer that he does it to avoid being mistaken for a waiter. You will then retire crushed. But you will leave behind you a mystery as yet unsolved and a tale worth telling.

If (to pursue the same vein of improbable conjecture) you were to meet a mild, hard-working little priest, named Father Brown, and were to ask him what he thought was the most singular luck of his life, he would

probably reply that upon the whole his best stroke was
at the Vernon Hotel, where he had averted a crime and,
perhaps, saved a soul, merely by listening to a few footsteps in a passage. He is perhaps a little proud of this
wild and wonderful guess of his, and it is possible that
he might refer to it. But since it is immeasurably unlikely that you will ever rise high enough in the social
world to find 'The Twelve True Fishermen,' or that you
will ever sink low enough among slums and criminals to
find Father Brown, I fear you will never hear the story
at all unless you hear it from me.

The Vernon Hotel, at which The Twelve True Fishermen held their annual dinners, was an institution such
as can only exist in an oligarchical society which has
almost gone mad on good manners. It was that topsy-
turvy product—an 'exclusive' commercial enterprise.
That is, it was a thing which paid, not by attracting
people, but actually by turning people away. In the heart
of a plutocracy tradesmen become cunning enough to be
more fastidious than their customers. They positively
create difficulties so that their wealthy and weary clients
may spend money and diplomacy in overcoming them.
If there were a fashionable hotel in London which no
man could enter who was under six foot, society would
meekly make up parties of six-foot men to dine in it. If
there were an expensive restaurant which by a mere
caprice of its proprietor was only open on Thursday
afternoon, it would be crowded on Thursday afternoon.
The Vernon Hotel stood, as if by accident, in the corner
of a square in Belgravia. It was a small hotel; and a very
inconvenient one. But its very inconveniences were considered as walls protecting a particular class. One incon-
venience, in particular, was held to be of vital importance: the fact that practically only twenty-four people
could dine in the place at once. The only big dinner table

was the celebrated terrace table, which stood open to the
air on a sort of veranda overlooking one of the most
exquisite old gardens in London. Thus it happened that
even the twenty-four seats at this table could only be
enjoyed in warm weather; and this making the enjoy-
ment yet more difficult made it yet more desired. The
existing owner of the hotel was a Jew named Lever; and
he made nearly a million out of it, by making it difficult
to get into. Of course he combined with this limitation
in the scope of his enterprise the most careful polish in
its performance. The wines and cooking were really as
good as any in Europe, and the demeanour of the attendants exactly mirrored the fixed mood of the English
upper class. The proprietor knew all his waiters like the
fingers on his hand; there were only fifteen of them all
told. It was much easier to become a Member of Parlia-
ment than to become a waiter in that hotel. Each waiter
was trained in terrible silence and smoothness, as if he
were a gentleman's servant. And, indeed, there was
generally at least one waiter to every gentleman who
dined.

The club of The Twelve True Fishermen would not
have consented to dine anywhere but in such a place,
for it insisted on a luxurious privacy; and would have
been quite upset by the mere thought that any other
club was even dining in the same building. On the occasion of their annual dinner the Fishermen were in the
habit of exposing all their treasures, as if they were in
a private house, especially the celebrated set of fish knives
and forks which were, as it were, the insignia of the
society, each being exquisitely wrought in silver in the
form of a fish, and each loaded at the hilt with one large
pearl. These were always laid out for the fish course, and
the fish course was always the most magnificent in that
magnificent repast. The society had a vast number of

ceremonies and observances, but it had no history and no object; that was where it was so very aristocratic. You did not have to be anything in order to be one of the Twelve Fishers; unless you were already a certain sort of person, you never even heard of them. It had been in existence twelve years. Its president was Mr. Audley. Its vice-president was the Duke of Chester.

If I have in any degree conveyed the atmosphere of this appalling hotel, the reader may feel a natural wonder as to how I came to know anything about it, and may even speculate as to how so ordinary a person as my friend Father Brown came to find himself in that golden gallery. As far as that is concerned, my story is simple, or even vulgar. There is in the world a very aged rioter and demagogue who breaks into the most refined retreats with the dreadful information that all men are brothers, and wherever this leveller went on his pale horse it was Father Brown's trade to follow. One of the waiters, an Italian, had been struck down with a paralytic stroke that afternoon; and his Jewish employer, marvelling mildly at such superstitions, had consented to send for the nearest Popish priest. With what the waiter confessed to Father Brown we are not concerned, for the excellent reason that the cleric kept it to himself; but apparently it involved him in writing out a note or statement for the conveying of some message or the righting of some wrong. Father Brown, therefore, with a meek impudence which he would have shown equally in Buckingham Palace, asked to be provided with a room and writing materials. Mr. Lever was torn in two. He was a kind man, and had also that bad imitation of kindness, the dislike of any difficulty or scene. At the same time the presence of one unusual stranger in his hotel that evening was like a speck of dirt on something just cleaned. There was never any borderland or ante-room in the Vernon Hotel, no people waiting in the hall, no customers coming in on chance. There were fifteen waiters. There were twelve guests. It would be as startling to find a new guest in the hotel that night as to find a new brother taking breakfast or tea in one's own family. Moreover, the priest's appearance was second-rate and his clothes muddy; a mere glimpse of him afar off might precipitate a crisis in the club. Mr. Lever at last hit on a plan to cover, since he might not obliterate, the disgrace. When you enter (as you never will) the Vernon Hotel, you pass down a short passage decorated with a few dingy but important pictures, and come to the main vestibule and lounge which opens on your right into passages leading to the public rooms, and on your left to a similar passage pointing to the kitchens and offices of the hotel. Immediately on your left hand is the corner of a glass office, which abuts upon the lounge—a house within a house, so to speak, like the old hotel bar which probably once occupied its place.

In this office sat the representative of the proprietor (nobody in this place ever appeared in person if he could help it), and just beyond the office, on the way to the servants' quarters, was the gentlemen's cloakroom, the last boundary of the gentlemen's domain. But between the office and the cloak-room was a small private room without other outlet, sometimes used by the proprietor for delicate and important matters, such as lending a duke a thousand pounds or declining to lend him sixpence. It is a mark of the magnificent tolerance of Mr. Lever that he permitted this holy place to be for about half an hour profaned by a mere priest, scribbling away on a piece of paper. The story which Father Brown was writing down was very likely a much better story than this one, only it will never be known. I can merely state that it was very nearly as long, and that the last two or three paragraphs of it were the least exciting and absorbing.

For it was by the time he had reached these that the priest began a little to allow his thoughts to wander and his animal senses, which were commonly keen, to awaken. The time of darkness and dinner was drawing on; his own forgotten little room was without a light, and perhaps the gathering gloom, as occasionally happens, sharpened the sense of sound. As Father Brown wrote the last and least essential part of his document, he caught himself writing to the rhythm of a recurrent noise outside, just as one sometimes thinks to the tune of a railway train. When he became conscious of the thing he found what it was: only the ordinary patter of feet passing the door, which in an hotel was no very unlikely matter. Nevertheless, he stared at the darkened ceiling, and listened to the sound. After he had listened for a few seconds dreamily, he got to his feet and listened intently, with his head a little on one side. Then he sat down again and buried his brow in his hands, now not merely listening, but listening and thinking also.

The footsteps outside at any given moment were such as one might hear in any hotel; and yet, taken as a whole, there was something very strange about them. There were no other footsteps. It was always a very silent house, for the few familiar guests went at once to their own apartments, and the well-trained waiters were told to be almost invisible until they were wanted. One could not conceive any place where there was less reason to apprehend anything irregular. But these footsteps were so odd that one could not decide to call them regular or irregular. Father Brown followed them with his finger on the edge of the table, like a man trying to learn a tune on the piano.

First, there came a long rush of rapid little steps, such

as a light man might make in winning a walking race. At a certain point they stopped and changed to a sort of slow-swinging stamp, numbering not a quarter of the steps, but occupying about the same time. The moment the last echoing stamp had died away would come again the run or ripple of light, hurrying feet, and then again the thud of the heavier walking. It was certainly the same pair of boots, partly because (as has been said) there were no other boots about, and partly because they had a small but unmistakable creak in them. Father Brown had the kind of head that cannot help asking questions; and on this apparently trivial question his head almost split. He had seen men run in order to jump. He had seen men run in order to slide. But why on earth should a man run in order to walk? Or, again, why should he walk in order to run? Yet no other description would cover the antics of this invisible pair of legs. The man was either walking very fast down one-half of the corridor in order to walk very slow down the other half; or he was walking very slow at one end to have the rapture of walking fast at the other. Neither suggestion seemed to make much sense. His brain was growing darker and darker, like his room.

Yet, as he began to think steadily, the very blackness of his cell seemed to make his thoughts more vivid; he began to see as in a kind of vision the fantastic feet capering along the corridor in unnatural or symbolic attitudes. Was it a heathen religious dance? Or some entirely new kind of scientific exercise? Father Brown began to ask himself with more exactness what the steps suggested. Taking the slow step first; it certainly was not the step of the proprietor. Men of his type walk with a rapid waddle, or they sit still. It could not be any servant or messenger waiting for directions. It did not sound like it. The poorer orders (in an oligarchy) sometimes lurch about when they are slightly drunk, but generally, and especially in such gorgeous scenes, they stand or sit in constrained attitudes. No; that heavy yet springy step, with a kind of careless emphasis, not specially noisy, yet not caring what noise it made, belonged to only one of the animals of this earth. It was a gentleman of western Europe, and probably one who had never worked for his living.

Just as he came to this solid certainty, the step changed to the quicker one, and ran past the door as feverishly as a rat. The listener remarked that though this step was much swifter it was also much more noiseless, almost as if the man were walking on tiptoe. Yet it was not associated in his mind with secrecy, but with something else —something that he could not remember. He was maddened by one of those half-memories that make a man feel half-witted. Surely he had heard that strange, swift walking somewhere. Suddenly he sprang to his feet with a new idea in his head, and walked to the door. His room had no direct outlet on the passage, but let on one side into the glass office, and on the other into the cloak-room beyond. He tried the door into the office, and found it locked. Then he looked at the window, now a square pane full of purple cloud cleft by livid sunset, and for an instant he smelt evil as a dog smells rats.

The rational part of him (whether the wiser or not) regained its supremacy. He remembered that the proprietor had told him that he should lock the door, and would come later to release him. He told himself that twenty things he had not thought of might explain the eccentric sounds outside; he reminded himself that there was just enough light left to finish his own proper work. Bringing his paper to the window so as to catch the last stormy evening light, he resolutely plunged once more into the almost completed record. He had written for about twenty minutes, bending closer and closer to his paper in the lessening light; then suddenly he sat upright. He had heard the strange feet once more.

This time they had a third oddity. Previously the unknown man had walked, with levity indeed and lightning quickness, but he had walked. This time he ran. One could hear the swift, soft, bounding steps coming along the corridor, like the pads of a fleeing and leaping panther Whoever was coming was a very strong, active man, in still yet tearing excitement. Yet, when the sound had swept up to the office like a sort of whispering whirlwind, it suddenly changed again to the old slow, swaggering stamp.

Father Brown flung down his paper, and, knowing the office door to be locked, went at once into the cloak-room on the other side. The attendant of this place was temporarily absent, probably because the only guests were at dinner, and his office was a sinecure. After groping through a grey forest of overcoats, he found that the dim cloak-room opened on the lighted corridor in the form of a sort of counter or half-door, like most of the counters across which we have all handed umbrellas and received tickets. There was a light immediately above the semi-circular arch of this opening. It threw little illumination on Father Brown himself, who seemed a mere dark outline against the dim sunset window behind him. But it threw an almost theatrical light on the man who stood outside the cloakroom in the corridor.

He was an elegant man in very plain evening-dress; tall, but with an air of not taking up much room; one felt that he could have slid along like a shadow where many smaller men would have been obvious and obstructive. His face, now flung back in the lamplight, was swarthy and vivacious, the face of a foreigner. His figure was good, his manners good-humoured and confident; a

critic could only say that his black coat was a shade below his figure and manners, and even bulged and bagged
in an odd way. The moment he caught sight of Brown's
black silhouette against the sunset, he tossed down a
scrap of paper with a number and called out with amiable authority: 'I want my hat and coat, please; I find I
have to go away at once.'

Father Brown took the paper without a word, and
obediently went to look for the coat; it was not the first
menial work he had done in his life. He brought it and
laid it on the counter; meanwhile, the strange gentleman
who had been feeling in his waistcoat pocket, said, laughing: 'I haven't got any silver; you can keep this.' And he
threw down half a sovereign, and caught up his coat.

Father Brown's figure remained quite dark and still;
but in that instant he had lost his head. His head was
always most valuable when he had lost it. In such moments he put two and two together and made four million. Often the Catholic Church (which is wedded to
common sense) did not approve of it. Often he did not
approve of it himself. But it was a real inspiration—
important at rare crises—when whosoever shall lose his
head the same shall save it.

'I think, sir,' he said civilly, 'that you have some silver
in your pocket.'

The tall gentleman stared. 'Hang it,' he cried. 'If I give
you gold, why should you complain?'

'Because silver is sometimes more valuable than gold,'
said the priest mildly; 'that is, in large quantities.'

The stranger looked at him curiously. Then he looked
still more curiously up the passage towards the main entrance. Then he looked back at Brown again, and then
he looked very carefully at the window beyond Brown's
head, still coloured with the after-glow of the storm.
Then he seemed to make up his mind. He put one hand

on the counter, vaulted over as easily as an acrobat and towered above the priest, putting one tremendous hand upon his collar.

'Stand still,' he said, in a hacking whisper. 'I don't want to threaten you, but——'

'I do want to threaten you,' said Father Brown, in a voice like a rolling drum. 'I want to threaten you with the worm that dieth not, and the fire that is not quenched.'

'You're a rum sort of cloak-room clerk,' said the other.

'I am a priest, Monsieur Flambeau,' said Brown, 'and I am ready to hear your confession.'

The other stood gasping for a few moments, and then staggered back into a chair.

The first two courses of the dinner of The Twelve True Fishermen had proceeded with placid success. I do not possess a copy of the menu; and if I did it would not convey anything to anybody. It was written in a sort of super-French employed by cooks, but quite unintelligible to Frenchmen. There was a tradition in the club that the *hors d'œuvres* should be various and manifold to the point of madness. They were taken seriously because they were avowedly useless extras, like the whole dinner and the whole club. There was also a tradition that the soup course should be light and unpretending —a sort of simple and austere vigil for the feast of fish that was to come. The talk was that strange, slight talk which governs the British Empire, which governs it in secret, and yet would scarcely enlighten an ordinary Englishman even if he could overhear it. Cabinet Ministers on both sides were alluded to by their Christian names with a sort of bored benignity. The Radical Chancellor of the Exchequer, whom the whole Tory party was supposed to be cursing for his extortions, was praised for his minor poetry, or his saddle in the hunting-field. The Tory leader, whom all Liberals were supposed to hate as a tyrant, was discussed and, on the whole, praised —as a Liberal. It seemed somehow that politicians were very important. And yet, anything seemed important about them except their politics. Mr. Audley, the chairman, was an amiable, elderly man who still wore Gladstone collars; he was a kind of symbol of all that phantasmal and yet fixed society. He had never done anything—not even anything wrong. He was not fast; he was not even particularly rich. He was simply in the thing; and there was an end of it. No party could ignore him, and if he had wished to be in the Cabinet he certainly would have been put there. The Duke of Chester, the vice-president, was a young and rising politician. That is to say, he was a pleasant youth, with flat, fair hair and a freckled face, with moderate intelligence and enormous estates. In public his appearances were always successful and his principle was simple enough. When he thought of a joke he made it, and was called brilliant. When he could not think of a joke he said that this was no time for trifling, and was called able. In private, in a club of his own class, he was simply quite pleasantly frank and silly, like a schoolboy. Mr. Audley, never having been in politics, treated them a little more seriously. Sometimes he even embarrassed the company by phrases suggesting that there was some difference between a Liberal and a Conservative. He, himself, was a Conservative, even in private life. He had a roll of grey hair over the back of his collar like certain old-fashioned statesmen, and seen from behind he looked like the man the empire wants. Seen from the front he looked like a mild, self-indulgent bachelor, with rooms in the Albany —which he was.

As has been remarked, there were twenty-four seats at the terrace table, and only twelve members of the club. Thus they could occupy the terrace in the most luxurious style of all, being ranged along the inner side of the table, with no one opposite, commanding an uninterrupted view of the garden, the colours of which were still vivid, though evening was closing in somewhat luridly for the time of year. The chairman sat in the centre of the line, and the vice-president at the right-hand end of it. When the twelve guests first trooped into their seats it was the custom (for some unknown reason) for all the fifteen waiters to stand lining the wall like troops presenting arms to the king, while the fat proprietor stood and bowed to the club with radiant surprise, as if he had never heard of them before. But before the first chink of knife and fork this army of retainers had vanished, only the one or two required to collect and distribute the plates darting about in deathly silence. Mr. Lever, the proprietor, of course had disappeared in convulsions of courtesy long before. It would be exaggerative, indeed irreverent, to say that he ever positively appeared again. But when the important course, the fish course, was being brought on, there was—how shall I put it?—a vivid shadow, a projection of his personality, which told that he was hovering near. The sacred fish course consisted (to the eyes of the vulgar) in a sort of monstrous pudding, about the size and shape of a wedding cake, in which some considerable number of interesting fishes had finally lost the shapes which God had given to them. The Twelve True Fishermen took up their celebrated fish knives and fish forks, and approached it as gravely as if every inch of the pudding cost as much as the silver fork it was eaten with. So it did, for all I know. This course was dealt with in eager and devouring silence; and it was only when his plate was nearly empty that the young duke made the ritual remark: 'They can't do this anywhere but here.'

'Nowhere,' said Mr. Audley, in a deep bass voice, turning to the speaker and nodding his venerable head a number of times. 'Nowhere, assuredly, except here. It was represented to me that at the Café Anglais——'

Here he was interrupted and even agitated for a moment by the removal of his plate, but he recaptured the valuable thread of his thoughts. 'It was represented to me that the same could be done at the Café Anglais. Nothing like it, sir,' he said, shaking his head ruthlessly, like a hanging judge. 'Nothing like it.'

'Overrated place,' said a certain Colonel Pound, speaking (by the look of him) for the first time for some months.

'Oh, I don't know,' said the Duke of Chester, who was an optimist, 'it's jolly good for some things. You can't beat it at——'

A waiter came swiftly along the room, and then stopped dead. His stoppage was as silent as his tread; but all those vague and kindly gentlemen were so used to the utter smoothness of the unseen machinery which surrounded and supported their lives, that a waiter doing anything unexpected was a start and a jar. They felt as you and I would feel if the inanimate world disobeyed —if a chair ran away from us.

The waiter stood staring a few seconds, while there deepened on every face at table a strange shame which is wholly the product of our time. It is the combination of modern humanitarianism with the horrible modern abyss between the souls of the rich and poor. A genuine historic aristocrat would have thrown things at the waiter, beginning with empty bottles, and very probably ending with money. A genuine democrat would have asked him, with a comrade-like clearness of speech, what the devil he was doing. But these modern plutocrats could not bear a poor man near to them, either as a slave or as a friend. That something had gone wrong with the servants was merely a dull, hot embarrassment. They did not want to be brutal, and they dreaded the need to be benevolent. They wanted the thing, whatever it was, to be over. It was over. The waiter, after standing for some seconds rigid, like a cataleptic, turned round and ran madly out of the room.

When he reappeared in the room, or rather in the doorway, it was in company with another waiter, with whom he whispered and gesticulated with southern fierceness. Then the first waiter went away, leaving the second waiter, and reappeared with a third waiter. By the time a fourth waiter had joined this hurried synod, Mr. Audley felt it necessary to break the silence in the interests of Tact. He used a very loud cough, instead of the presidential hammer, and said: 'Splendid work young Moocher's doing in Burmah. Now, no other nation in the world could have——'

A fifth waiter had sped towards him like an arrow, and was whispering in his ear: 'So sorry. Important! Might the proprietor speak to you?'

The chairman turned in disorder, and with a dazed stare saw Mr. Lever coming towards them with his lumbering quickness. The gait of the good proprietor was indeed his usual gait, but his face was by no means usual. Generally it was a genial copper-brown; now it was a sickly yellow.

'You will pardon me, Mr. Audley,' he said, with asthmatic breathlessness. 'I have great apprehensions. Your fish-plates, they are cleared away with the knife and fork on them!'

'Well, I hope so,' said the chairman, with some warmth.

'You see him?' panted the excited hotel keeper; 'you see the waiter who took them away? You know him?'

'Know the waiter?' answered Mr. Audley indignantly. 'Certainly not!'

Mr. Lever opened his hands with a gesture of agony. 'I never send him,' he said. 'I know not when or why he come. I send my waiter to take away the plates, and he find them already away.'

Mr. Audley still looked rather too bewildered to be really the man the empire wants; none of the company could say anything except the man of wood—Colonel Pound—who seemed galvanized into an unnatural life. He rose rigidly from his chair, leaving all the rest sitting, screwed his eyeglass into his eye, and spoke in a raucous undertone as if he had half-forgotten how to speak. 'Do you mean,' he said, 'that somebody has stolen our silver fish service?'

The proprietor repeated the open-handed gesture with even greater helplessness; and in a flash all the men at the table were on their feet.

'Are all your waiters here?' demanded the colonel, in his low, harsh accent.

'Yes; they're all here. I noticed it myself,' cried the young duke, pushing his boyish face into the inmost ring. 'Always count 'em as I come in; they look so queer standing up against the wall.'

'But surely one cannot exactly remember,' began Mr. Audley, with heavy hesitation.

'I remember exactly, I tell you,' cried the duke excitedly. 'There never have been more than fifteen waiters at this place, and there were no more than fifteen to-night, I'll swear; no more and no less.'

The proprietor turned upon him, quaking in a kind of palsy of surprise. 'You say—you say,' he stammered, 'that you see all my fifteen waiters?'

'As usual,' assented the duke. 'What is the matter with that?'

'Nothing,' said Lever, with a deepening accent, 'only you did not. For one of zem is dead upstairs.'

There was a shocking stillness for an instant in that room. It may be (so supernatural is the word death) that each of those idle men looked for a second at his soul, and saw it as a small dried pea. One of them—the duke, I think—even said with the idiotic kindness of wealth: 'Is there anything we can do?'

'He has had a priest,' said the Jew, not untouched.

Then, as to the clang of doom, they awoke to their own position. For a few weird seconds they had really felt as if the fifteenth waiter might be the ghost of the dead man upstairs. They had been dumb under that oppression, for ghosts were to them an embarrassment, like beggars. But the remembrance of the silver broke the spell of the miraculous; broke it abruptly and with a brutal reaction. The colonel flung over his chair and strode to the door. 'If there was a fifteenth man here, friends,' he said, 'that fifteenth fellow was a thief. Down at once to the front and back doors and secure everything; then we'll talk. The twenty-four pearls are worth recovering.'

Mr. Audley seemed at first to hesitate about whether it was gentlemanly to be in such a hurry about anything; but, seeing the duke dash down the stairs with youthful energy, he followed with a more mature motion.

At the same instant a sixth waiter ran into the room, and declared that he had found the pile of fish plates on a sideboard, with no trace of the silver.

The crowd of diners and attendants that tumbled helter-skelter down the passages divided into two groups. Most of the Fishermen followed the proprietor to the front room to demand news of any exit. Colonel Pound, with the Chairman, the vice-president, and one or two others, darted down the corridor leading to the servants' quarters, as the more likely line of escape. As they did so they passed the dim alcove or cavern of the cloak-room, and saw a short, black-coated figure, presumably an attendant, standing a little way back in the shadow of it.

'Hallo there!' called out the duke. 'Have you seen anyone pass?'

The short figure did not answer the question directly, but merely said: 'Perhaps I have got what you are looking for, gentlemen.'

They paused, wavering and wondering, while he quietly went to the back of the cloak-room, and came back with both hands full of shining silver, which he laid out on the counter as calmly as a salesman. It took the form of a dozen quaintly shaped forks and knives.

'You—you——' began the colonel, quite thrown off his balance at last. Then he peered into the dim little room and saw two things: first, that the short, black-clad man was dressed like a clergyman; and, second, that the window of the room behind him was burst, as if someone had passed violently through.

'Valuable things to deposit in a cloak-room, aren't they?' remarked the clergyman, with cheerful composure.

'Did—did you steal those things?' stammered Mr. Audley, with staring eyes.

'If I did,' said the cleric pleasantly, 'at least I am bringing them back again.'

'But you didn't,' said Colonel Pound, still staring at the broken window.

'To make a clean breast of it, I didn't,' said the other, with some humour. And he seated himself quite gravely on a stool.

'But you know who did,' said the colonel.

'I don't know his real name,' said the priest placidly; 'but I know something of his fighting weight, and a great deal about his spiritual difficulties. I formed the physical estimate when he was trying to throttle me, and the moral estimate when he repented.'

'Oh, I say—repented!' cried young Chester, with a sort of crow of laughter.

Father Brown got to his feet, putting his hands behind him. 'Odd, isn't it,' he said, 'that a thief and a vagabond should repent, when so many who are rich and secure remain hard and frivolous, and without fruit for God or man? But there, if you will excuse me, you trespass a little upon my province. If you doubt the penitence as a practical fact, there are your knives and forks. You are The Twelve True Fishers, and there are all your silver fish. But He has made me a fisher of men.'

'Did you catch this man?' asked the colonel, frowning.

Father Brown looked him full in his frowning face. 'Yes,' he said, 'I caught him, with an unseen hook and an invisible line which is long enough to let him wander to the ends of the world, and still to bring him back with a twitch upon the thread.'

There was a long silence. All the other men present drifted away to carry the recovered silver to their comrades, or to consult the proprietor about the queer condition of affairs. But the grim-faced colonel still sat sideways on the counter, swinging his long, lank legs and biting his dark moustache.

At last he said quietly to the priest: 'He must have been a clever fellow, but I think I know a cleverer.'

'He was a clever fellow,' answered the other, 'but I am not quite sure of what other you mean.'

'I mean you,' said the colonel, with a short laugh. 'I don't want to get the fellow jailed; make yourself easy about that. But I'd give a good many silver forks to know exactly how you fell into this affair, and how you got the stuff out of him. I reckon you're the most up-to-date devil of the present company.'

Father Brown seemed rather to like the saturnine candour of the soldier. 'Well,' he said, smiling, 'I mustn't tell you anything of the man's identity, or his own story, of course; but there's no particular reason why I shouldn't tell you of the mere outside facts which I found out for myself.'

He hopped over the barrier with unexpected activity, and sat beside Colonel Pound, kicking his short legs like a little boy on a gate. He began to tell the story as easily as if he were telling it to an old friend by a Christmas fire.

'You see, colonel,' he said, 'I was shut up in that small room there doing some writing, when I heard a pair of feet in this passage doing a dance that was as queer as the dance of death. First came quick, funny little steps, like a man walking on tiptoe for a wager; then came slow, careless, creaking steps, as of a big man walking about with a cigar. But they were both made by the same feet, I swear, and they came in rotation; first the run and then the walk, and then the run again. I wondered at first idly, and then wildly why a man should act these two parts at once. One walk I knew; it was just like yours, colonel. It was the walk of a well-fed gentleman waiting for something, who strolls about rather because he is physically alert than because he is mentally impatient. I knew that I knew the other walk, too, but I could not remember what it was. What wild creature had I met on my travels that tore along on tiptoe in that extraordinary style? Then I heard a clink of plates somewhere; and the answer stood up as plain as St. Peter's. It was the walk of a waiter—that walk with the body slanted forward, the eyes looking down, the ball of the toe spurning away the ground, the coat tails and napkin flying. Then I thought for a minute and a half more. And I believe I saw the manner of the crime, as clearly as if I were going to commit it.'

Colonel Pound looked at him keenly, but the speaker's mild grey eyes were fixed upon the ceiling with almost empty wistfulness.

'A crime,' he said slowly, 'is like any other work of art. Don't look surprised; crimes are by no means the only works of art that come from an infernal workshop. But every work of art, divine or diabolic, has one indispensable mark—I mean, that the centre of it is simple, however much the fulfilment may be complicated. Thus, in *Hamlet*, let us say, the grotesqueness of the grave-digger, the flowers of the mad girl, the fantastic finery of Osric, the pallor of the ghost and the grin of the skull are all oddities in a sort of tangled wreath round one plain tragic figure of a man in black. Well, this also,' he said, getting slowly down from his seat with a smile, 'this also is the plain tragedy of a man in black. Yes,' he went on, seeing the colonel look up in some wonder, 'the whole of this tale turns on a black coat. In this, as in *Hamlet*, there are the rococo excrescences—yourselves, let us say. There is the dead waiter, who was there when he could not be there. There is the invisible hand that swept your table clear of silver and melted into air. But every clever crime is founded ultimately on some one quite simple fact—some fact that is not itself mysterious. The mystification comes in covering it up, in leading men's thoughts away from it. This large and subtle and (in the ordinary course) most profitable crime, was built on the plain fact that a gentleman's evening dress is the same as a waiter's. All the rest was acting, and thundering good acting, too.'

'Still,' said the colonel, getting up and frowning at his boots. 'I am not sure that I understand.'

'Colonel,' said Father Brown, 'I tell you that this arch-angel of impudence who stole your forks walked up and down this passage twenty times in the blaze of all the lamps, in the glare of all the eyes. He did not go and hide in dim corners where suspicion might have searched for him. He kept constantly on the move in the lighted corridors, and everywhere that he went he seemed to be there by right. Don't ask me what he was like; you have seen him yourself six or seven times to-night. You were waiting with all the other grand people in the reception room at the end of the passage there, with the terrace just beyond. Whenever he came among you gentlemen, he came in the lightning style of a waiter, with bent head, flapping napkin and flying feet. He shot out on to the terrace, did something to the table-cloth, and shot back again towards the office and the waiters' quarters. By the time he had come under the eye of the office clerk and the waiters he had become another man in every inch of his body, in every instinctive gesture. He strolled among the servants with the absent-minded insolence which they have all seen in their patrons. It was no new thing to them that a swell from the dinner party should pace all parts of the house like an animal at the Zoo; they know that nothing marks the Smart Set more than a habit of walking where one chooses. When he was magnificently weary of walking down that particular passage he would wheel round and pace back past the office; in the shadow of the arch just be-yond he was altered as by a blast of magic, and went hurrying forward again among the Twelve Fishermen, an obsequious attendant. Why should the gentlemen look at a chance waiter? Why should the waiters suspect a first-rate walking gentleman? Once or twice he played the coolest tricks. In the proprietor's private quarters he called out breezily for a syphon of soda water, saying he was thirsty. He said genially that he would carry it himself, and he did; he carried it quickly and correctly through the thick of you, a waiter with an obvious errand. Of course, it could not have been kept up long, but it only had to be kept up till the end of the fish course.

'His worst moment was when the waiters stood in a row; but even then he contrived to lean against the wall just around the corner in such a way that for that important instant the waiters thought him a gentleman, while the gentlemen thought him a waiter. The rest went like winking. If any waiter caught him away from the table, that waiter caught a languid aristocrat. He had only to time himself two minutes before the fish was cleared, become a swift servant, and clear it himself. He put the plates down on a sideboard, stuffed the silver in his breast pocket, giving it a bulgy look, and ran like a hare (I heard him coming) till he came to the cloakroom. There he had only to be a plutocrat again—a plutocrat called away suddenly on business. He had only to give his ticket to the cloak-room attendant, and go out again elegantly as he had come in. Only—only I happened to be the cloak-room attendant.'

'What did you do to him?' cried the colonel, with unusual intensity. 'What did he tell you?'

'I beg your pardon,' said the priest immovably, 'that is where the story ends.'

'And the interesting story begins,' muttered Pound. 'I think I understand his professional trick. But I don't seem to have got hold of yours.'

'I must be going,' said Father Brown.

They walked together along the passage to the entrance hall, where they saw the fresh, freckled face of the Duke of Chester, who was bounding buoyantly along towards them.

'Come along, Pound,' he cried breathlessly. 'I've been looking for you everywhere. The dinner's going again in spanking style, and old Audley has got to make a speech in honour of the forks being saved. We want to start some new ceremony, don't you know, to commemorate the occasion. I say, you really got the goods back, what do you suggest?'

'Why,' said the colonel, eyeing him with a certain sardonic approval. 'I should suggest that henceforward we wear green coats instead of black. One never knows what mistakes may arise when one looks so like a waiter.'

'Oh, hang it all!' said the young man, 'a gentleman never looks like a waiter.'

'Nor a waiter like a gentleman, I suppose,' said Colonel Pound, with the same lowering laughter on his face. 'Reverend sir, your friend must have been very smart to act the gentleman.'

Father Brown buttoned up his commonplace overcoat to the neck, for the night was stormy, and took his commonplace umbrella from the stand.

'Yes,' he said; 'it must be very hard work to be a gentleman; but, do you know, I have sometimes thought that it may be almost as laborious to be a waiter.'

And saying 'Good evening,' he pushed open the heavy doors of that palace of pleasures. The golden gates closed behind him, and he went at a brisk walk through the damp, dark streets in search of a penny omnibus.

The Invisible Man

In the cool blue twilight of two steep streets in Camden Town, the shop at the corner, a confectioner's, glowed like the butt of a cigar. One should rather say, perhaps, like the butt of a firework, for the light was of many colours and some complexity, broken up by many mirrors and dancing on many gilt and gaily-coloured cakes and sweetmeats. Against this one fiery glass were glued the noses of many gutter-snipes, for the chocolates were all wrapped in those red and gold and green metallic colours which are almost better than chocolate itself; and the huge white wedding-cake in the window was somehow at once remote and satisfying, just as if the whole North Pole were good to eat. Such rainbow provocations could naturally collect the youth of the neighbourhood up to the ages of ten or twelve. But this corner was also attractive to youth at a later stage; and a young man, not less than twenty-four, was staring into the same shop window. To him, also, the shop was of fiery charm, but this attraction was not wholly to be explained by chocolates; which, however, he was far from despising.

He was a tall, burly, red-haired young man, with a resolute face but a listless manner. He carried under his arm a flat, grey portfolio of black-and-white sketches which he had sold with more or less success to publishers ever since his uncle (who was an admiral) had disinherited him for Socialism, because of a lecture which he had delivered against that economic theory. His name was John Turnbull Angus.

Entering at last, he walked through the confectioner's shop into the back room, which was a sort of pastry-

cook restaurant, merely raising his hat to the young
lady who was serving there. She was a dark, elegant,
alert girl in black, with a high colour and very quick,
dark eyes; and after the ordinary interval she followed
him into the inner room to take his order.

His order was evidently a usual one. 'I want, please,'
he said with precision, 'one halfpenny bun and a small
cup of black coffee.' An instant before the girl could
turn away he added, 'Also, I want you to marry me.'

The young lady of the shop stiffened suddenly, and
said: 'Those are jokes I don't allow.'

The red-haired young man lifted grey eyes of an
unexpected gravity.

'Really and truly,' he said, 'it's as serious—as serious
as the halfpenny bun. It is expensive, like the bun; one
pays for it. It is indigestible, like the bun. It hurts.'

The dark young lady had never taken her dark eyes
off him, but seemed to be studying him with almost
tragic exactitude. At the end of her scrutiny she had
something like the shadow of a smile, and she sat down
in a chair.

'Don't you think,' observed Angus, absently, 'that it's
rather cruel to eat these halfpenny buns? They might
grow up into penny buns. I shall give up these brutal
sports when we are married.'

The dark young lady rose from her chair and walked
to the window, evidently in a state of strong but not un-
sympathetic cogitation. When at last she swung round
again with an air of resolution, she was bewildered to
observe that the young man was carefully laying out on
the table various objects from the shop-window. They
included a pyramid of highly coloured sweets, several
plates of sandwiches, and the two decanters containing
that mysterious port and sherry which are peculiar to
pastry-cooks. In the middle of this neat arrangement

he had carefully let down the enormous load of white sugared cake which had been the huge ornament of the window.

'What on earth are you doing?' she asked.

'Duty, my dear Laura,' he began.

'Oh, for the Lord's sake, stop a minute,' she cried, 'and don't talk to me in that way. I mean what is all that?'

'A ceremonial meal, Miss Hope.'

'And what is *that*?' she asked impatiently, pointing to the mountain of sugar.

'The wedding-cake, Mrs. Angus,' he said

The girl marched to that article, removed it with some clatter, and put it back in the shop-window; she then returned, and, putting her elegant elbows on the table, regarded the young man not unfavourably, but with considerable exasperation.

'You don't give me any time to think,' she said.

'I'm not such a fool,' he answered; 'that's my Christian humility.'

She was still looking at him; but she had grown considerably graver behind the smile.

'Mr. Angus,' she said steadily, 'before there is a minute more of this nonsense I must tell you something about myself as shortly as I can.'

'Delighted,' replied Angus gravely. 'You might tell me something about myself, too, while you are about it.'

'Oh, do hold your tongue and listen,' she said. 'It's nothing that I'm ashamed of, and it isn't even anything that I'm specially sorry about. But what would you say if there were something that is no business of mine and yet is my nightmare?'

'In that case,' said the man seriously, 'I should suggest that you bring back the cake.'

'Well, you must listen to the story first,' said Laura.

persistently. 'To begin with, I must tell you that my father owned the inn called the "Red Fish" at Ludbury, and I used to serve people in the bar.'

'I have often wondered,' he said, 'why there was a kind of a Christian air about this one confectioner's shop.'

'Ludbury is a sleepy, grassy little hole in the Eastern Counties, and the only kind of people who ever came to the "Red Fish" were occasional commercial travellers, and for the rest, the most awful people you can see, only you've never seen them. I mean little, loungy men, who had just enough to live on, and had nothing to do but lean about in bar-rooms and bet on horses, in bad clothes that were just too good for them. Even these wretched young rotters were not very common at our house; but there were two of them that were a lot too common—common in every sort of way. They both lived on money of their own, and were wearisomely idle and over-dressed. But yet I was a bit sorry for them, because I half believe they slunk into our little empty bar because each of them had a slight deformity; the sort of thing that some yokels laugh at. It wasn't exactly a deformity either; it was more an oddity. One of them was a surprisingly small man, something like a dwarf, or at least like a jockey. He was not at all jockeyish to look at, though, he had a round black head and a well-trimmed black beard, bright eyes like a bird's; he jingled money in his pockets; he jangled a great gold watch chain; and he never turned up except dressed just too much like a gentleman to be one. He was no fool, though, though a futile idler; he was curiously clever at all kinds of things that couldn't be the slightest use; a sort of impromptu conjuring; making fifteen matches set fire to each other like a regular firework; or cutting a banana or some such thing into a dancing doll. His name was Isidore Smythe; and I can see him still, with his little dark face, just coming up to the counter, making a jumping kangaroo out of five cigars.

'The other fellow was more silent and more ordinary; but somehow he alarmed me much more than poor little Smythe. He was very tall and slight, and light-haired; his nose had a high bridge, and he might almost have been handsome in a spectral sort of way; but he had one of the most appalling squints I have ever seen or heard of. When he looked straight at you, you didn't know where you were yourself, let alone what he was looking at. I fancy this sort of disfigurement embittered the poor chap a little; for while Smythe was ready to show off his monkey tricks anywhere, James Welkin (that was the squinting man's name) never did anything except soak in our bar parlour, and go for great walks by himself in the flat, grey country all round. All the same, I think Smythe, too, was a little sensitive about being so small, though he carried it off more smartly. And so it was that I was really puzzled, as well as startled, and very sorry, when they both offered to marry me in the same week.

'Well, I did what I've since thought was perhaps a silly thing. But, after all, these freaks were my friends in a way; and I had a horror of their thinking I refused them for the real reason, which was that they were so impossibly ugly. So I made up some gas of another sort, about never meaning to marry anyone who hadn't carved his way in the world. I said it was a point of principle with me not to live on money that was just inherited like theirs. Two days after I had talked in this well-meaning sort of way, the whole trouble began. The first thing I heard was that both of them had gone off to seek their fortunes, as if they were in some silly fairy tale.

'Well, I've never seen either of them from that day to this. But I've had two letters from the little man called Smythe, and really they were rather exciting.'

'Ever heard of the other man?' asked Angus.

'No, he never wrote,' said the girl, after an instant's hesitation. 'Smythe's first letter was simply to say that he had started out walking with Welkin to London; but Welkin was such a good walker that the little man dropped out of it, and took a rest by the roadside. He happened to be picked up by some travelling show, and, partly because he was nearly a dwarf, and partly because he was really a clever little wretch, he got on quite well in the show business, and was soon sent up to the Aquarium, to do some tricks that I forgot. That was his first letter. His second was much more of a startler, and I only got it last week.'

The man called Angus emptied his coffee-cup and regarded her with mild and patient eyes. Her own mouth took a slight twist of laughter as she resumed: 'I suppose you've seen on the hoardings all about this "Smythe's Silent Service"? Or you must be the only person that hasn't. Oh, I don't know much about it, it's some clockwork invention for doing all the housework by machinery. You know the sort of thing: 'Press a button —A Butler who Never Drinks." "Turn a handle—Ten Housemaids who Never Flirt." You must have seen the advertisements. Well, whatever these machines are, they are making pots of money; and they are making it all for that little imp whom I knew down in Ludbury. I can't help feeling pleased the poor little chap has fallen on his feet; but the plain fact is, I'm in terror of his turning up any minute and telling me he's carved his way in the world—as he certainly has.'

'And the other man?' repeated Angus with a sort of obstinate quietude.

Laura Hope got to her feet suddenly. 'My friend,' she said: 'I think you are a witch. Yes, you are quite right. I have not seen a line of the other man's writing; and I have no more notion than the dead of what or where he is. But it is of him that I am frightened. It is he who is all about my path. It is he who has half driven me mad. Indeed, I think he has driven me mad; for I have felt him where he could not have been, and I have heard his voice when he could not have spoken.'

'Well, my dear,' said the young man, cheerfully, 'if he were Satan himself, he is done for now you have told somebody. One goes mad all alone, old girl. But when was it you fancied you felt and heard our squinting friend?'

'I heard James Welkin laugh as plainly as I hear you speak,' said the girl, steadily. 'There was nobody there, for I stood just outside the shop at the corner, and could see down both streets at once. I had forgotten how he laughed, though his laugh was as odd as his squint. I had not thought of him for nearly a year. But it's a solemn truth that a few seconds later the first letter came from his rival.'

'Did you ever make the spectre speak or squeak, or anything?' asked Angus, with some interest.

Laura suddenly shuddered, and then said with an unshaken voice: 'Yes. Just when I had finished reading the second letter from Isidore Smythe announcing his success, just then, I heard Welkin say: "He shan't have you, though." It was quite plain, as if he were in the room. It is awful; I think I must be mad.'

'If you really were mad,' said the young man, 'you would think you must be sane. But certainly there seems to me to be something a little rum about this unseen gentleman. Two heads are better than one—I spare you allusions to any other organs—and really, if you would allow me, as a sturdy, practical man, to bring back the wedding-cake out of the window——'

Even as he spoke, there was a sort of steely shriek in the street outside, and a small motor, driven at devilish speed, shot up to the door of the shop and stuck there. In the same flash of time a small man in a shiny top hat stood stamping in the outer room.

Angus, who had hitherto maintained hilarious ease from motives of mental hygiene, revealed the strain of his soul by striding abruptly out of the inner room and confronting the new-comer. A glance at him was quite sufficient to confirm the savage guesswork of a man in love. This very dapper but dwarfish figure, with the spike of black beard carried insolently forward, the clever unrestful eyes, the neat but very nervous fingers, could be none other than the man just described to him: Isidore Smythe, who made dolls out of banana skins and matchboxes: Isidore Smythe, who made millions out of undrinking butlers and unflirting house-maids of metal. For a moment the two men, instinctively understanding each other's air of possession, looked at each other with that curious cold generosity which is the soul of rivalry.

Mr. Smythe, however, made no allusion to the ultimate ground of their antagonism, but said simply and explosively: 'Has Miss Hope seen that thing on the window?'

'On the window?' repeated the staring Angus.

'There's no time to explain other things,' said the small millionaire shortly. 'There's some tomfoolery going on here that has to be investigated.'

He pointed his polished walking-stick at the window, recently depleted by the bridal preparations of Mr. Angus; and that gentleman was astonished to see along the front of the glass a long strip of paper pasted, which had certainly not been on the window when he had looked through it some time before. Following the energetic Smythe outside into the street, he found that some yard and a half of stamp paper had been carefully gummed along the glass outside, and on this was written in straggly characters: 'If you marry Smythe, he will die.'

'Laura,' said Angus, putting his big red head into the shop, 'you're not mad.'

'It's the writing of that fellow Welkin,' said Smythe gruffly. 'I haven't seen him for years, but he's always bothering me. Five times in the last fortnight he's had threatening letters left at my flat, and I can't even find out who leaves them, let alone if it is Welkin himself. The porter of the flats swears that no suspicious characters have been seen, and here he has pasted up a sort of dado on a public shop window, while the people in the shop——'

'Quite so,' said Angus modestly, 'while the people in the shop were having tea. Well, sir, I can assure you I appreciate your common sense in dealing so directly with the matter. We can talk about other things afterwards. The fellow cannot be very far off yet, for I swear there was no paper there when I went last to the window, ten or fifteen minutes ago. On the other hand, he's too far off to be chased, as we don't even know the direction. If you'll take my advice, Mr. Smythe, you'll put this at once in the hands of some energetic inquiry man, private rather than public. I know an extremely clever fellow, who has set up in business five minutes from here in your car. His name's Flambeau, and though his youth was a bit stormy, he's a strictly honest man now, and his brains are worth money. He lives in Lucknow Mansions, Hampstead.'

'That is odd,' said the little man, arching his black

eyebrows. 'I live myself in Himalaya Mansions round the corner. Perhaps you might care to come with me; I can go to my rooms and sort out these queer Welkin documents, while you run round and get your friend the detective.'

'You are very good,' said Angus politely. 'Well, the sooner we act the better.'

Both men, with a queer kind of impromptu fairness, took the same sort of formal farewell of the lady, and both jumped into the brisk little car. As Smythe took the wheel and they turned the great corner of the street, Angus was amused to see a gigantesque poster of 'Smythe's Silent Service,' with a picture of a huge headless iron doll, carrying a saucepan with the legend, 'A Cook Who is Never Cross.'

'I use them in my own flat,' said the little black-bearded man, laughing, 'partly for advertisement, and partly for real convenience. Honestly, and all above board, those big clockwork dolls of mine do bring you coals or claret or a time-table quicker than any live servants I've ever known, if you know which knob to press. But I'll never deny, between ourselves, that such servants have their disadvantages, too.'

'Indeed' said Angus; 'is there something they can't do?'

'Yes,' replied Smythe coolly; 'they can't tell me who left those threatening letters at my flat.'

The man's motor was small and swift like himself; in fact, like his domestic service, it was of his own invention. If he was an advertising quack, he was one who believed in his own wares. The sense of something tiny and flying was accentuated as they swept up long white curves of road in the dead but open daylight of evening. Soon the white curves came sharper and dizzier; they were upon ascending spirals, as they say in the modern religions. For, indeed, they were cresting a corner of London which is almost as precipitous as Edinburgh, if not quite so picturesque. Terrace rose above terrace, and the special tower of flats they sought, rose above them all to almost Egyptian height, gilt by the level sunset. The change, as they turned the corner and entered the crescent known as Himalaya Mansions, was as abrupt as the opening of a window; for they found that pile of flats sitting above London as above a green sea of slate. Opposite to the mansions, on the other side of the gravel crescent, was a bushy enclosure more like a steep hedge or dyke than a garden, and some way below that ran a strip of artificial water, a sort of canal, like the moat of that embowered fortress. As the car swept round the crescent it passed, at one corner, the stray stall of a man selling chestnuts; and right away at the other end of the curve, Angus could see a dim blue policeman walking slowly. These were the only human shapes in that high suburban solitude; but he had an irrational sense that they expressed the speechless poetry of London. He felt as if they were figures in a story.

The little car shot up to the right house like a bullet, and shot out its owner like a bomb shell. He was immediately inquiring of a tall commissionaire in shining braid, and a short porter in shirt sleeves, whether anybody or anything had been seeking his apartments. He was assured that nobody and nothing had passed these officials since his last inquiries; whereupon he and the slightly bewildered Angus were shot up in the lift like a rocket, till they reached the top floor.

'Just come in for a minute,' said the breathless Smythe. 'I want to show you those Welkin letters. Then you might run round the corner and fetch your friend.' He pressed a button concealed in the wall, and the door opened of itself.

It opened on a long, commodious ante-room, of which the only arresting features, ordinarily speaking, were the rows of tall half-human mechanical figures that stood up on both sides like tailors' dummies. Like tailors' dummies they were headless; and like tailors' dummies they had a handsome unnecessary humpiness in the shoulders, and a pigeon-breasted protuberance of chest; but barring this, they were not much more like a human figure than any automatic machine at a station that is about the human height. They had two great hooks like arms, for carrying trays; and they were painted pea-green, or vermilion, or black for convenience of distinction; in every other way they were only automatic machines and nobody would have looked twice at them. On this occasion, at least, nobody did. For between the two rows of these domestic dummies lay something more interesting than most of the mechanics of the world. It was a white, tattered scrap of paper scrawled with red ink; and the agile inventor had snatched it up almost as soon as the door flew open. He handed it to Angus without a word. The red ink on it actually was not dry, and the message ran: 'If you have been to see her to-day, I shall kill you.'

There was a short silence, and then Isidore Smythe said quietly: 'Would you like a little whisky? I rather feel as if I should.'

'Thank you; I should like a little Flambeau,' said Angus, gloomily. 'This business seems to me to be getting rather grave. I'm going round at once to fetch him.'

'Right you are,' said the other, with admirable cheerfulness. 'Bring him round here as quick as you can.'

But as Angus closed the front door behind him he saw Smythe push back a button, and one of the clockwork images glided from its place and slid along a groove in the floor carrying a tray with syphon and decanter. There did seem something a trifle weird about leaving the little man alone among those dead servants, who were coming to life as the door closed.

Six steps down from Smythe's landing the man in shirt sleeves was doing something with a pail. Angus stopped to extract a promise, fortified with a prospective bribe, that he would remain in that place until the return with the detective, and would keep count of any kind of stranger coming up those stairs. Dashing down to the front hall he then laid similar charges of vigilance on the commissionaire at the front door, from whom he learned the simplifying circumstance that there was no back door. Not content with this, he captured the floating policeman and induced him to stand opposite the entrance and watch it; and finally paused an instant for a pennyworth of chestnuts, and an inquiry as to the probable length of the merchant's stay in the neighbourhood.

The chestnut seller, turning up the collar of his coat, told him he should probably be moving shortly, as he thought it was going to snow. Indeed, the evening was growing grey and bitter, but Angus, with all his eloquence, proceeded to nail the chestnut man to his post.

'Keep yourself warm on your own chestnuts,' he said earnestly. 'Eat up your whole stock; I'll make it worth your while. I'll give you a sovereign if you'll wait here till I come back, and then tell me whether any man, woman, or child has gone into that house where the commissionaire is standing.'

He then walked away smartly, with a last look at the besieged tower.

'I've made a ring round that room, anyhow,' he said. 'They can't all four of them be Mr. Welkin's accomplices.'

Lucknow Mansions were, so to speak, on a lower platform of that hill of houses, of which Himalaya Mansions might be called the peak. Mr. Flambeau's semi-official flat was on the ground floor, and presented in every way a marked contrast to the American machinery and cold hotel-like luxury of the flat of the Silent Service. Flambeau, who was a friend of Angus, received him in a rococo artistic den behind his office, of which the ornaments were sabres, harque-buses, Eastern curiosities, flasks of Italian wine, savage cooking-pots, a plumy Persian cat, and a small dusty-looking Roman Catholic priest, who looked particularly out of place.

'This is my friend, Father Brown,' said Flambeau. 'I've often wanted you to meet him. Splendid weather, this; a little cold for Southerners like me.'

'Yes, I think it will keep clear,' said Angus, sitting down on a violet-striped Eastern ottoman.

'No,' said the priest quietly; 'it has begun to snow.'

And indeed, as he spoke, the first few flakes, foreseen by the man of chestnuts, began to drift across the darkening window-pane.

'Well,' said Angus heavily. 'I'm afraid I've come on business, and rather jumpy business at that. The fact is, Flambeau, within a stone's throw of your house is a fellow who badly wants your help; he's perpetually being haunted and threatened by an invisible enemy— a scoundrel whom nobody has even seen.' As Angus proceeded to tell the whole tale of Smythe and Welkin beginning with Laura's story, and going on with his own, the supernatural laugh at the corner of two empty streets, the strange distinct words spoken in an empty room, Flambeau grew more and more vividly concerned, and the little priest seemed to be left out of it, like a piece of furniture. When it came to the scribbled stamp-paper pasted on the window, Flambeau rose, seeming to fill the room with his huge shoulders.

'If you don't mind,' he said, 'I think you had better tell me the rest on the nearest road to this man's house. It strikes me, somehow, that there is no time to be lost.'

'Delighted,' said Angus, rising also, 'though he's safe enough for the present, for I've set four men to watch the only hole to his burrow.'

They turned out into the street, the small priest trundling after them with the docility of a small dog. He merely said, in a cheerful way, like one making conversation: 'How quick the snow gets thick on the ground.'

As they threaded the steep side streets already powdered with silver, Angus finished his story; and by the time they reached the crescent with the towering flats, he had leisure to turn his attention to the four sentinels. The chestnut seller, both before and after receiving a sovereign, swore stubbornly that he had watched the door and seen no visitor enter. The policeman was even more emphatic. He said he had had experience of crooks of all kinds, in top hats and in rags; he wasn't so green as to expect suspicious characters to look suspicious; he looked out for anybody, and, so help him, there had been nobody. And when all three men gathered round the gilded commissionaire, who still stood smiling astride of the porch, the verdict was more final still.

'I've got a right to ask any man, duke or dustman, what he wants in these flats,' said the genial and gold-laced giant, 'and I'll swear there's been nobody to ask since this gentleman went away.'

The unimportant Father Brown, who stood back, looking modestly at the pavement, here ventured to say meekly: 'Has nobody been up and down stairs, then, since the snow began to fall? It began while we were all round at Flambeau's.'

'Nobody's been in here, sir, you can take it from me,' said the official, with beaming authority.

'Then I wonder what that is?' said the priest, and stared at the ground blankly like a fish.

The others all looked down also; and Flambeau used a fierce exclamation and a French gesture. For it was unquestionably true that down the middle of the entrance guarded by the man in gold lace, actually between the arrogant, stretched legs of that colossus, ran a stringy pattern of grey footprints stamped upon the white snow.

'God!' cried Angus involuntarily; 'the Invisible Man!'

Without another word he turned and dashed up the stairs, with Flambeau following; but Father Brown still stood looking about him in the snow-clad street as if he had lost interest in his query.

Flambeau was plainly in a mood to break down the door with his big shoulder; but the Scotsman, with more reason, if less intuition, fumbled about on the frame of the door till he found the invisible button; and the door swung slowly open.

It showed substantially the same serried interior; the hall had grown darker, though it was still struck here and there with the last crimson shafts of sunset, and one or two of the headless machines had been moved from their places for this or that purpose, and stood here and there about the twilit place. The green and red of their coats were all darkened in the dusk, and their likeness to human shapes slightly increased by their very shapelessness. But in the middle of them all, exactly where the paper with the red ink had lain, there lay something that looked very like red ink spilled out of its bottle. But it was not red ink.

With a French combination of reason and violence Flambeau simply said 'Murder!' and, plunging into the flat, had explored every corner and cupboard of it in five minutes. But if he expected to find a corpse he found none. Isidore Smythe simply was not in the place, either dead or alive. After the most tearing search the two men met each other in the outer hall with streaming faces and staring eyes. 'My friend,' said Flambeau, talking French in his excitement, 'not only is your murderer invisible, but he makes invisible also the murdered man.'

Angus looked round at the dim room full of dummies, and in some Celtic corner of his Scotch soul a shudder started. One of the life-size dolls stood immediately overshadowing the blood stain, summoned, perhaps, by the slain man an instant before he fell. One of the high-shouldered hooks that served the thing for arms, was a little lifted and Angus had suddenly the horrid fancy that poor Smythe's own iron child had struck him down. Matter had rebelled, and these machines had killed their master. But even so, what had they done with him?

'Eaten him?' said the nightmare at his ear; and he sickened for an instant at the idea of rent, human remains absorbed and crushed into all the acephalous clockwork.

He recovered his mental health by an emphatic effort, and said to Flambeau: 'Well, there it is. The poor fellow has evaporated like a cloud and left a red streak on the floor. The tale does not belong to this world.'

'There is only one thing to be done,' said Flambeau, 'whether it belongs to this world or the other, I must go down and talk to my friend.'

They descended, passing the man with the pail, who again asseverated that he had let no intruder pass, down to the commissionaire and the hovering chestnut man, who rightly reasserted their own watchfulness. But when Angus looked round for his fourth confirmation he could not see it, and called out with some nervousness: 'Where is the policeman?'

'I beg your pardon,' said Father Brown; 'that is my fault. I just sent him down the road to investigate something—that I just thought worth investigating.'

'Well, we want him back pretty soon,' said Angus abruptly, 'for the wretched man upstairs has not only been murdered, but wiped out.'

'How?' asked the priest.

'Father,' said Flambeau, after a pause, 'upon my soul I believe it is more in your department than mine. No friend or foe has entered the house, but Smythe is gone, as if stolen by the fairies. If that is not supernatural, I——'

As he spoke they were all checked by an unusual sight; the big blue policeman came round the corner of the crescent running. He came straight up to Brown.

'You're right, sir,' he panted, 'they've just found poor Mr. Smythe's body in the canal down below.'

Angus put his hand wildly to his head. 'Did he run down and drown himself?' he asked.

'He never came down, I'll swear,' said the constable, 'and he wasn't drowned either, for he died of a great stab over the heart.'

'And yet you saw no one enter?' said Flambeau in a grave voice.

'Let us walk down the road a little,' said the priest.

As they reached the other end of the crescent he observed abruptly: 'Stupid of me! I forgot to ask the policeman something. I wonder if they found a light brown sack.'

'Why a light brown sack?' asked Angus, astonished.

'Because if it was any other coloured sack, the case must begin over again,' said Father Brown; 'but if it was a light brown sack, why, the case is finished.'

'I am pleased to hear it,' said Angus with hearty irony. 'It hasn't begun, so far as I am concerned.'

'You must tell us all about it,' said Flambeau, with a strange heavy simplicity, like a child.

Unconsciously they were walking with quickening steps down the long sweep of road on the other side of the high crescent, Father Brown leading briskly, though in silence. At last he said with an almost touching vagueness: 'Well, I'm afraid you'll think it so prosy. We always begin at the abstract end of things, and you can't begin this story anywhere else.

'Have you ever noticed this—that people never answer what you say? They answer what you mean—or what they think you mean. Suppose one lady says to another in a country house, "Is anybody staying with you?" the lady doesn't answer "Yes; the butler, the three footmen, the parlour-maid, and so on," though the parlour-maid may be in the room, or the butler behind her chair. She says: "There is *nobody* staying with us," meaning nobody of the sort you mean. But suppose a doctor inquiring into an epidemic asks, "Who is staying in the house?" then the lady will remember the butler, the parlour-maid, and the rest. All language is used like that; you never get a question answered literally, even when you get it answered truly. When those four quite honest men said that no man had gone into the Mansions, they did not really mean that *no man* had gone into them. They meant no man whom they could suspect of being your man. A man did go into the house, and did come out of it, but they never noticed him.'

'An invisible man?' inquired Angus, raising his red eyebrows.

'A mentally invisible man,' said Father Brown.

A minute or two after he resumed in the same unassuming voice, like a man thinking his way. 'Of course, you can't think of such a man, until you do think of him. That's where his cleverness comes in. But I came to think of him through two or three little things in the tale Mr. Angus told us. First, there was the fact that this Welkin went for long walks. And then there was the vast lot of stamp paper on the window. And then, most of all, there were the two things the young lady said—things that couldn't be true. Don't get annoyed,' he added hastily, noting a sudden movement of the Scotsman's head; 'she thought they were true all right, but they couldn't be true. A person *can't* be quite alone in a street a second before she receives a letter. She can't be quite alone in a street when she starts reading a letter just received. There must be somebody pretty near her; he must be mentally invisible.'

'Why must there be somebody near her?' asked Angus.

'Because,' said Father Brown: 'barring carrier-pigeons, somebody must have brought her the letter.'

'Do you really mean to say,' asked Flambeau, with energy, 'that Welkin carried his rival's letters to his lady?'

'Yes,' said the priest. 'Welkin carried his rival's letters to his lady. You see, he had to.'

'Oh, I can't stand much more of this,' exploded Flambeau. 'Who is this fellow? What does he look like. What is the usual get-up of a mentally invisible man?'

'He is dressed rather handsomely in red, blue and

gold,' replied the priest promptly with decision, 'and in this striking, and even showy costume he entered Himalaya Mansions under eight human eyes; he killed Smythe in cold blood, and came down into the street again carrying the dead body in his arms——'

'Reverend sir,' cried Angus, standing still, 'are you raving mad, or am I?'

'You are not mad,' said Brown, 'only a little unobservant. You have not noticed such a man as this, for example.'

He took three quick strides forward, and put his hand on the shoulder of an ordinary passing postman who had bustled by them unnoticed under the shade of the trees.

'Nobody ever notices postmen, somehow,' he said thoughtfully; 'yet they have passions like other men, and even carry large bags where a small corpse can be stowed quite easily.'

The postman, instead of turning naturally, had ducked and tumbled against the garden fence. He was a lean fair-bearded man of very ordinary appearance, but as he turned an alarmed face over his shoulder, all three men were fixed with an almost fiendish squint.

Flambeau went back to his sabres, purple rugs and Persian cat, having many things to attend to. John Turnbull Angus went back to the lady at the shop, with whom that imprudent young man contrives to be extremely comfortable. But Father Brown walked those snow-covered hills under the stars for many hours with a murderer, and what they said to each other will never be known.

The Honour of Israel Gow

A STORMY evening of olive and silver was closing in, as Father Brown, wrapped in a grey Scotch plaid, came to the end of a grey Scotch valley and beheld the strange castle of Glengyle. It stopped one end of the glen or hollow like a blind alley; and it looked like the end of the world. Rising in steep roofs and spires of seagreen slate in the manner of the old French-Scottish châteaux, it reminded an Englishman of the sinister steeple-hats of witches in fairy tales; and the pine woods that rocked round the green turrets looked, by comparison, as black as numberless flocks of ravens. This note of a dreamy, almost a sleepy devilry, was no mere fancy from the landscape. For there did rest on the place one of those clouds of pride and madness and mysterious sorrow which lie more heavily on the noble houses of Scotland than on any other of the children of men. For Scotland has a double dose of the poison called heredity; the sense of blood in the aristocrat, and the sense of doom in the Calvinist.

The priest had snatched a day from his business at Glasgow to meet his friend Flambeau, the amateur detective, who was at Glengyle Castle with another more formal officer investigating the life and death of the late Earl of Glengyle. That mysterious person was the last representative of a race whose valour, insanity, and violent cunning had made them terrible even among the sinister nobility of their nation in the sixteenth century. None were deeper in that labyrinthine ambition, in chamber within chamber of that palace of lies that was built up around Mary Queen of Scots.

95

The rhyme in the country-side attested the motive and the result of their machinations candidly:

> As green sap to the simmer trees
> Is red gold to the Ogilvies.

For many centuries there had never been a decent lord in Glengyle Castle; and with the Victorian era one would have thought that all eccentricities were exhausted. The last Glengyle, however, satisfied his tribal tradition by doing the only thing that was left for him to do; he disappeared. I do not mean that he went abroad; by all accounts he was still in the castle, if he was anywhere. But though his name was in the church register and the big red Peerage, nobody ever saw him under the sun.

If anyone saw him it was a solitary man-servant, something between a groom and a gardener. He was so deaf that the more business-like assumed him to be dumb; while the more penetrating declared him to be half-witted. A gaunt, red-haired labourer, with a dogged jaw and chin, but quite black blue eyes, he went by the name of Israel Gow, and was the one silent servant on that deserted estate. But the energy with which he dug potatoes, and the regularity with which he disappeared into the kitchen gave people an impression that he was providing for the meals of a superior, and that the strange earl was still concealed in the castle. If society needed any further proof that he was there, the servant persistently asserted that he was not at home. One morning the provost and the minister (for the Glengyles were Presbyterian) were summoned to the castle. There they found that the gardener, groom and cook had added to his many professions that of an undertaker, and had nailed up his noble master in a coffin. With how much or how little further inquiry this odd fact was passed, did not as yet very plainly appear; for the thing had never been legally investigated till Flambeau had gone north two or three days before. By then the body of Lord Glengyle (if it was the body) had lain for some time in the little churchyard on the hill.

As Father Brown passed through the dim garden and came under the shadow of the château, the clouds were thick and the whole air damp and thundery. Against the last stripe of the green-gold sunset he saw a black human silhouette; a man in a chimney-pot hat, with a big spade over his shoulder. The combination was queerly suggestive of a sexton; but when Brown remembered the deaf servant who dug potatoes, he thought it natural enough. He knew something of the Scotch peasant; he knew the respectability which might well feel it necessary to wear 'blacks' for an official inquiry; he knew also the economy that would not lose an hour's digging for that. Even the man's start and suspicious stare as the priest went by were consonant enough with the vigilance and jealousy of such a type.

The great door was opened by Flambeau himself, who had with him a lean man with iron-grey hair and papers in his hand: Inspector Craven from Scotland Yard. The entrance hall was mostly stripped and empty; but the pale, sneering faces of one or two of the wicked Ogilvies looked down out of the black periwigs and blackening canvas.

Following them into an inner room, Father Brown found that the allies had been seated at a long oak table, of which their end was covered with scribbled papers, flanked with whisky and cigars. Through the whole of its remaining length it was occupied by detached objects arranged at intervals; objects about as inexplicable as any objects could be. One looked like a small heap of glittering broken glass. Another looked like a high heap of brown dust. A third appeared to be a plain stick of wood.

'You seem to have a sort of geological museum here,' he said, as he sat down, jerking his head briefly in the direction of the brown dust and the crystalline fragments.

'Not a geological museum,' replied Flambeau; 'say a psychological museum.'

'Oh, for the Lord's sake,' cried the police detective, laughing, 'don't let's begin with such long words.'

'Don't you know what psychology means?' asked Flambeau with friendly surprise. 'Psychology means being off your chump.'

'Still I hardly follow,' replied the official.

'Well,' said Flambeau, with decision; 'I mean that we've only found out one thing about Lord Glengyle. He was a maniac.'

The black silhouette of Gow with his top hat and spade passed the window, dimly outlined against the darkening sky. Father Brown stared passively at it and answered:

'I can understand there must have been something odd about the man, or he wouldn't have buried himself alive—nor been in such a hurry to bury himself dead. But what makes you think it was lunacy?'

'Well,' said Flambeau; 'you just listen to the list of things Mr. Craven has found in the house.'

'We must get a candle,' said Craven, suddenly. 'A storm is getting up, and it's too dark to read.'

'Have you found any candles,' asked Brown smiling, 'among your oddities?'

Flambeau raised a grave face, and fixed his dark eyes on his friend.

'That is curious, too,' he said. 'Twenty-five candles, and not a trace of a candlestick.'

In the rapidly darkening room and rapidly rising

wind, Brown went along the table to where a bundle of wax candles lay among the other scrappy exhibits. As he did so he bent accidentally over the heap of red-brown dust; and a sharp sneeze cracked the silence.

'Hullo!' he said; 'snuff!'

He took one of the candles, lit it carefully, came back and stuck it in the neck of the whisky bottle. The unrestful night air, blowing through the crazy window, waved the long flame like a banner. And on every side of the castle they could hear the miles and miles of black pine wood seething like a black sea around a rock.

'I will read the inventory,' began Craven gravely, picking up one of the papers, 'the inventory of what we found loose and unexplained in the castle. You are to understand that the place generally was dismantled and neglected; but one or two rooms had plainly been inhabited in a simple but not squalid style by somebody; somebody who was not the servant Gow. The list is as follows:

'First item. A very considerable hoard of precious stones, nearly all diamonds, and all of them loose, without any setting whatever. Of course, it is natural that the Ogilvies should have family jewels; but those are exactly the jewels that are almost aways set in particular articles of ornament. The Ogilvies would seem to have kept theirs loose in their pockets, like coppers.

'Second item. Heaps and heaps of loose snuff, not kept in a horn, or even a pouch, but lying in heaps on the mantelpieces, on the sideboard, on the piano, anywhere. It looks as if the old gentleman would not take the trouble to look in a pocket or lift a lid.

'Third item. Here and there about the house curious little heaps of minute pieces of metal, some like steel springs and some in the form of microscopic wheels. As if they had gutted some mechanical toy.

'Fourth item. The wax candles, which have to be stuck in bottle necks because there is nothing else to stick them in. Now I wish you to note how very much queerer all this is than anything we anticipated. For the central riddle we are prepared; we have all seen at a glance that there was something wrong about the last earl. We have come here to find out whether he really lived here, whether he really died here, whether that red-haired scarecrow who did his burying had anything to do with his dying. But suppose the worst in all this, the most lurid or melodramatic solution you like. Suppose the servant really killed the master, or suppose the master isn't really dead, or suppose the master is dressed up as the servant, or suppose the servant is buried for the master; invent what Wilkie Collins's tragedy you like, and you still have not explained a candle without a candlestick, or why an elderly gentleman of good family should habitually spill snuff on the piano. The core of the tale we could imagine; it is the fringes that are mysterious. By no stretch of fancy can the human mind connect together snuff and diamonds and wax and loose clockwork.'

'I think I see the connexion,' said the priest. 'This Glengyle was mad against the French Revolution. He was an enthusiast for the *ancien régime*, and was trying to re-enact literally the family life of the last Bourbons. He had snuff because it was the eighteenth century luxury; wax candles, because they were the eighteenth century lighting; the mechanical bits of iron represent the locksmith hobby of Louis XVI; the diamonds are for the Diamond Necklace of Marie Antoinette.'

Both the other men were staring at him with round eyes. 'What a perfectly extraordinary notion!' cried Flambeau. 'Do you really think that is the truth?'

'I am perfectly sure it isn't,' answered Father Brown,

'only you said that nobody could connect snuff and diamonds and clockwork and candles. I give you that connexion off-hand. The real truth, I am very sure, lies deeper.'

He paused a moment and listened to the wailing of the wind in the turrets. Then he said: 'The late Earl of Glengyle was a thief. He lived a second and darker life as a desperate house-breaker. He did not have any candlesticks because he only used these candles cut short in the lantern he carried. The snuff he employed as the fiercest French criminals have used pepper: to fling it suddenly in dense masses in the face of a captor or pursuer. But the final proof is in the curious coincidence of the diamonds and the small steel wheels. Surely that makes everything plain to you? Diamonds and small steel wheels are the only two instruments with which you can cut out a pane of glass.'

The bough of a broken pine tree lashed heavily in the blast against the window-pane behind them, as if in parody of a burglar, but they did not turn round. Their eyes were fastened on Father Brown.

'Diamonds and small wheels,' repeated Craven ruminating. 'Is that all that makes you think it the true explanation?'

'I don't think it the true explanation,' replied the priest placidly; 'but you said that nobody could connect the four things. The true tale, of course, is something much more humdrum. Glengyle had found, or thought he had found, precious stones on his estate. Somebody had bamboozled him with those loose brilliants, saying they were found in the castle caverns. The little wheels are some diamond-cutting affair. He had to do the thing very roughly and in a small way, with the help of a few shepherds or rude fellows on these hills. Snuff is the one great luxury of such Scotch shepherds; it's the one thing with which you can bribe them. They didn't have candlesticks because they didn't want them; they held the candles in their hands when they explored the caves.'

'Is that all?' asked Flambeau after a long pause. 'Have we got to the dull truth at last?'

'Oh, no,' said Father Brown.

As the wind died in the most distant pine woods with a long hoot as of mockery, Father Brown, with an utterly impassive face, went on:

'I only suggested that because you said one could not plausibly connect snuff with clockwork or candles with bright stones. Ten false philosophies will fit the universe; ten false theories will fit Glengyle Castle. But we want the real explanation of the castle and the universe. But are there no other exhibits?'

Craven laughed, and Flambeau rose smiling to his feet and strolled down the long table.

'Items five, six, seven, etc.,' he said, 'are certainly more varied than instructive. A curious collection, not of lead pencils, but of the lead out of lead pencils. A senseless stick of bamboo, with the top rather splintered. It might be the instrument of the crime. Only, there isn't any crime. The only other things are a few old missals and little Catholic pictures, which the Ogilvies kept, I suppose, from the Middle Ages—their family pride being stronger than their Puritanism. We only put them in the museum because they seem curiously cut about and defaced.'

The heady tempest without drove a dreadful wrack of clouds across Glengyle and threw the long room into darkness as Father Brown picked up the little illuminated pages to examine them. He spoke before the drift of darkness had passed; but it was the voice of an utterly new man.

'Mr. Craven,' said he, talking like a man ten years younger: 'you have got a legal warrant, haven't you, to go up and examine that grave? The sooner we do it the better, and get to the bottom of this horrible affair. If I were you I should start now.'

'Now,' repeated the astonished detective, 'and why now?'

'Because this is serious,' answered Brown; 'this is not spilt snuff or loose pebbles, that might be there for a hundred reasons. There is only one reason I know of for *this* being done; and the reason goes down to the roots of the world. These religious pictures are not just dirtied or torn or scrawled over, which might be done in idleness or bigotry, by children or by Protestants. These have been treated very carefully—and very queerly. In every place where the great ornamented name of God comes in the old illuminations it has been elaborately taken out. The only other thing that has been removed is the halo round the head of the Child Jesus. Therefore, I say, let us get our warrant and our spade and our hatchet, and go up and break open that coffin.'

'What *do* you mean?' demanded the London officer.

'I mean,' answered the little priest, and his voice seemed to rise slightly in the roar of the gale. 'I mean that the great devil of the universe may be sitting on the top tower of this castle at this moment, as big as a hundred elephants, and roaring like the Apocalypse. There is black magic somewhere at the bottom of this.'

'Black magic,' repeated Flambeau in a low voice, for he was too enlightened a man not to know of such things; 'but what can these other things mean?'

'Oh, something damnable, I suppose,' replied Brown impatiently. 'How should I know? How can I guess all their mazes down below? Perhaps you can make a torture out of snuff and bamboo. Perhaps lunatics lust after

wax and steel filings. Perhaps there is a maddening drug
made of lead pencils! Our shortest cut to the mystery is
up the hill to the grave.'

His comrades hardly knew that they had obeyed and
followed him till a blast of the night wind nearly flung
them on their faces in the garden. Nevertheless they had
obeyed him like automata; for Craven found a hatchet
in his hand, and the warrant in his pocket; Flambeau
was carrying the heavy spade of the strange gardener;
Father Brown was carrying the little gilt book from
which had been torn the name of God.

The path up the hill to the churchyard was crooked
but short; only under the stress of wind it seemed
laborious and long. Far as the eye could see, farther and
farther as they mounted the slope, were seas beyond seas
of pines, now all aslope one way under the wind. And
that universal gesture seemed as vain as it was vast,
as vain as if that wind were whistling about some un-
peopled and purposeless planet. Through all that infinite growth of grey-blue forests sang, shrill and high,
that ancient sorrow that is in the heart of all heathen
things. One could fancy that the voices from the under-
world of unfathomable foliage were cries of the lost and
wandering pagan gods: gods who had gone roaming in
that irrational forest, and who will never find their way
back to heaven.

'You see,' said Father Brown in low but easy tone,
'Scotch people before Scotland existed were a curious
lot. In fact, they're a curious lot still. But in the pre-
historic times I fancy they really worshipped demons.
That,' he added genially, 'is why they jumped at the
Puritan theology.'

'My friend,' said Flambeau, turning in a kind of fury,
'what does all that snuff mean?'

'My friend,' replied Brown, with equal seriousness,

'there is one mark of all genuine religions: materialism. Now, devil-worship is a perfectly genuine religion.'

They had come up on the grassy scalp of the hill, one of the few bald spots that stood clear of the crashing and roaring pine forest. A mean enclosure, partly timber and partly wire, rattled in the tempest to tell them the border of the graveyard. But by the time Inspector Craven had come to the corner of the grave, and Flambeau had planted his spade point downwards and leaned on it, they were both almost as shaken as the shaky wood and wire. At the foot of the grave grew great tall thistles, grey and silver in their decay. Once or twice, when a ball of thistledown broke under the breeze and flew past him, Craven jumped slightly as if it had been an arrow.

Flambeau drove the blade of his spade through the whistling grass into the wet clay below. Then he seemed to stop and lean on it as on a staff.

'Go on,' said the priest very gently. 'We are only trying to find the truth. What are you afraid of?'

'I am afraid of finding it,' said Flambeau.

The London detective spoke suddenly in a high crowing voice that was meant to be conversational and cheery. 'I wonder why he really did hide himself like that. Something nasty, I suppose; was he a leper?'

'Something worse than that,' said Flambeau.

'And what do you imagine,' asked the other, 'would be worse than a leper?'

'I don't imagine it,' said Flambeau.

He dug for some dreadful minutes in silence, and then said in a choked voice: 'I'm afraid of his not being the right shape.'

'Nor was that piece of paper, you know,' said Father Brown quietly, 'and we survived even that piece of paper.'

Flambeau dug on with a blind energy. But the tempest had shouldered away the choking grey clouds that clung to the hills like smoke and revealed grey fields of faint starlight before he cleared the shape of a rude timber coffin, and somehow tipped it up upon the turf. Craven stepped forward with his axe; a thistle-top touched him, and he flinched. Then he took a firmer stride, and hacked and wrenched with an energy like Flambeau's till the lid was torn off, and all that was there lay glimmering in the grey starlight.

'Bones,' said Craven; and then he added, 'but it is a man,' as if that were something unexpected.

'Is he,' asked Flambeau in a voice that went oddly up and down, 'is he all right?'

'Seems so,' said the officer huskily, bending over the obscure and decaying skeleton in the box. 'Wait a minute.'

A vast heave went over Flambeau's huge figure. 'And now I come to think of it,' he cried, 'why in the name of madness shouldn't he be all right? What is it gets hold of a man on these cursed cold mountains? I think it's the black, brainless repetition; all these forests, and over all an ancient horror of unconsciouness. It's like the dream of an atheist. Pine-trees and more pine-trees and millions more pine-trees——'

'God!' cried the man by the coffin; 'but he hasn't got a head.'

While the others stood rigid the priest, for the first time, showed a leap of startled concern.

'No head!' he repeated, *'No head?'* as if he had almost expected some other deficiency.

Half-witted visions of a headless baby born to Glengyle, of a headless youth hiding himself in the castle, of a headless man pacing those ancient halls or that gorgeous garden, passed in panorama through their minds.

But even in that stiffened instant the tale took no root in them and seemed to have no reason in it. They stood listening to the loud woods and the shrieking sky quite foolishly, like exhausted animals. Thought seemed to be something enormous that had suddenly slipped out of their grasp.

'There are three headless men,' said Father Brown: 'standing round this open grave.'

The pale detective from London opened his mouth to speak, and left it open like a yokel, while a long scream of wind tore the sky; then he looked at the axe in his hands as if it did not belong to him, and dropped it.

'Father,' said Flambeau in that infantile and heavy voice he used very seldom, 'what are we to do?'

His friend's reply came with the pent promptitude of a gun going off.

'Sleep!' cried Father Brown. 'Sleep. We have come to the end of the ways. Do you know what sleep is? Do you know that every man who sleeps believes in God? It is a sacrament; for it is an act of faith and it is a food. And we need a sacrament, if only a natural one. Something has fallen on us that falls very seldom on men; perhaps the worst thing that can fall on them.'

Craven's parted lips came together to say: 'What do you mean?'

The priest turned his face to the castle as he answered:

'We have found the truth; and the truth makes no sense.'

He went down the path in front of them with a plunging and reckless step very rare with him, and when they reached the castle again he threw himself upon sleep with the simplicity of a dog.

Despite his mystic praise of slumber, Father Brown was up earlier than anyone else except the silent gardener; and was found smoking a big pipe and watching that expert at his speechless labours in the kitchen garden. Towards daybreak the rocking storm had ended in roaring rains, and the day came with a curious freshness. The gardener seemed even to have been conversing, but at sight of the detectives he planted his spade sullenly in a bed and, saying something about his breakfast, shifted along the lines of cabbages and shut himself in the kitchen. 'He's a valuable man, that,' said Father Brown. 'He does the potatoes amazingly. Still,' he added, with a dispassionate charity, 'he has his faults; which of us hasn't? He doesn't dig this bank quite regularly. There, for instance,' and he stamped suddenly on one spot. 'I'm really very doubtful about that potato.'

'And why?' asked Craven, amused with the little man's new hobby.

'I'm doubtful about it,' said the other, 'because old Gow was doubtful about it himself. He put his spade in methodically in every place but just this. There must be a mighty fine potato just there.'

Flambeau pulled up the spade and impetuously drove it into the place. He turned up, under a load of soil, something that did not look like a potato, but rather like a monstrous, over-domed mushroom. But it struck the spade with a cold click; it rolled over like a ball, and grinned up at them.

'The Earl of Glengyle,' said Brown sadly, and looked down heavily at the skull.

Then, after a momentary meditation, he plucked the spade from Flambeau, and, saying: 'We must hide it again,' clamped the skull down in the earth. Then he leaned his little body and huge head on the great handle of the spade, that stood up stiffly in the earth, and his eyes were empty and his forehead full of wrinkles. 'If one could only conceive,' he muttered, 'the meaning of this last monstrosity.' And leaning on the large spade handle, he buried his brows in his hands, as men do in church.

All the corners of the sky were brightening into blue and silver; the birds were chattering in the tiny garden trees; so loud it seemed as if the trees themselves were talking. But the three men were silent enough.

'Well, I give it all up,' said Flambeau at last boisterously. 'My brain and this world don't fit each other; and there's an end of it. Snuff, spoilt Prayer Books, and the insides of musical boxes—what——'

Brown threw up his bothered brow and rapped on the spade handle with an intolerance quite unusual with him. 'Oh, tut, tut, tut, tut, tut!' he cried. 'All that is as plain as a pikestaff. I understood the snuff and clockwork, and so on, when I first opened my eyes this morning. And since then I've had it out with old Gow, the gardener, who is neither so deaf nor so stupid as he pretends. There's something amiss about the loose items. I was wrong about the torn mass-book, too; there's no harm in that. But it's this last business. Desecrating graves and stealing dead men's heads—surely there's harm in that? Surely there's black magic still in that? That doesn't fit in to the quite simple story of the snuff and the candles.' And, striding about again, he smoked moodily.

'My friend,' said Flambeau, with a grim humour, 'you must be careful with me and remember I was once a criminal. The great advantage of that estate was that I always made up the story myself, and acted it as quick as I chose. This detective business of waiting about is too much for my French impatience. All my life, for good or evil, I have done things at the instant; I always fought duels the next morning; I always paid bills on the nail; I never even put off a visit to the dentist——'

Father Brown's pipe fell out of his mouth and broke into three pieces on the gravel path. He stood rolling his eyes, the exact picture of an idiot. 'Lord, what a turnip I am!' he kept saying. 'Lord, what a turnip!' Then, in a somewhat groggy kind of way, he began to laugh.

'The dentist!' he repeated. 'Six hours in the spiritual abyss, and all because I never thought of the dentist! Such a simple, such a beautiful and peaceful thought! Friends, we have passed a night in hell; but now the sun is risen, the birds are singing, and the radiant form of the dentist consoles the world.'

'I will get some sense out of this,' cried Flambeau, striding forward, 'if I use the tortures of the Inquisition.'

Father Brown repressed what appeared to be a momentary disposition to dance on the now sunlit lawn and cried quite piteously, like a child: 'Oh, let me be silly a little. You don't know how unhappy I have been. And now I know that there has been no deep sin in this business at all. Only a little lunacy, perhaps—and who minds that?'

He spun round once, then faced them with gravity.

'This is not a story of crime,' he said; 'rather it is the story of a strange and crooked honesty. We are dealing with the one man on earth, perhaps, who has taken no more than his due. It is a study in the savage living logic that has been the religion of this race.

'That old local rhyme about the house of Glengyle——

> "As green sap to the simmer trees
> Is red gold to the Ogilvies"——

was literal as well as metaphorical. It did not merely mean that the Glengyles sought for wealth; it was also true that they literally gathered gold; they had a huge collection of ornaments and utensils in that metal. They were, in fact, misers whose mania took that turn. In the light of that fact, run through all the things we found in the castle. Diamonds without their gold rings; candles without their gold candlesticks; snuff without the gold snuff-boxes; pencil-leads without the gold pencil-cases; a walking-stick without its gold top; clockwork without the gold clocks—or rather watches. And, mad as it sounds, because the halos and the name of God in the old missals were of real gold, these also were taken away.'

The garden seemed to brighten, the grass to grow gayer in the strengthening sun, as the crazy truth was told. Flambeau lit a cigarette as his friend went on.

'Were taken away,' continued Father Brown; 'were taken away—but not stolen. Thieves would never have left this mystery. Thieves would have taken the gold snuff-boxes, snuff and all; the gold pencil-cases, lead and all. We have to deal with a man with a peculiar conscience, but certainly a conscience. I found that mad moralist this morning in the kitchen garden yonder, and I heard the whole story.

'The late Archbishop Ogilvie was the nearest approach to a good man ever born at Glengyle. But his bitter virtue took the turn of the misanthrope; he moped over the dishonesty of his ancestors, from which, somehow, he generalized a dishonesty of all men. More especially he distrusted philanthropy or free-giving; and he swore if he could find one man who took his exact rights he should have all the gold of Glengyle. Having delivered this defiance to humanity he shut himself up, without the smallest expectation of its being answered. One day, however, a deaf and seemingly senseless lad from a distant village brought him a belated telegram;

and Glengyle, in his acrid pleasantry, gave him a new farthing. At least he thought he had done so, but when he turned over his change he found the new farthing still there and a sovereign gone. The accident offered him vistas of sneering speculation. Either way, the boy would show the greasy greed of the species. Either he would vanish, a thief stealing a coin; or he would sneak back with it virtuously, a snob seeking a reward. In the middle of the night Lord Glengyle was knocked up out of his bed—for he lived alone—and forced to open the door to the deaf idiot. The idiot brought with him, not the sovereign, but exactly nineteen shillings and eleven-pence three-farthings in change.

'Then the wild exactitude of this action took hold on the mad lord's brain like fire. He swore he was Diogenes, that had long sought an honest man, and at last had found one. He made a new will, which I have seen. He took the literal youth into his huge, neglected house, and trained him up as his solitary servant and—after an odd manner—his heir. And whatever that queer creature understands, he understood absolutely his lord's two fixed ideas: first, that the letter of right is everything; and second, that he himself was to have the gold of Glengyle. So far, that is all; and that is simple. He has stripped the house of gold, and taken not a grain that was not gold; not so much as a grain of snuff. He lifted the gold leaf off an old illumination, fully satisfied that he left the rest unspoilt. All that I understood; but I could not understand this skull business. I was really uneasy about that human head buried among the potatoes. It distressed me—till Flambeau said the word.

'It will be all right. He will put the skull back in the grave, when he has taken the gold out of the tooth.'

And, indeed, when Flambeau crossed the hill that

morning, he saw that strange being, the just miser,
digging at the desecrated grave, the plaid round his
throat thrashing out in the mountain wind; the sober
top hat on his head.

The Hammer of God

THE little village of Bohun Beacon was perched on a hill
so steep that the tall spire of its church seemed only like
the peak of a small mountain. At the foot of the church
stood a smithy, generally red with fires and always littered with hammers and scraps of iron; opposite to this,
over a rude cross of cobbled paths, was 'The Blue Boar,'
the only inn of the place. It was upon this crossway, in
the lifting of a leaden and silver daybreak, that two
brothers met in the street and spoke; though one was
beginning the day and the other finishing it. The Rev.
and Hon. Wilfred Bohun was very devout, and was
making his way to some austere exercises of prayer or
contemplation at dawn. Colonel the Hon. Norman
Bohun, his elder brother, was by no means devout, and
was sitting in evening-dress on the bench outside 'The
Blue Boar,' drinking what the philosophic observer was
free to regard either as his last glass on Tuesday or his
first on Wednesday. The colonel was not particular.

The Bohuns were one of the very few aristocratic
families really dating from the Middle Ages, and their
pennon had actually seen Palestine. But it is a great
mistake to suppose that such houses stand high in
chivalric traditions. Few except the poor preserve traditions. Aristocrats live not in traditions but in fashions.
The Bohuns had been Mohocks under Queen Anne and
Mashers under Queen Victoria. But, like more than one

of the really ancient houses, they had rotted in the last two centuries into mere drunkards and dandy degenerates, till there had even come a whisper of insanity. Certainly there was something hardly human about the colonel's wolfish pursuit of pleasure, and his chronic resolution not to go home till morning had a touch of the hideous charity of insomnia. He was a tall, fine animal, elderly, but with hair startlingly yellow. He would have looked merely blond and leonine, but his blue eyes were sunk so deep in his face that they looked black. They were a little too close together. He had very long yellow moustaches: on each side of them a fold or furrow from nostril to jaw, so that a sneer seemed to cut into his face. Over his evening clothes he wore a curiously pale yellow coat that looked more like a very light dressing gown than an overcoat, and on the back of his head was stuck an extraordinary broad-brimmed hat of a bright green colour, evidently some oriental curiosity caught up at random. He was proud of appearing in such incongruous attires—proud of the fact that he always made them look congruous.

His brother the curate had also the yellow hair and the elegance, but he was buttoned up to the chin in black, and his face was clean-shaven, cultivated and a little nervous. He seemed to live for nothing but his religion; but there were some who said (notably the blacksmith, who was a Presbyterian) that it was a love of Gothic architecture rather than of God, and that his haunting of the church like a ghost was only another and purer turn of the almost morbid thirst for beauty which sent his brother raging after women and wine. This charge was doubtful, while the man's practical piety was indubitable. Indeed, the charge was mostly an ignorant misunderstanding of the love of solitude and secret prayer, and was founded on his being often found kneeling, not before the altar, but in peculiar places, in the crypts or gallery, or even in the belfry. He was at the moment about to enter the church through the yard of the smithy, but stopped and frowned a little as he saw his brother's cavernous eyes staring in the same direction. On the hypothesis that the colonel was interested in the church he did not waste any speculations. There only remained the blacksmith's shop, and though the blacksmith was a Puritan and none of his people, Wilfred Bohun had heard some scandals about a beautiful and rather celebrated wife. He flung a suspicious look across the shed, and the colonel stood up laughing to speak to him.

'Good morning, Wilfred,' he said. 'Like a good landlord I am watching sleeplessly over my people. I am going to call on the blacksmith.'

Wilfred looked at the ground and said: 'The blacksmith is out. He is over at Greenford.'

'I know,' answered the other with silent laughter; 'that is why I am calling on him.'

'Norman,' said the cleric, with his eye on a pebble in the road, 'are you ever afraid of thunderbolts?'

'What do you mean?' asked the colonel. 'Is your hobby meteorology?'

'I mean,' said Wilfred, without looking up, 'do you ever think that God might strike you in the street?'

'I beg your pardon,' said the colonel; 'I see your hobby is folklore.'

'I know your hobby is blasphemy,' retorted the religious man, stung in the one live place of his nature. 'But if you do not fear God, you have good reason to fear man.'

The elder raised his eyebrows politely. 'Fear man?' he said.

'Barnes the blacksmith is the biggest and strongest man for forty miles round,' said the clergyman sternly. 'I know you are no coward or weakling, but he could throw you over the wall.'

This struck home, being true, and the lowering line by mouth and nostril darkened and deepened. For a moment he stood with the heavy sneer on his face. But in an instant Colonel Bohun had recovered his own cruel good humour and laughed, showing two dog-like front teeth under his yellow moustache. 'In that case, my dear Wilfred,' he said quite carelessly, 'it was wise for the last of the Bohuns to come out partially in armour.'

And he took off the queer round hat covered with green, showing that it was lined within with steel. Wilfred recognized it indeed as a light Japanese or Chinese helmet torn down from a trophy that hung in the old family hall.

'It was the first to hand,' explained his brother airily; 'always the nearest hat—and the nearest woman.'

'The blacksmith is away at Greenford,' said Wilfred quietly; 'the time of his return is unsettled.'

And with that he turned and went into the church with bowed head, crossing himself like one who wishes to be quit of an unclean spirit. He was anxious to forget such grossness in the cool twilight of his tall Gothic cloisters; but on that morning it was fated that his still round of religious exercises should be everywhere arrested by small shocks. As he entered the church, hitherto always empty at that hour, a kneeling figure rose hastily to its feet and came towards the full daylight of the doorway. When the curate saw it he stood still with surprise. For the early worshipper was none other than the village idiot, a nephew of the blacksmith, one who neither would nor could care for the church or for anything else. He was always called 'Mad Joe,' and seemed to have no other name; he was a dark, strong, slouching lad, with a heavy white face, dark straight hair, and a mouth always open. As he passed the priest, his moon-calf countenance gave no hint of what he had been doing or thinking of. He had never been known to pray before. What sort of prayers was he saying now? Extraordinary prayers surely.

Wilfred Bohun stood rooted to the spot long enough to see the idiot go out into the sunshine, and even to see his dissolute brother hail him with a sort of avuncular jocularity. The last thing he saw was the colonel throwing pennies at the open mouth of Joe, with the serious appearance of trying to hit it.

This ugly sunlight picture of the stupidity and cruelty of the earth sent the ascetic finally to his prayers for purification and new thoughts. He went up to a pew in the gallery, which brought him under a coloured window which he loved and which always quieted his spirit; a blue window with an angel carrying lilies. There he began to think less about the half-wit, with his livid face and mouth like a fish. He began to think less of his evil brother, pacing like a lean lion in his horrible hunger. He sank deeper and deeper into those cold and sweet colours of silver blossoms and sapphire sky.

In this place half an hour afterwards he was found by Gibbs, the village cobbler, who had been sent for him in some haste. He got to his feet with promptitude, for he knew that no small matter would have brought Gibbs into such a place at all. The cobbler was, as in many villages, an atheist, and his appearance in church was a shade more extraordinary than Mad Joe's. It was a morning of theological enigmas.

'What is it?' asked Wilfred Bohun rather stiffly, but putting out a trembling hand for his hat.

The atheist spoke in a tone that, coming from him,

was quite startlingly respectful, and even, as it were, huskily sympathetic.

'You must excuse me, sir,' he said in a hoarse whisper, 'but we didn't think it right not to let you know at once. I'm afraid a rather dreadful thing has happened, sir. I'm afraid your brother——'

Wilfred clenched his frail hands. 'What devilry has he done now?' he cried in involuntary passion.

'Why, sir,' said the cobbler, coughing, 'I'm afraid he's done nothing, and won't do anything. I'm afraid he's done for. You had really better come down, sir.'

The curate followed the cobbler down a short winding stair which brought them out at an entrance rather higher than the street. Bohun saw the tragedy in one glance, flat underneath him like a plan. In the yard of the smithy were standing five or six men, mostly in black, one in an inspector's uniform. They included the doctor, the Presbyterian minister, and the priest from the Roman Catholic chapel to which the blacksmith's wife belonged. The latter was speaking to her, indeed, very rapidly, in an undertone, as she, a magnificent woman with red-gold hair, was sobbing blindly on a bench. Between these two groups, and just clear of the main heap of hammers, lay a man in evening dress, spread-eagled and flat on his face. From the height above Wilfred could have sworn to every item of his costume and appearance, down to the Bohun rings upon his fingers; but the skull was only a hideous splash, like a star of blackness and blood.

Wilfred Bohun gave but one glance, and ran down the steps into the yard. The doctor, who was the family physician, saluted him, but he scarcely took any notice. He could only stammer out: 'My brother is dead. What does it mean? What is this horrible mystery?' There was an unhappy silence; and then the cobbler, the most outspoken man present, answered: 'Plenty of horror, sir,' he said, 'but not much mystery.'

'What do you mean?' asked Wilfred, with a white face.

'It's plain enough,' answered Gibbs. 'There is only one man for forty miles round that could have struck such a blow as that, and he's the man that had most reason to.'

'We must not prejudge anything,' put in the doctor, a tall, black-bearded man, rather nervously; 'but it is competent for me to corroborate what Mr. Gibbs says about the nature of the blow, sir; it is an incredible blow. Mr. Gibbs says that only one man in this district could have done it. I should have said myself that nobody could have done it.'

A shudder of superstition went through the slight figure of the curate. 'I can hardly understand,' he said.

'Mr. Bohun,' said the doctor in a low voice, 'metaphors literally fail me. It is inadequate to say that the skull was smashed to bits like an egg-shell. Fragments of bone were driven into the body and the ground like bullets into a mud wall. It was the hand of a giant.'

He was silent a moment, looking grimly through his glasses; then he added: 'The thing has one advantage—that it clears most people of suspicion at one stroke. If you or I or any normally made man in the country were accused of this crime, we should be acquitted as an infant would be acquitted of stealing the Nelson Column.'

'That's what I say,' repeated the cobbler obstinately, 'there's only one man that could have done it, and he's the man that would have done it. Where's Simeon Barnes, the blacksmith?'

'He's over at Greenford,' faltered the curate.

'More likely over in France,' muttered the cobbler.

'No; he is in neither of those places,' said a small and

colourless voice, which came from the little Roman priest who had joined the group. 'As a matter of fact, he is coming up the road at this moment.'

The little priest was not an interesting man to look at, having stubbly brown hair and a round and stolid face. But if he had been as splendid as Apollo no one would have looked at him at that moment. Everyone turned round and peered at the pathway which wound across the plain below, along which was indeed walking, at his own huge stride and with a hammer on his shoulder, Simeon the smith. He was a bony and gigantic man, with deep, dark, sinister eyes and a dark chin beard. He was walking and talking quietly with two other men; and though he was never specially cheerful, he seemed quite at his ease.

'My God!' cried the atheistic cobbler; 'and there's the hammer he did it with.'

'No,' said the inspector, a sensible-looking man with a sandy moustache, speaking for the first time. 'There's the hammer he did it with, over there by the church wall. We have left it and the body exactly as they are.'

All glanced round, and the short priest went across and looked down in silence at the tool where it lay. It was one of the smallest and the lightest of the hammers, and would not have caught the eye among the rest; but on the iron edge of it were blood and yellow hair.

After a silence the short priest spoke without looking up, and there was a new note in his dull voice. 'Mr. Gibbs was hardly right,' he said, 'in saying that there is no mystery. There is at least the mystery of why so big a man should attempt so big a blow with so little a hammer.'

'Oh, never mind that,' cried Gibbs, in a fever. 'What are we to do with Simeon Barnes?'

'Leave him alone,' said the priest quietly. 'He is

coming here of himself. I know these two men with him. They are very good fellows from Greenford, and they have come over about the Presbyterian chapel.'

Even as he spoke the tall smith swung round the corner of the church and strode into his own yard. Then he stood there quite still, and the hammer fell from his hand. The inspector, who had preserved impenetrable propriety, immediately went up to him.

'I won't ask you, Mr. Barnes,' he said, 'whether you know anything about what has happened here. You are not bound to say. I hope you don't know, and that you will be able to prove it. But I must go through the form of arresting you in the King's name for the murder of Colonel Norman Bohun.'

'You are not bound to say anything,' said the cobbler in officious excitement. 'They've got to prove everything. They haven't proved yet that it is Colonel Bohun, with the head all smashed up like that.'

'That won't wash,' said the doctor aside to the priest. 'That's out of detective stories. I was the colonel's medical man, and I knew his body better than he did. He had very fine hands, but quite peculiar ones. The second and third fingers were the same in length. Oh, that's the colonel right enough.'

As he glanced at the brained corpse upon the ground the iron eyes of the motionless blacksmith followed them and rested there also.

'Is Colonel Bohun dead?' said the smith quite calmly. 'Then he's damned.'

'Don't say anything! Oh, don't say anything!' cried the atheist cobbler, dancing about in an ecstasy of admiration of the English legal system. For no man is such a legalist as the good Secularist.

The blacksmith turned on him over his shoulder the august face of a fanatic.

'It is well for you infidels to dodge like foxes because the world's law favours you,' he said; 'but God guards His own in His pocket, as you shall see this day.'

Then he pointed to the colonel and said: 'When did this dog die in his sins?'

'Moderate your language,' said the doctor.

'Moderate the Bible's language, and I'll moderate mine. When did he die?'

'I saw him alive at six o'clock this morning,' stammered Wilfred Bohun.

'God is good,' said the smith. 'Mr. Inspector, I have not the slightest objection to being arrested. It is you who may object to arresting me. I don't mind leaving the court without a stain on my character. You do mind, perhaps, leaving the court with a bad set-back in your career.'

The solid inspector for the first time looked at the blacksmith with a lively eye—as did everybody else, except the short, strange priest, who was still looking down at the little hammer that had dealt the dreadful blow.

'There are two men standing outside this shop,' went on the blacksmith with ponderous lucidity, 'good tradesmen in Greenford whom you all know, who will swear that they saw me from before midnight till daybreak and long after in the committee-room of our Revival Mission, which sits all night, we save souls so fast. In Greenford itself twenty people could swear to me for all that time. If I were a heathen, Mr. Inspector, I would let you walk on to your downfall; but, as a Christian man, I feel bound to give you your chance and ask you whether you will hear my alibi now or in court.'

The inspector seemed for the first time disturbed and said. 'Of course I should be glad to clear you altogether now.'

The smith walked out of his yard with the same long and easy stride, and returned to his two friends from Greenford, who were indeed friends of nearly everyone present. Each of them said a few words which no one ever thought of disbelieving. When they had spoken the innocence of Simeon stood up as solid as the great church above them.

One of those silences struck the group which are more strange and insufferable than any speech. Madly, in order to make conversation, the curate said to the Catholic priest:

'You seem very much interested in that hammer, Father Brown.'

'Yes, I am,' said Father Brown; 'why is it such a small hammer?'

The doctor swung round on him.

'By George, that's true,' he cried; 'who would use a little hammer with ten larger hammers lying about?'

Then he lowered his voice in the curate's ear and said: 'Only the kind of person that can't lift a large hammer. It is not a question of force or courage between the sexes. It's a question of lifting power in the shoulders. A bold woman could commit ten murders with a light hammer and never turn a hair. She could not kill a beetle with a heavy one.'

Wilfred Bohun was staring at him with a sort of hypnotized horror, while Father Brown listened with his head a little on one side, really interested and attentive. The doctor went on with more hissing emphasis:

'Why do those idiots always assume that the only person who hates the wife's lover is the wife's husband? Nine times out of ten the person who most hates the wife's lover is the wife. Who knows what insolence or treachery he had shown her—look there?'

He made a momentary gesture towards the red-haired

woman on the bench. She had lifted her head at last and the tears were drying on her splendid face. But the eyes were fixed on the corpse with an electric glare that had in it something of idiocy.

The Rev. William Bohun made a limp gesture as if waving away all desire to know; but Father Brown, dusting off his sleeve some ashes blown from the furnace, spoke in his indifferent way.

'You are like so many doctors,' he said; 'your mental science is really suggestive. It is your physical science that is utterly impossible. I agree that the woman wants to kill the co-respondent much more than the petitioner does. And I agree that a woman will always pick up a small hammer instead of a big one. But the difficulty is one of physical impossibility. No woman ever born could have smashed a man's skull out flat like that.' Then he added reflectively, after a pause: 'These people haven't grasped the whole of it. The man was actually wearing an iron helmet, and the blow scattered it like broken glass. Look at that woman. Look at her arms.'

Silence held them all up again, and then the doctor said rather sulkily: 'Well, I may be wrong; there are objections to everything. But I stick to the main point. No man but an idiot would pick up that little hammer if he could use a big hammer.'

With that the lean and quivering hands of Wilfred Bohun went up to his head and seemed to clutch his scanty yellow hair. After an instant they dropped, and he cried: 'That was the word I wanted; you have said the word.'

Then he continued, mastering his discomposure: 'The words you said were, "No man but an idiot would pick up the small hammer."'

'Yes,' said the doctor, 'Well?'

'Well,' said the curate, 'no man but an idiot did.' The

rest stared at him with eyes arrested and riveted, and he went on in a febrile and feminine agitation.

'I am a priest,' he cried unsteadily, 'and a priest should be no shedder of blood. I—I mean that he should bring no one to the gallows. And I thank God that I see the criminal clearly now—because he is a criminal who cannot be brought to the gallows.'

'You will not denounce him?' inquired the doctor.

'He would not be hanged if I did denounce him,' answered Wilfred, with a wild but curiously happy smile. 'When I went into the church this morning I found a madman praying there—that poor Joe, who has been wrong all his life. God knows what he prayed; but with such strange folk it is not incredible to suppose that their prayers are all upside down. Very likely a lunatic would pray before killing a man. When I last saw poor Joe he was with my brother. My brother was mocking him.'

'By Jove!' cried the doctor, 'this is talking at last. But how do you explain——'

The Rev. Wilfred was almost trembling with the excitement of his own glimpse of the truth. 'Don't you see; don't you see,' he cried feverishly, 'that is the only theory that covers both the queer things, that answers both the riddles. The two riddles are the little hammer and the big blow. The smith might have struck the big blow, but he would not have chosen the little hammer. His wife would have chosen the little hammer, but she could not have struck the big blow. But the madman might have done both. As for the little hammer—why, he was mad and might have picked up anything. And for the big blow, have you never heard, doctor, that a maniac in his paroxysm may have the strength of ten men?'

The doctor drew a deep breath and then said: 'By golly, I believe you've got it.'

Father Brown had fixed his eyes on the speaker so long and steadily as to prove that his large grey, ox-like eyes were not quite so insignificant as the rest of his face. When silence had fallen he said with marked respect: 'Mr. Bohun, yours is the only theory yet propounded which holds water every way and is essentially unassailable. I think, therefore, that you deserve to be told, on my positive knowledge, that it is not the true one.' And with that the odd little man walked away and stared again at the hammer.

'That fellow seems to know more than he ought to,' whispered the doctor peevishly to Wilfred. 'Those popish priests are deucedly sly.'

'No, no,' said Bohun, with a sort of wild fatigue. 'It was the lunatic. It was the lunatic.'

The group of the two clerics and the doctor had fallen away from the more official group containing the inspector and the man he had arrested. Now, however, that their own party had broken up, they heard voices from the others. The priest looked up quietly and then looked down again as he heard the blacksmith say in a loud voice:

'I hope I've convinced you, Mr. Inspector. I'm a strong man, as you say, but I couldn't have flung my hammer bang here from Greenford. My hammer hasn't any wings that it should come flying half a mile over hedges and fields.'

The inspector laughed amicably and said: 'No; I think you can be considered out of it, though it's one of the rummiest coincidences I ever saw. I can only ask you to give us all the assistance you can in finding a man as big and strong as yourself. By George! you might be useful, if only to hold him! I suppose you yourself have no guess at the man?'

'I may have a guess,' said the pale smith, 'but it is not

at a man.' Then, seeing the sacred eyes turn towards his wife on the bench, he put his huge hand on her shoulder and said: 'Nor a woman either.'

'What do you mean?' asked the inspector jocularly. 'You don't think cows use hammers, do you?'

'I think no thing of flesh held that hammer,' said the blacksmith in a stifled voice; 'mortally speaking, I think the man died alone.'

Wilfred made a sudden forward movement and peered at him with burning eyes.

'Do you mean to say, Barnes,' came the sharp voice of the cobbler, 'that the hammer jumped up of itself and knocked the man down?'

'Oh, you gentlemen may stare and snigger,' cried Simeon; 'you clergymen who tell us on Sunday in what a stillness the Lord smote Sennacherib. I believe that One who walks invisible in every house defended the honour of mine, and laid the defiler dead before the door of it. I believe the force in that blow was just the force there is in earthquakes, and no force less.'

Wilfred said, with a voice utterly undescribable: 'I told Norman myself to beware of the thunderbolt.'

'That agent is outside my jurisdiction,' said the inspector with a slight smile.

'You are not outside His,' answered the smith; 'see you to it.' And, turning his broad back, he went into the house.

The shaken Wilfred was led away by Father Brown, who had an easy and friendly way with him. 'Let us get out of this horrid place, Mr. Bohun,' he said. 'May I look inside your church? I hear it's one of the oldest in England. We take some interest, you know,' he added with a comical grimace, 'in old English churches.'

Wilfred Bohun did not smile, for humour was never his strong point. But he nodded rather eagerly, being only too ready to explain the Gothic splendours to some-one more likely to be sympathetic than the Presbyterian blacksmith or the atheist cobbler.

'By all means,' he said; 'let us go in at this side.' And he led the way into the high side entrance at the top of the flight of steps. Father Brown was mounting the first step to follow him when he felt a hand on his shoulder, and turned to behold the dark, thin figure of the doctor, his face darker yet with suspicion.

'Sir,' said the physician harshly, 'you appear to know some secrets in this black business. May I ask if you are going to keep them to yourself?'

'Why, doctor,' answered the priest, smiling quite pleasantly, 'there is one very good reason why a man of my trade would keep things to himself when he is not sure of them, and that is that it is so constantly his duty to keep them to himself when he is sure of them. But if you think I have been discourteously reticent with you or anyone, I will go to the extreme limit of my custom. I will give you two very large hints.'

'Well, sir?' said the doctor gloomily.

'First,' said Father Brown quietly, 'the thing is quite in your own province. It is a matter of physical science. The blacksmith is mistaken, not perhaps in saying that the blow was divine, but certainly in saying that it came by a miracle. It was no miracle, doctor, except in so far as man is himself a miracle, with his strange and wicked and yet half-heroic heart. The force that smashed that skull was a force well known to scientists—one of the most frequently debated of the laws of nature.'

The doctor, who was looking at him with frowning intentness, only said: 'And the other hint?'

'The other hint is this,' said the priest: 'Do you re-member the blacksmith, though he believes in miracles, talking scornfully of the impossible fairy tale that his hammer had wings and flew half a mile across country?'

'Yes,' said the doctor, 'I remember that.'

'Well,' added Father Brown, with a broad smile, 'that fairy tale was the nearest thing to the real truth that has been said to-day.' And with that he turned his back and stumped up the steps after the curate.

The Reverend Wilfred, who had been waiting for him, pale and impatient, as if this little delay were the last straw for his nerves, led him immediately to his favourite corner of the church, that part of the gallery closest to the carved roof and lit by the wonderful window with the angel. The little Latin priest explored and admired everything exhaustively, talking cheerfully but in a low voice all the time. When in the course of his investigation he found the side exit and the winding stair down which Wilfred had rushed to find his brother dead, Father Brown ran not down but up, with the agility of a monkey, and his clear voice came from an outer platform above.

'Come up here, Mr. Bohun,' he called. 'The air will do you good.'

Bohun followed him, and came out on a kind of stone gallery or balcony outside the building, from which one could see the illimitable plain in which their small hill stood, wooded away to the purple horizon and dotted with villages and farms. Clear and square, but quite small beneath them, was the blacksmith's yard, where the inspector still stood taking notes and the corpse still lay like a smashed fly.

'Might be the map of the world, mightn't it?' said Father Brown.

'Yes,' said Bohun very gravely, and nodded his head.

Immediately beneath and about them the lines of the Gothic building plunged outwards into the void with a

sickening swiftness akin to suicide. There is that element
of Titan energy in the architecture of the Middle Ages
that, from whatever aspect it be seen, it always seems to
be rushing away, like the strong back of some maddened
horse. This church was hewn out of ancient and silent
stone, bearded with old fungoids and stained with the
nests of birds. And yet, when they saw it from below, it
sprang like a fountain at the stars; and when they saw
it, as now, from above, it poured like a cataract into a
voiceless pit. For these two men on the tower were left
alone with the most terrible aspect of the Gothic: the
monstrous foreshortening and disproportion, the dizzy
perspectives, the glimpses of great things small and small
things great; a topsy-turvydom of stone in the mid-air.
Details of stone, enormous by their proximity, were
relieved against a pattern of fields and farms, pygmy in
their distance. A carved bird or beast at a corner seemed
like some vast walking or flying dragon wasting the pas-
tures and villages below. The whole atmosphere was
dizzy and dangerous, as if men were upheld in air amid
the gyrating wings of colossal genii; and the whole of
that old church, as tall and rich as a cathedral, seemed
to sit upon the sunlit country like a cloudburst.

'I think there is something rather dangerous about
standing on these high places even to pray,' said Father
Brown. 'Heights were made to be looked at, not to be
looked from.'

'Do you mean that one may fall over,' asked Wilfred.

'I mean that one's soul may fall if one's body doesn't,'
said the other priest.

'I scarcely understand you,' remarked Bohun indis-
tinctly.

'Look at that blacksmith, for instance,' went on Father
Brown calmly; 'a good man, but not a Christian—hard,
imperious, unforgiving. Well, his Scotch religion was

made up by men who prayed on hills and high crags, and learnt to look down on the world more than to look up at heaven. Humility is the mother of giants. One sees great things from the valley; only small things from the peak.'

'But he—he didn't do it,' said Bohun tremulously.

'No,' said the other in an odd voice; 'we know he didn't do it.'

After a moment he resumed, looking tranquilly out over the plain with his pale grey eyes. 'I knew a man,' he said, 'who began by worshipping with others before the altar, but who grew fond of high and lonely places to pray from, corners or niches in the belfry or the spire. And once in one of those dizzy places, where the whole world seemed to turn under him like a wheel, his brain turned also, and he fancied he was God. So that though he was a good man, he committed a great crime.'

Wilfred's face was turned away, but his bony hands turned blue and white as they tightened on the parapet of stone.

'He thought it was given to *him* to judge the world and strike down the sinner. He would never have had such a thought if he had been kneeling with other men upon a floor. But he saw all men walking about like insects. He saw one especially strutting just below him, insolent and evident by a bright green hat—a poisonous insect.'

Rooks cawed round the corners of the belfry; but there was no other sound till Father Brown went on.

'This also tempted him, that he had in his hand one of the most awful engines of nature; I mean gravitation, that mad and quickening rush by which all earth's creatures fly back to her heart when released. See, the inspector is strutting just below us in the smithy. If I were to toss a pebble over this parapet it would be something

like a bullet by the time it struck him. If I were to drop
a hammer—even a small hammer——'

Wilfred Bohun threw one leg over the parapet, and
Father Brown had him in a minute by the collar.

'Not by that door,' he said quite gently; 'that door
leads to hell.'

Bohun staggered back against the wall, and stared at
him with frightful eyes.

'How do you know all this?' he cried. 'Are you a
devil?'

'I am a man,' answered Father Brown gravely; 'and
therefore have all devils in my heart. Listen to me,' he
said after a short pause. 'I know what you did—at least,
I can guess the great part of it. When you left your
brother you were racked with no unrighteous rage to the
extent even that you snatched up the small hammer, half
inclined to kill him with his foulness on his mouth. Re-
coiling, you thrust it under your buttoned coat instead,
and rushed into the church. You pray wildly in many
places, under the angel window, upon the platform
above, and on a higher platform still, from which you
could see the colonel's Eastern hat like the back of a
green beetle crawling about. Then something snapped
in your soul, and you let God's thunderbolt fall.'

Wilfred put a weak hand to his head, and asked in a
low voice: 'How did you know that his hat looked like
a green beetle?'

'Oh, that,' said the other with the shadow of a smile,
'that was common sense. But hear me further. I say I
know all this; but no one else shall know it. The next
step is for you; I shall take no more steps; I will seal this
with the seal of confession. If you ask me why, there are
many reasons, and only one that concerns you. I leave
things to you because you have not yet gone very far
wrong, as assassins go. You did not help to fix the crime

on the smith when it was easy; or on his wife, when that was easy. You tried to fix it on the imbecile, because you knew that he could not suffer. That was one of the gleams that it is my business to find in assassins. And now come down into the village, and go your own way as free as the wind; for I have said my last word.'

They went down the winding stairs in utter silence, and came out into the sunlight by the smithy. Wilfred Bohun carefully unlatched the wooden gate of the yard, and going up to the inspector, said: 'I wish to give myself up; I have killed my brother.'

The Sign of the Broken Sword

THE thousand arms of the forest were grey, and its million fingers silver. In a sky of dark green-blue-like slate the stars were bleak and brilliant like splintered ice. All that thickly wooded and sparsely tenanted country-side was stiff with a bitter and brittle frost. The black hollows between the trunks of the trees looked like bottomless, black caverns of that heartless Scandinavian hell, a hell of incalculable cold. Even the square stone tower of the church looked northern to the point of heathenry, as if it were some barbaric tower among the sea rocks of Iceland. It was a queer night for anyone to explore a churchyard. But, on the other hand, perhaps it was worth exploring.

It rose abruptly out of the ashen wastes of forest in a sort of hump or shoulder of green turf that looked grey in the starlight. Most of the graves were on a slant, and the path leading up to the church was as steep as a staircase. On the top of the hill, in the one flat and prominent place, was the monument for which the place was famous. It contrasted strangely with the featureless graves all round, for it was the work of one of the greatest sculptors of modern Europe; and yet his fame was at once forgotten in the fame of the man whose image he had made. It showed, by touches of the small silver pencil of starlight, the massive metal figure of a soldier recumbent, the strong hands sealed in an everlasting worship, the great head pillowed upon a gun. The venerable face was bearded, or rather whiskered, in the old, heavy Colonel Newcome fashion. The uniform, though suggested with the few strokes of simplicity, was that of modern war. By his right side lay a sword, of which the tip was broken off; on the left side lay a Bible. On glowing summer afternoons wagonettes came full of Americans and cultured suburbans to see the sepulchre; but even then they felt the vast forest land with its one dumpy dome of churchyard and church as a place oddly dumb and neglected. In this freezing darkness of mid-winter one would think he might be left alone with the stars. Nevertheless, in the stillness of those stiff woods a wooden gate creaked, and two dim figures dressed in black climbed up the little path to the tomb.

So faint was that frigid starlight that nothing could have been traced about them except that while they both wore black, one man was enormously big, and the other (perhaps by contrast) almost startlingly small. They went up to the great graven tomb of the historic warrior, and stood for a few minutes staring at it. There was no human, perhaps no living, thing for a wide circle; and a morbid fancy might well have wondered if they were human themselves. In any case, the beginning of their conversation might have seemed strange. After the first silence the small man said to the other:

'Where does a wise man hide a pebble?'

And the tall man answered in a low voice: 'On the beach.'

The small man nodded, and after a short silence said: 'Where does a wise man hide a leaf?'

And the other answered: 'In the forest.'

There was another stillness, and then the tall man resumed: 'Do you mean that when a wise man has to hide a real diamond he has been known to hide it among sham ones?'

'No, no,' said the little man with a laugh, 'we will let bygones be bygones.'

He stamped his cold feet for a second or two and then said: 'I'm not thinking of that at all, but of something else; something rather peculiar. Just strike a match, will you?'

The big man fumbled in his pocket, and soon a scratch and a flare painted gold the whole flat side of the monument. On it was cut in black letters the well-known words which so many Americans had reverently read: 'Sacred to the Memory of General Sir Arthur St. Clare, Hero and Martyr, who Always Vanquished his Enemies and Always Spared Them, and Was Treacherously Slain by Them at Last. May God in Whom he Trusted both Reward and Revenge him.'

The match burnt the big man's fingers, blackened, and dropped. He was about to strike another, but his small companion stopped him. 'That's all right, Flambeau, old man; I saw what I wanted. Or, rather, I didn't see what I didn't want. And now we must walk a mile and a half along the road to the next inn, and I will try to tell you all about it. For Heaven knows a man should have fire and ale when he dares tell such a story.'

They descended the precipitous path, they re-latched the rusty gate, and set off at a stamping, ringing walk down the frozen forest road. They had gone a full quarter of a mile before the smaller man spoke again. He said: 'Yes; the wise man hides a pebble on the beach. But what does he do if there is no beach? Do you know anything of the great St. Clare trouble?'

'I know nothing about English generals, Father Brown,' answered the large man, laughing, 'though a little about English policemen. I only know that you have dragged me a precious long dance to all the shrines of this fellow, whoever he is. One would think he got buried in six different places. I've seen a memorial to General St. Clare in Westminster Abbey; I've seen a ramping equestrian statue of General St. Clare on the Embankment; I've seen a medallion of General St. Clare in the street he was born in; and another in the street he lived in; and now you drag me after dark to his coffin in the village churchyard. I am beginning to be a bit tired of his magnificent personality, especially as I don't in the least know who he was. What are you hunting for in all these crypts and effigies?'

'I am only looking for one word,' said Father Brown. 'A word that isn't there.'

'Well,' asked Flambeau, 'are you going to tell me anything about it?'

'I must divide it into two parts,' remarked the priest. 'First there is what everybody knows; and then there is what I know. Now, what everybody knows is short and plain enough. It is also entirely wrong.'

'Right you are,' said the big man called Flambeau cheerfully. 'Let's begin at the wrong end. Let's begin with what everybody knows, which isn't true.'

'If not wholly untrue, it is at least very inadequate,' continued Brown; 'for in point of fact, all that the public knows amounts precisely to this: The public knows that Arthur St. Clare was a great and successful English general. It knows that after splendid yet careful campaigns both in India and Africa he was in command against Brazil when the great Brazilian patriot Olivier issued his ultimatum. It knows that on that occasion St. Clare with a very small force attacked Olivier with a very large one, and was captured after heroic resistance. And it knows that after his capture, and to the abhorrence of the civilized world, St. Clare was hanged on the nearest tree. He was found swinging there after the Brazilians had retired, with his broken sword hung round his neck.'

'And that popular story is untrue?' suggested Flambeau.

'No,' said his friend quietly; 'that story is quite true, so far as it goes.'

'Well, I think it goes far enough!' said Flambeau, 'but if the popular story is true, what is the mystery?'

They had passed many hundreds of grey and ghostly trees before the little priest answered. Then he bit his finger reflectively and said: 'Why, the mystery is a mystery of psychology. Or, rather, it is a mystery of two psychologies. In that Brazilian business two of the most famous men of modern history acted flat against their characters. Mind you, Olivier and St. Clare were both heroes—the old thing, and no mistake; it was like the fight between Hector and Achilles. Now, what would you say to an affair in which Achilles was timid and Hector was treacherous?'

'Go on,' said the large man impatiently as the other bit his finger again.

'Sir Arthur St. Clare was a soldier of the old religious type—the type that saved us during the Mutiny,' continued Brown. 'He was always more for duty than for dash; and with all his personal courage was decidedly a prudent commander, particularly indignant at any needless waste of soldiers. Yet, in this last battle, he attempted something that a baby could see was absurd. One need not be a strategist to see it was as wild as wind; just as one need not be a strategist to keep out of the way of a motor-bus. Well, that is the first mystery; what had become of the English general's head? The second riddle is, what had become of the Brazilian general's heart? President Olivier might be called a visionary or a nuisance; but even his enemies admitted that he was magnanimous to the point of knight errantry. Almost every other prisoner he had ever captured had been set free, or even loaded with benefits. Men who had really wronged him came away touched by his simplicity and sweetness. Why the deuce should he diabolically revenge himself only once in his life; and then for the one particular blow that could not have hurt him? Well, there you have it. One of the wisest men in the world acted like an idiot for no reason. One of the best men in the world acted like a fiend for no reason. That's the long and short of it; and I leave it to you, my boy.'

'No, you don't,' said the other with a snort. 'I leave it to you; and you jolly well tell me all about it.'

'Well,' resumed Father Brown, 'it's not fair to say that the public impression is just what I've said, without adding that two things have happened since. I can't say they threw a new light, for nobody can make sense of them. But they threw a new kind of darkness, they threw the darkness in new directions. The first was this. The family physician of the St. Clares quarrelled with that family and began publishing a violent series of articles, in which he said that the late general was a religious maniac; but as far as the tale went, this seemed to mean little more than a religious man. Anyhow, the story fizzled out. Everyone knew, of course, that St. Clare had some of the eccentricities of puritan piety. The second incident was much more arresting. In the luckless and unsupported regiment which made that rash attempt at the Black River there was a certain Captain Keith, who was at that time engaged to St. Clare's daughter, and who afterwards married her. He was one of those who were captured by Olivier, and, like all the rest except the general, appears to have been bounteously treated and promptly set free. Some twenty years afterwards this man, then Lieutenant-Colonel Keith, published a sort of autobiography called "A British Officer in Burmah and Brazil." In the place where the reader looks eagerly for some account of the mystery of St. Clare's disaster may be found the following words: "Everywhere else in this book I have narrated things exactly as they occurred, holding as I do the old-fashioned opinion that the glory of England is old enough to take care of itself. The exception I shall make is in this matter of the defeat by the Black River; and my reasons, though private, are honourable and compelling. I will, however, add this in justice to the memories of two distinguished men. General St. Clare has been accused of incapacity on this occasion; I can at least testify that this action, properly understood, was one of the most brilliant and sagacious of his life. President Olivier by similar report is charged with savage injustice. I think it due to the honour of an enemy to say that he acted on this occasion with even more than his characteristic good feeling. To put the matter popularly, I can assure my countrymen that St. Clare was by no means such a fool, nor Olivier such a brute as he looked. This is all I have to say; nor shall any earthly consideration induce me to add a word."'

A large frozen moon like a lustrous snowball began to show through the tangle of twigs in front of them, and by its light the narrator had been able to refresh his memory of Captain Keith's text from a scrap of

printed paper. As he folded it up and put it back in his
pocket Flambeau threw up his hand with a French
gesture.

'Wait a bit, wait a bit,' he cried excitedly. 'I believe I
can guess it at the first go.'

He strode on, breathing hard, his black head and bull
neck forward, like a man winning a walking race. The
little priest, amused and interested, had some trouble in
trotting beside him. Just before them the trees fell back
a little to left and right, and the road swept downwards
across a clear, moonlit valley, till it dived again like a
rabbit into the wall of another wood. The entrance to
the farther forest looked small and round, like the black
hole of a remote railway tunnel. But it was within some
hundred yards, and gaped like a cavern before Flambeau spoke again.

'I've got it,' he cried at last, slapping his thigh with
his great hand. 'Four minutes' thinking, and I can tell
you the whole story myself.'

'All right,' assented his friend. 'You tell it.'

Flambeau lifted his head, but lowered his voice.
'General Sir Arthur St. Clare,' he said, 'came of a family
in which madness was hereditary; and his whole aim
was to keep this from his daughter, and even, if possible,
from his future son-in-law. Rightly or wrongly, he
thought the final collapse was close, and resolved on
suicide. Yet ordinary suicide would blazon the very idea
he dreaded. As the campaign approached the clouds
came thicker on his brain, and at last in a mad moment
he sacrificed his public duty to his private. He rushed
rashly into battle, hoping to fall by the first shot. When
he found that he had only attained capture and dis-
credit, the sealed bomb in his brain burst, and he broke
his own sword and hanged himself.'

He stared firmly at the grey façade of forest in front

of him, with the one black gap in it, like the mouth of the grave, into which their path plunged. Perhaps something menacing in the road thus suddenly swallowed reinforced his vivid vision of the tragedy, for he shuddered.

'A horrid story,' repeated the priest with bent head; 'but not the real story.'

Then he threw back his head with a sort of despair and cried: 'Oh, I wish it had been.'

The tall Flambeau faced round and stared at him.

'Yours is a clean story,' cried Father Brown, deeply moved. 'A sweet, pure, honest story, as open and white as that moon. Madness and despair are innocent enough. There are worse things, Flambeau.'

Flambeau looked up wildly at the moon thus invoked; and from where he stood one black tree-bough curved across it exactly like a devil's horn.

'Father—Father,' cried Flambeau with the French gesture and stepping yet more rapidly forward, 'do you mean it was worse than that?'

'Worse than that,' said the other like a grave echo. And they plunged into the black cloister of the woodland, which ran by them in a dim tapestry of trunks, like one of the dark corridors in a dream.

They were soon in the most secret entrails of the wood, and felt close about them the foliage that they could not see, when the priest said again:

'Where does a wise man hide a leaf? In the forest. But what does he do if there is no forest?'

'Well—well,' cried Flambeau irritably, 'what does he do?'

'He grows a forest to hide it in,' said the priest in an obscure voice. 'A fearful sin.'

'Look here,' cried his friend impatiently, for the dark wood and the dark sayings got a little on his nerves;

'will you tell me this story or not? What other evidence is there to go on?'

'There are three more bits of evidence,' said the other, 'that I have dug up in holes and corners, and I will give them in logical rather than chronological order. First of all, of course, our authority for the issue and event of the battle is in Olivier's own despatches, which are lucid enough. He was entrenched with two or three regiments on the heights that swept down to the Black River, on the other side of which was lower and more marshy ground. Beyond this again was gently rising country, on which was the first English outpost, supported by others which lay, however, considerably in its rear. The British forces as a whole were greatly superior in numbers; but this particular regiment was just far enough from its base to make Olivier consider the project of crossing the river to cut it off. By sunset, however, he had decided to retain his own position, which was a specially strong one. At daybreak next morning he was thunderstruck to see that this stray handful of English, entirely unsupported from their rear, had flung themselves across the river, half by the bridge to the right, and the other half by a ford higher up, and were massed upon the marshy bank below him.

'That they should attempt an attack with such numbers against such a position was incredible enough; but Olivier noticed something yet more extraordinary. For instead of attempting to seize more solid ground, this mad regiment, having put the river in its rear by one wild charge, did nothing more, but stuck there in the mire like flies in treacle. Needless to say, the Brazilians blew great gaps in them with artillery, which they could only return with spirited but lessening rifle fire. Yet they never broke; and Olivier's curt account ends with a strong tribute of admiration for the mystic valour of these imbeciles. "Our line then advanced finally," writes Olivier, "and drove them into the river; we captured General St. Clare himself and several other officers. The colonel and the major had both fallen in the battle. I cannot resist saying that few finer sights can have been seen in history than the last stand of this extraordinary regiment; wounded officers picking up the rifles of dead soldiers, and the general himself facing us on horseback bare-headed and with a broken sword." On what happened to the general afterwards Olivier is as silent as Captain Keith.'

'Well,' grunted Flambeau, 'get on to the next bit of evidence.'

'The next evidence,' said Father Brown, 'took some time to find, but it will not take long to tell. I found at last, in an almshouse down in the Lincolnshire Fens, an old soldier who not only was wounded at the Black River, but had actually knelt beside the colonel of the regiment when he died. This latter was a certain Colonel Clancy, a big bull of an Irishman; and it would seem that he died almost as much of rage as of bullets. He, at any rate, was not responsible for that ridiculous raid; it must have been imposed on him by the general. His last edifying words, according to my informant, were these: "And there goes the damned old donkey with the end of his sword knocked off. I wish it was his head." You will remark that everyone seems to have noticed this detail about the broken sword blade, though most people regard it somewhat more reverently than did the late Colonel Clancy. And now for the third fragment.'

Their path through the woodland began to go upward, and the speaker paused a little for breath before he went on. Then he continued in the same business-like tone:

'Only a month or two ago a certain Brazilian official died in England, having quarrelled with Olivier and left his country. He was a well-known figure both here and on the Continent, a Spaniard named Espado; I knew him myself, a yellow-faced old dandy, with a hooked nose. For various private reasons I had permission to see the documents he had left; he was a Catholic, of course, and I had been with him towards the end. There was nothing of his that lit up any corner of the black St. Clare business, except five or six common exercise books filled with the diary of some English soldier. I can only suppose that it was found by the Brazilians on one of those that fell. Anyhow, it stopped abruptly the night before the battle.

'But the account of that last day in the poor fellow's life was certainly worth reading. I have it on me; but it's too dark to read it here, and I will give you a résumé. The first part of that entry is full of jokes, evidently flung about among the men, about somebody called the Vulture. It does not seem as if this person, whoever he was, was one of themselves, nor even an Englishman; neither is he exactly spoken of as one of the enemy. It sounds rather as if he were some local go-between and non-combatant; perhaps a guide or a journalist. He has been closeted with old Colonel Clancy; but is more often seen talking to the major. Indeed, the major is somewhat prominent in this soldier's narrative; a lean, dark-haired man, apparently, of the name of Murray—a north of Ireland man and a Puritan. There are continual jests about the contrast between this Ulsterman's austerity and the conviviality of Colonel Clancy. There is also some joke about the Vulture wearing bright-coloured clothes.

'But all these levities are scattered by what may well be called the note of a bugle. Behind the English camp, and almost parallel to the river, ran one of the few great roads of that district. Westward the road curved round towards the river, which it crossed by the bridge before mentioned. To the east the road swept backwards into the wilds, and some two miles along it was the next English outpost. From this direction there came along the road that evening a glitter and clatter of light cavalry, in which even the simple diarist could recognize with astonishment the general with his staff. He rode the great white horse which you have seen so often in illustrated papers and Academy pictures; and you may be sure that the salute they gave him was not merely ceremonial. He, at least, wasted no time on ceremony, but, springing from the saddle immediately, mixed with the group of officers, and fell into emphatic though confidential speech. What struck our friend the diarist most was his special disposition to discuss matters with Major Murray; but, indeed, such a selection, so long as it was not marked, was in no way unnatural. The two men were made for sympathy; they were men who "read their Bibles"; they were both the old Evangelical type of officer. However this may be, it is certain that when the general mounted again he was still talking earnestly to Murray; and that as he walked his horse slowly down the road towards the river, the tall Ulsterman still walked by his bridle-rein in earnest debate. The soldiers watched the two until they vanished behind a clump of trees where the road turned towards the river. The colonel had gone back to his tent, and the men to their pickets; the man with the diary lingered for another four minutes, and saw a marvellous sight.

'The great white horse which had marched slowly down the road, as it had marched in so many processions, flew back, galloping up the road towards them as if it were mad to win a race. At first they thought it had run away with the man on its back; but they soon saw that the general, a fine rider, was himself urging it to full speed. Horse and man swept up to them like a whirlwind; and then, reining up the reeling charger, the general turned on them a face like flame, and called for the colonel like the trumpet that wakes the dead.

'I conceive that all the earthquake events of that catastrophe tumbled on top of each other rather like lumber in the minds of men such as our friend with the diary. With the dazed excitement of a dream, they found themselves falling—literally falling—into their ranks, and learned that an attack was to be led at once across the river. The general and the major, it was said, had found out something at the bridge, and there was only just time to strike for life. The major had gone back at once to call up the reserve along the road behind; it was doubtful if even with that prompt appeal help could reach them in time. But they must pass the stream that night, and seize the heights by morning. It is with the very stir and throb of that romantic nocturnal march that the diary suddenly ends.'

Father Brown had mounted ahead; for the woodland path grew smaller, steeper, and more twisted, till they felt as if they were ascending a winding staircase. The priest's voice came from above out of the darkness.

'There was one other little and enormous thing. When the general urged them to their chivalric charge he drew half his sword from the scabbard; and then, as if ashamed of such melodrama, thrust it back again. The sword again, you see.'

A half-light broke through the network of boughs above them, flinging the ghost of a net about their feet; for they were mounting again to the faint luminosity of the naked light. Flambeau felt truth all round him as an atmosphere, but not as an idea. He answered with bewildered brain: 'Well, what's the matter with the sword? Officers generally have swords, don't they?'

'They are not often mentioned in modern war,' said the other dispassionately; 'but in this affair one falls over the blessed sword everywhere.'

'Well, what is there in that?' growled Flambeau; 'it was a twopence coloured sort of incident; the old man's blade breaking in his last battle. Anyone might bet the papers would get hold of it, as they have. On all these tombs and things it's shown broken at the point. I hope you haven't dragged me through this Polar expedition merely because two men with an eye for a picture saw St. Clare's broken sword.'

'No,' cried Father Brown, with a sharp voice like a pistol shot; 'but who saw his unbroken sword?'

'What do you mean?' cried the other, and stood still under the stars. They had come abruptly out of the grey gates of the wood.

'I say, who saw his unbroken sword?' repeated Father Brown obstinately. 'Not the writer of the diary, anyhow; the general sheathed it in time.'

Flambeau looked about him in the moonlight, as a man struck blind might look in the sun; and his friend went on for the first time with eagerness:

'Flambeau,' he cried, 'I cannot prove it, even after hunting through the tombs. But I am sure of it. Let me add just one more tiny fact that tips the whole thing over. The colonel, by a strange chance, was one of the first struck by a bullet. He was struck long before the troops came to close quarters. But he saw St. Clare's sword broken. Why was it broken? How was it broken? My friend, it was broken before the battle.'

'Oh!' said his friend, with a sort of forlorn jocularity; 'and pray where is the other piece?'

'I can tell you,' said the priest promptly. 'In the north-east corner of the cemetery of the Protestant Cathedral at Belfast.'

'Indeed?' inquired the other. 'Have you looked for it?'

'I couldn't,' replied Brown, with frank regret. 'There's a great marble monument on top of it; a monument to the heroic Major Murray, who fell fighting gloriously at the famous Battle of the Black River.'

Flambeau seemed suddenly galvanized into existence. 'You mean,' he cried hoarsely, 'that General St. Clare hated Murray, and murdered him on the field of battle because——'

'You are still full of good and pure thoughts,' said the other. 'It was worse than that.'

'Well,' said the large man, 'my stock of evil imagination is used up.'

The priest seemed really doubtful where to begin, and at last he said again:

'Where would a wise man hide a leaf? In the forest.'

The other did not answer.

'If there were no forest, he would make a forest. And if he wished to hide a dead leaf, he would make a dead forest.'

There was still no reply, and the priest added still more mildly and quietly:

'And if a man had to hide a dead body, he would make a field of dead bodies to hide it in.'

Flambeau began to stamp forward with an intolerance of delay in time or space; but Father Brown went on as if he were continuing the last sentence:

'Sir Arthur St. Clare, as I have already said, was a man who read his Bible. That was what was the matter with *him*. When will people understand that it is useless for a man to read his Bible unless he also reads every-body else's Bible? A printer reads a Bible for misprints.

A Mormon reads his Bible and finds polygamy; a Christian Scientist reads his and finds we have no arms and legs. St. Clare was an old Anglo-Indian Protestant soldier. Now, just think what that might mean; and, for Heaven's sake, don't cant about it. It might mean a man physically formidable living under a tropic sun in an Oriental society, and soaking himself without sense or guidance in an Oriental book. Of course, he read the Old Testament rather than the New. Of course, he found in the Old Testament anything that he wanted —lust, tyranny, treason. Oh, I dare say he was honest, as you call it. But what is the good of a man being honest in his worship of dishonesty?

'In each of the hot and secret countries to which that man went he kept a harem, he tortured witnesses, he amassed shameful gold; but certainly he would have said with steady eyes that he did it to the glory of the Lord. My own theology is sufficiently expressed by asking which Lord? Anyhow, there is this about such evil, that it opens door after door in hell, and always into smaller and smaller chambers. This is the real case against crime, that a man does not become wilder and wilder, but only meaner and meaner. St. Clare was soon suffocated by difficulties of bribery and blackmail; and needed more and more cash. And by the time of the battle of the Black River he had fallen from world to world to that place which Dante makes the lowest floor of the universe.'

'What do you mean?' asked his friend again.

'I mean *that*,' retorted the cleric, and suddenly pointed at a puddle sealed with ice that shone in the moon. 'Do you remember whom Dante put in the last circle of ice?'

'The traitors,' said Flambeau, and shuddered. As he looked round at the inhuman landscape of trees, with taunting and almost obscene outlines, he could almost fancy he was Dante, and the priest with the rivulet of a voice was, indeed, a Virgil leading him through a land of eternal sins.

The voice went on: 'Olivier, as you know, was quixotic, and would not permit a secret service and spies. The thing, however, was done, like many other things, behind his back. It was managed by my old friend Espado; he was the bright-clad fop, whose hook nose got him called the Vulture. Posing as a sort of philanthropist at the front, he felt his way through the English Army, and at last got his fingers on its one corrupt man —please God!—and that man at the top. St. Clare was in foul need of money, and mountains of it. The discredited family doctor was threatening those extraordinary exposures that afterwards began and were broken off; tales of monstrous and prehistoric things in Park Lane; things done by an English Evangelical that smelt like human sacrifice and hordes of slaves. Money was wanted, too, for his daughter's dowry; for to him the fame of wealth was as sweet as wealth itself. He snapped the last thread, whispered the word to Brazil, and wealth poured in from the enemies of England. But another man had talked to Espado the Vulture as well as he. Somehow the dark, grim young major from Ulster had guessed the hideous truth; and when they walked slowly together down that road towards the bridge Murray was telling the general that he must resign instantly, or be court-martialled and shot. The general temporized with him till they came to the fringe of tropic trees by the bridge; and there by the singing river and the sunlit palms (for I can see the picture) the general drew his sabre and plunged it through the body of the major.'

The wintry road curved over a ridge in cutting frost,

with cruel black shapes of bush and thicket; but Flambeau fancied that he saw beyond it faintly the edge of an aureole that was not starlight and moonlight, but some fire such as is made by men. He watched it as the tale drew to its close.

'St. Clare was a hell-hound, but he was a hound of breed. Never, I'll swear, was he so lucid and so strong as when poor Murray lay a cold lump at his feet. Never in all his triumphs, as Captain Keith said truly, was the great man so great as he was in this last world-despised defeat. He looked coolly at his weapon to wipe off the blood; he saw the point he had planted between his victim's shoulders had broken off in the body. He saw quite calmly, as through a club window-pane, all that must follow. He saw that men must find the unaccountable corpse; must extract the unaccountable sword-point; must notice the unaccountable broken sword—or absence of sword. He had killed, but not silenced. But his imperious intellect rose against the facer—there was one way yet. He could make the corpse less unaccountable. He could create a hill of corpses to cover this one. In twenty minutes eight hundred English soldiers were marching down to their death.'

The warmer glow behind the black winter wood grew richer and brighter, and Flambeau strode on to reach it. Father Brown also quickened his stride; but he seemed merely absorbed in his tale.

'Such was the valour of that English thousand, and such the genius of their commander, that if they had at once attacked the hill, even their mad march might have met some luck. But the evil mind that played with them like pawns had other aims and reasons. They must remain in the marshes by the bridge at least till British corpses should be a common sight there. Then for the last grand scene: the silver-haired soldier-saint would give up his shattered sword to save further slaughter. Oh, it was well organized for an impromptu. But I think (I cannot prove), I think that it was while they stuck there in the bloody mire that someone doubted—and someone guessed.'

He was mute a moment, and then said: 'There is a voice from nowhere that tells me the man who guessed was the lover . . . the man to wed the old man's child.'

'But what about Olivier and the hanging?' asked Flambeau.

'Olivier, partly from chivalry, partly from policy, seldom encumbered his march with captives,' explained the narrator. 'He released everybody in most cases. He released everybody in this case.'

'Everybody but the general,' said the tall man.

'Everybody,' said the priest.

Flambeau knitted his black brows. 'I don't grasp it all yet,' he said.

'There is another picture, Flambeau,' said Brown in his more mystical undertone. 'I can't prove it; but I can do more—I can see it. There is a camp breaking up on the bare, torrid hills at morning, and Brazilian uniforms massed in blocks and columns to march. There is the red shirt and long black beard of Olivier, which blows as he stands, his broad-brimmed hat in his hand. He is saying farewell to the great enemy he is setting free— the simple, snow-headed English veteran, who thanks him in the name of his men. The English remnant stand behind at attention; beside them are stores and vehicles for the retreat. The drums roll; the Brazilians are moving; the English are still like statues. So they abide till the last hum and flash of the enemy have faded from the tropic horizon. Then they alter their postures all at once, like dead men coming to life; they turn their fifty faces upon the general—faces not to be forgotten.'

Flambeau gave a great jump. 'Ah,' he cried. 'You don't mean——'

'Yes,' said Father Brown in a deep, moving voice. 'It was an English hand that put the rope round St. Clare's neck; I believe the hand that put the ring on his daughter's finger. They were English hands that dragged him up to the tree of shame; the hands of men that had adored him and followed him to victory. And they were English souls (God pardon and endure us all!) who stared at him swinging in that foreign sun on the green gallows of palm, and prayed in their hatred that he might drop off it into hell.'

As the two topped the ridge there burst on them the strong scarlet light of a red-curtained English inn. It stood sideways in the road, as if standing aside in the amplitude of hospitality. Its three doors stood open with invitation; and even where they stood they could hear the hum and laughter of humanity happy for a night.

'I need not tell you more,' said Father Brown. 'They tried him in the wilderness and destroyed him; and then, for the honour of England and of his daughter, they took an oath to seal up for ever the story of the traitor's purse and the assassin's sword blade. Perhaps —Heaven help them—they tried to forget it. Let us try to forget it, anyhow; here is our inn.'

'With all my heart,' said Flambeau, and was just striding into the bright, noisy bar when he stepped back and almost fell on the road.

'Look there, in the devil's name!' he cried, and pointed rigidly at the square wooden sign that overhung the road. It showed dimly the crude shape of a sabre hilt and a shortened blade; and was inscribed in false archaic lettering, 'The Sign of the Broken Sword.'

'Were you not prepared?' asked Father Brown gently.

'He is the god of this country; half the inns and parks and streets are named after him and his story.'

'I thought we had done with the leper,' cried Flambeau, and spat on the road.

'You will never have done with him in England,' said the priest, looking down, 'while brass is strong and stone abides. His marble statues will erect the souls of proud, innocent boys for centuries, his village tomb will smell of loyalty as of lilies. Millions who never knew him shall love him like a father—this man whom the last few that knew him dealt with like dung. He shall be a saint; and the truth shall never be told of him, because I have made up my mind at last. There is so much good and evil in breaking secrets, that I put my conduct to a test. All these newspapers will perish; the anti-Brazil boom is already over; Olivier is already honoured everywhere. But I told myself that if anywhere, by name, in metal or marble that will endure like the pyramids, Colonel Clancy, or Captain Keith, or President Olivier, or any innocent man was wrongly blamed, then I would speak. If it were only that St. Clare was wrongly praised, I would be silent. And I will.'

They plunged into the red-curtained tavern, which was not only cosy, but even luxurious inside. On a table stood a silver model of the tomb of St. Clare, the silver head bowed, the silver sword broken. On the walls were coloured photographs of the same scene, and of the system of wagonettes that took tourists to see it. They sat down on the comfortable padded benches.

'Come, it's cold,' cried Father Brown; 'let's have some wine or beer.'

'Or brandy,' said Flambeau.

THE WISDOM OF
FATHER BROWN

The Paradise of Thieves

THE great Muscari, most original of the young Tuscan poets, walked swiftly into his favourite restaurant, which overlooked the Mediterranean, was covered by an awning and fenced by little lemon and orange trees. Waiters in white aprons were already laying out on white tables the insignia of an early and elegant lunch; and this seemed to increase a satisfaction that already touched the top of swagger. Muscari had an eagle nose like Dante; his hair and neckerchief were dark and flowing; he carried a black cloak, and might almost have carried a black mask, so much did he bear with him a sort of Venetian melodrama. He acted as if a troubadour had still a definite social office, like a bishop. He went as near as his century permitted to walking the world literally like Don Juan, with rapier and guitar.

For he never travelled without a case of swords, with which he had fought many brilliant duels, or without a corresponding case for his mandolin, with which he had actually serenaded Miss Ethel Harrogate, the highly-conventional daughter of a Yorkshire banker on a holiday. Yet he was neither a charlatan nor a child; but a hot, logical Latin who liked a certain thing and was it. His poetry was as straightforward as anyone else's prose. He desired fame or wine or the beauty of women with a torrid directness inconceivable among the cloudy ideals or cloudy compromises of the north; to vaguer races his intensity smelt of danger or even crime. Like fire or the sea, he was too simple to be trusted.

The banker and his beautiful English daughter were staying at the hotel attached to Muscari's restaurant; that was why it was his favourite restaurant. A glance flashed round the room told him at once, however, that the English party had not descended. The restaurant was glittering, but still comparatively empty. Two priests were talking at a table in a corner, but Muscari (an ardent Catholic) took no more notice of them than of a couple of crows. But from a yet farther seat, partly concealed behind a dwarf tree golden with oranges, there rose and advanced towards the poet a person whose costume was the most aggressively opposite to his own.

This figure was clad in tweeds of a piebald check, with a pink tie, a sharp collar and protuberant yellow boots. He contrived, in the true tradition of 'Arry at Margate, to look at once startling and commonplace. But as the Cockney apparition drew nearer, Muscari was astounded to observe that the head was distinctly different from the body. It was an Italian head: fuzzy, swarthy and very vivacious, that rose abruptly out of the standing collar like cardboard and the comic pink tie. In fact it was a head he knew. He recognised it, above all the dire erection of English holiday array, as the face of an old but forgotten friend named Ezza. This youth had been a prodigy at college, and European fame was promised him when he was barely fifteen; but when he appeared in the world he failed, first publicly as a dramatist and a demagogue, and then privately for years on end as an actor, a traveller, a commission agent or a journalist. Muscari had known him last behind the footlights; he was but too well attuned to the excitements of that profession, and it was believed that some moral calamity had swallowed him up.

'Ezza!' cried the poet, rising and shaking hands in a pleasant astonishment. 'Well! I've seen you in many costumes in the green room; but I never expected to see you dressed up as an Englishman.'

'This,' answered Ezza gravely: 'is not the costume of an Englishman, but of the Italian of the future.'

'In that case,' remarked Muscari, 'I confess I prefer the Italian of the past.'

'That is your old mistake, Muscari,' said the man in tweeds, shaking his head; 'and the mistake of Italy. In the sixteenth century we Tuscans made the morning: we had the newest steel, the newest carving, the newest chemistry. Why should we not now have the newest factories, the newest motors, the newest finance—and the newest clothes?'

'Because they are not worth having,' answered Muscari. 'You cannot make Italians really progressive; they are too intelligent. Men who see the short cut to good living will never go by the new elaborate roads.'

'Well, to me Marconi, or D'Annunzio, is the star of Italy,' said the other. 'That is why I have become a Futurist—and a courier.'

'A courier!' cried Muscari, laughing. 'Is that the last of your list of trades? And whom are you conducting?'

'Oh, a man of the name of Harrogate, and his family, I believe.'

'Not the banker in this hotel?' inquired the poet, with some eagerness.

'That's the man,' answered the courier.

'Does it pay well?' asked the troubadour innocently.

'It will pay me,' said Ezza, with a very enigmatic smile. 'But I am a rather curious sort of courier.' Then, as if changing the subject, he said abruptly: 'He has a daughter—and a son.'

'The daughter is divine,' affirmed Muscari, 'the father and son are, I suppose, human. But granted his harmless qualities, doesn't that banker strike you as a splendid instance of my argument? Harrogate has millions in his safes, and I have—the hole in my pocket. But you daren't say—you can't say—that he's cleverer than I, or bolder than I, or even more energetic. He's not clever; he's got eyes like blue buttons; he's not energetic, he moves from chair to chair like a paralytic. He's a conscientious, kindly old blockhead; but he's got money simply because he collects money, as a boy collects stamps. You're too strong-minded for business, Ezza. You won't get on. To be clever enough to get all that money, one must be stupid enough to want it.'

'I'm stupid enough for that,' said Ezza gloomily. 'But I should suggest a suspension of your critique of the banker, for here he comes.'

Mr. Harrogate, the great financier, did indeed enter the room, but nobody looked at him. He was a massive elderly man with a boiled blue eye and faded greysandy moustaches; but for his heavy stoop he might have been a colonel. He carried several unopened letters in his hand. His son Frank was a really fine lad, curly-haired, sun-burnt and strenuous; but nobody looked at him either. All eyes, as usual, were riveted, for the moment at least, upon Ethel Harrogate, whose golden Greek head and colour of the dawn seemed set purposely above that sapphire sea, like a goddess's. The poet Muscari drew a deep breath as if he were drinking something, as indeed he was. He was drinking the Classic; which his fathers made. Ezza studied her with a gaze equally intense and far more baffling.

Miss Harrogate was specially radiant and ready for conversation on this occasion; and her family had fallen into the easier Continental habit, allowing the stranger Muscari and even the courier Ezza to share their table and their talk. In Ethel Harrogate conventionality crowned itself with a perfection and splendour of its own. Proud of her father's prosperity, fond of her fashionable pleasures, a fond daughter but an arrant flirt, she was all these things with a sort of golden good-nature that made her very pride pleasing and her worldly respectability a fresh and hearty thing.

They were in an eddy of excitement about some alleged peril in the mountain path they were to attempt that week. The danger was not from rock and avalanche, but from something yet more romantic. Ethel had been earnestly assured that brigands, the true cut-throats of the modern legend, still haunted that ridge and held that pass of the Apennines.

'They say,' she cried, with the awful relish of a schoolgirl, 'that all that country isn't ruled by the King of Italy, but by the King of Thieves. Who is the King of Thieves?'

'A great man,' replied Muscari, 'worthy to rank with your own Robin Hood, signorina. Montano, the King of Thieves, was first heard of in the mountains some ten years ago, when people said brigands were extinct. But his wild authority spread with the swiftness of a silent revolution. Men found his fierce proclamations nailed in every mountain village; his sentinels, gun in hand, in every mountain ravine. Six times the Italian Government tried to dislodge him, and was defeated in six pitched battles as if by Napoleon.'

'Now that sort of thing,' observed the banker weightily, 'would never be allowed in England; perhaps, after all, we had better choose another route. But the courier thought it perfectly safe.'

'It is perfectly safe,' said the courier contemptuously, 'I have been over it twenty times. There may have been some old jail-bird called a King in the time of our grandmothers; but he belongs to history if not to fable. Brigandage is utterly stamped out.'

'It can never be utterly stamped out,' Muscari answered; 'because armed revolt is a reaction natural to southerners. Our peasants are like their mountains, rich in grace and green gaiety, but with the fires beneath. There is a point of human despair where the northern poor take to drink—and our own poor take to daggers.'

'A poet is privileged,' replied Ezza, with a sneer. 'If Signor Muscari were English he would still be looking for highwaymen in Wandsworth. Believe me, there is no more danger of being captured in Italy than of being scalped in Boston.'

'Then you propose to attempt it?' asked Mr. Harrogate, frowning.

'Oh, it sounds rather dreadful,' cried the girl, turning her glorious eyes on Muscari. 'Do you really think the pass is dangerous?'

Muscari threw back his black mane. 'I know it is dangerous,' he said. 'I am crossing it to-morrow.'

The young Harrogate was left behind for a moment emptying a glass of white wine and lighting a cigarette, as the beauty retired with the banker, the courier and the poet, distributing peals of silvery satire. At about the same instant the two priests in the corner rose; the taller, a white-haired Italian, taking his leave. The shorter priest turned and walked towards the banker's son, and the latter was astonished to realize that though a Roman priest the man was an Englishman. He vaguely remembered meeting him at the social crushes of some of his Catholic friends. But the man spoke before his memories could collect themselves.

'Mr. Frank Harrogate, I think,' he said. 'I have had an introduction, but I do not mean to presume on it. The odd thing I have to say will come far better from a stranger. Mr. Harrogate, I say one word and go: take care of your sister in her great sorrow.'

Even for Frank's truly fraternal indifference the radiance and derision of his sister still seemed to sparkle and ring; he could hear her laughter still from the garden of the hotel, and he stared at his sombre adviser in puzzledom.

'Do you mean the brigands?' he asked; and then, remembering a vague fear of his own, 'or can you be thinking of Muscari?'

'One is never thinking of the real sorrow,' said the strange priest. 'One can only be kind when it comes.'

And he passed promptly from the room, leaving the other almost with his mouth open.

A day or two afterwards a coach containing the company was really crawling and staggering up the spurs of the menacing mountain range. Between Ezza's cheery denial of the danger and Muscari's boisterous defiance of it, the financial family were firm in their original purpose; and Muscari made his mountain journey coincide with theirs. A more surprising feature was the appearance at the coast-town station of the little priest of the restaurant; he alleged merely that business led him also to cross the mountains of the midland. But young Harrogate could not but connect his presence with the mystical fears and warnings of yesterday.

The coach was a kind of commodious wagonette, invented by the modernist talent of the courier, who dominated the expedition with his scientific activity and breezy wit. The theory of danger from thieves was banished from thought and speech; though so far conceded in formal act that some slight protection was employed. The courier and the young banker carried loaded revolvers, and Muscari (with much boyish gratification) buckled on a kind of cutlass under his black cloak.

He had planted his person at a flying leap next to the lovely Englishwoman; on the other side of her sat the priest, whose name was Brown and who was fortunately a silent individual; the courier and the father and son were on the *banc* behind. Muscari was in towering spirits, seriously believing in the peril, and his talk to Ethel might well have made her think him a maniac. But there was something in the crazy and gorgeous ascent, amid crags like peaks loaded with woods like orchards, that dragged her spirit up alone with his into purple preposterous heavens with wheeling suns. The white road climbed like a white cat; it spanned sunless chasms like a tight-rope; it was flung round far-off headlands like a lasso.

And yet, however high they went, the desert still blossomed like the rose. The fields were burnished in sun and wind with the colour of kingfisher and parrot and humming-bird; the hues of a hundred flowering flowers. There are no lovelier meadows and woodlands than the English; no nobler crests or chasms than those of Snowdon and Glencoe. But Ethel Harrogate had never before seen the southern parks tilted on the splintered northern peaks; the gorge of Glencoe laden with the fruits of Kent. There was nothing here of that chill and desolation that in Britain one associates with high and wild scenery. It was rather like a mosaic palace, rent with earthquakes; or like a Dutch tulip garden blown to the stars with dynamite.

'It's like Kew Gardens on Beachy Head,' said Ethel.

'It is our secret,' answered he, 'the secret of the volcano; that is also the secret of the revolution—that a thing can be violent and yet fruitful.'

'You are rather violent yourself,' and she smiled at him.

'And yet rather fruitless,' he admitted; 'if I die to-night I die unmarried and a fool.'

'It is not my fault if you have come,' she said after a difficult silence.

'It is never your fault,' answered Muscari; 'it was not your fault that Troy fell.'

As he spoke they came under overwhelming cliffs that spread almost like wings above a corner of peculiar peril. Shocked by the big shadow on the narrow ledge, the horses stirred doubtfully. The driver leapt to the earth to hold their heads, and they became ungovernable. One horse reared up to his full height—the titanic and terrifying height of a horse when he becomes a biped. It was just enough to alter the equilibrium; the whole coach heeled over like a ship and crashed through the fringe of bushes over the cliff. Muscari threw an arm round Ethel, who clung to him, and shouted aloud. It was for such moments that he lived.

At the moment when the gorgeous mountain walls went round the poet's head like a purple windmill a thing happened which was superficially even more startling. The elderly and lethargic banker sprang erect in the coach and leapt over the precipice before the tilted vehicle could take him there. In the first flash it looked as wild as suicide; but in the second it was as sensible as a safe investment. The Yorkshireman had evidently more promptitude, as well as more sagacity, than Muscari had given him credit for; for he landed in a lap of land which might have been specially padded with turf and clover to receive him. As it happened, indeed, the whole company were equally lucky, if less dignified in their form of ejection. Immediately under this abrupt turn of the road was a grassy and flowery hollow like a sunken meadow; a sort of green velvet pocket in the long, green, trailing garments of the hills. Into this they were all tipped or tumbled with little damage, save that their smallest baggage and even the contents of their pockets were scattered in the grass around them. The wrecked coach still hung above, entangled in the tough hedge, and the horses plunged painfully down the slope. The first to sit up was the little priest, who scratched his head with a face of foolish wonder. Frank Harrogate heard him say to himself: 'Now why on earth have we fallen just here?'

He blinked at the litter around him, and recovered his own very clumsy umbrella. Beyond it lay the broad sombrero fallen from the head of Muscari, and beside it a sealed business letter which, after a glance at the address, he returned to the elder Harrogate. On the other side of him the grass partly hid Miss Ethel's sunshade, and just beyond it lay a curious little glass bottle hardly two inches long. The priest picked it up; in a quick, unobtrusive manner he uncorked and sniffed it, and his heavy face turned the colour of clay.

'Heaven deliver us!' he muttered; 'it can't be hers! Has her sorrow come on her already?' He slipped it into his own waistcoat pocket. 'I think I'm justified,' he said, 'till I know a little more.'

He gazed painfully at the girl, at that moment being raised out of the flowers by Muscari, who was saying: 'We have fallen into heaven; it is a sign. Mortals climb up and they fall down; but it is only gods and goddesses who can fall upwards.'

And indeed she rose out of the sea of colours so beautiful and happy a vision that the priest felt his suspicion shaken and shifted. 'After all,' he thought, 'perhaps the poison isn't hers; perhaps it's one of Muscari's melodramatic tricks.'

Muscari set the lady lightly on her feet, made her an absurdly theatrical bow, and then, drawing his cutlass, hacked hard at the taut reins of the horses, so that they scrambled to their feet and stood in the grass trembling. When he had done so, a most remarkable thing occurred. A very quiet man, very poorly dressed and extremely sunburnt, came out of the bushes and took hold of the horses' heads. He had a queer-shaped knife, very broad and crooked, buckled on his belt; there was nothing else remarkable about him, except his sudden and silent appearance. The poet asked him who he was, and he did not answer.

Looking around him at the confused and startled group in the hollow, Muscari then perceived that another tanned and tattered man, with a short gun under his arm, was looking at them from the ledge just below, leaning his elbows on the edge of the turf. Then he looked up at the road from which they had fallen and saw, looking down on them, the muzzles of four other carbines and four other brown faces with bright but quite motionless eyes.

'The brigands!' cried Muscari, with a kind of monstrous gaiety. 'This was a trap. Ezza, if you will oblige me by shooting the coachman first, we can cut our way out yet. There are only six of them.'

'The coachman,' said Ezza, who was standing grimly with his hands in his pockets, 'happens to be a servant of Mr. Harrogate's.'

'Then shoot him all the more,' cried the poet impatiently; 'he was bribed to upset his master. Then put the lady in the middle, and we will break the line up there—with a rush.'

And, wading in wild grass and flowers, he advanced fearlessly on the four carbines; but finding that no one followed except young Harrogate, he turned, brandishing his cutlass to wave the others on. He beheld the courier still standing slightly astride in the centre of the grassy ring, his hands in his pockets; and his lean, ironical Italian face seemed to grow longer and longer in the evening light.

'You thought, Muscari, I was the failure among our

schoolfellows,' he said, 'and you thought you were the success. But I have succeeded more than you and fill a bigger place in history. I have been acting epics while you have been writing them.'

'Come on, I tell you!' thundered Muscari from above. 'Will you stand there talking nonsense about yourself with a woman to save and three strong men to help you? What do you call yourself?'

'I call myself Montano,' cried the strange courier in a voice equally loud and full. 'I am the King of Thieves, and I welcome you all to my summer palace.'

And even as he spoke five more silent men with weapons ready came out of the bushes, and looked towards him for their orders. One of them held a large paper in his hand.

'This pretty little nest where we are all picknicking,' went on the courier-brigand, with the same easy yet sinister smile, 'is, together with some caves underneath it, known by the name of the Paradise of Thieves. It is my principal stronghold on these hills; for (as you have doubtless noticed) the eyrie is invisible both from the road above and from the valley below. It is something better than impregnable; it is unnoticeable. Here I mostly live, and here I shall certainly die, if the gendarmes ever track me here. I am not the kind of criminal that "reserves his defence," but the better kind that reserves his last bullet.'

All were staring at him thunderstruck and still, except Father Brown, who heaved a huge sigh as of relief and fingered the little phial in his pocket. 'Thank God!' he muttered; 'that's much more probable. The poison belongs to this robber-chief, of course. He carries it so that he may never be captured, like Cato.'

The King of Thieves was, however, continuing his address with the same kind of dangerous politeness. 'It only remains for me,' he said, 'to explain to my guests the social conditions upon which I have the pleasure of entertaining them. I need not expound the quaint old ritual of ransom, which it is incumbent upon me to keep up; and even this only applies to a part of the company. The Reverend Father Brown and the celebrated Signor Muscari I shall release to-morrow at dawn and escort to my outposts. Poets and priests, if you will pardon my simplicity of speech, never have any money. And so (since it is impossible to get anything out of them), let us seize the opportunity to show our admiration for classic literature and our reverence for Holy Church.'

He paused with an unpleasing smile; and Father Brown blinked repeatedly at him, and seemed suddenly to be listening with great attention. The brigand captain took the large paper from the attendant brigand and, glancing it over, continued: 'My other intentions are clearly set forth in this public document, which I will hand round in a moment; and which after that will be posted on a tree by every village in the valley, and every cross-road in the hills. I will not weary you with the verbalism, since you will be able to check it; the substance of my proclamation is this: I announce first that I have captured the English millionaire, the colossus of finance, Mr. Samuel Harrogate. I next announce that I have found on his person notes and bonds for two thousand pounds, which he has given up to me. Now since it would be really immoral to announce such a thing to a credulous public if it had not occurred, I suggest it should occur without further delay. I suggest that Mr. Harrogate senior should now give me the two thousand pounds in his pocket.'

The banker looked at him under lowering brows, red-faced and sulky, but seemingly cowed. That leap from the falling carriage seemed to have used up his last virility. He had held back in a hang-dog style when his son and Muscari had made a bold movement to break out of the brigand trap. And now his red and trembling hand went reluctantly to his breast-pocket, and passed a bundle of papers and envelopes to the brigand.

'Excellent!' cried that outlaw gaily; 'so far we are all cosy. I resume the points of my proclamation, so soon to be published to all Italy. The third item is that of ransom. I am asking from the friends of the Harrogate family a ransom of three thousand pounds, which I am sure is almost insulting to that family in its moderate estimate of their importance. Who would not pay triple this sum for another day's association with such a domestic circle? I will not conceal from you that the document ends with certain legal phrases about the unpleasant things that may happen if the money is not paid; but meanwhile ladies and gentlemen, let me assure you that I am comfortably off here for accommodation, wine and cigars, and bid you for the present a sportsmanlike welcome to the luxuries of the Paradise of Thieves.'

All the time that he had been speaking, the dubious-looking men with carbines and dirty slouch hats had been gathering silently in such preponderating numbers that even Muscari was compelled to recognize his sally with the sword as hopeless. He glanced around him; but the girl had already gone over to soothe and comfort her father, for her natural affection for his person was as strong or stronger than her somewhat snobbish pride in his success. Muscari, with the illogicality of a lover, admired this filial devotion, and yet was irritated by it. He slapped his sword back in the scabbard and went and flung himself somewhat sulkily on one of the green banks. The priest sat down within a yard or two, and Muscari turned his aquiline eye and nose on him in an instantaneous irritation.

'Well,' said the poet tartly, 'do people still think me too romantic? Are there, I wonder, any brigands left in the mountains?'

'There may be,' said Father Brown agnostically.

'What do you mean?' asked the other sharply.

'I mean I am puzzled,' replied the priest. 'I am puzzled about Ezza or Montano, or whatever his name is. He seems to me much more inexplicable as a brigand even than he was as a courier.'

'But in what way?' persisted his companion. 'Santa Maria! I should have thought the brigand was plain enough.'

'I find three curious difficulties,' said the priest in a quiet voice. 'I should like to have your opinion on them. First of all I must tell you I was lunching in that restaurant at the seaside. As four of you left the room, you and Miss Harrogate went ahead, talking and laughing; the banker and the courier came behind, speaking sparely and rather low. But I could not help hearing Ezza say these words—"Well, let her have a little fun; you know the blow may smash her any minute." Mr. Harrogate answered nothing; so the words must have had some meaning. On the impulse of the moment I warned her brother that she might be in peril; I said nothing of its nature, for I did not know. But if it meant this capture in the hills, the thing is nonsense. Why should the brigand-courier warn his patron, even by a hint, when it was his whole purpose to lure him into the mountain-mousetrap? It could not have meant that. But if not, what is this other disaster, known both to courier and banker, which hangs over Miss Harrogate's head?'

'Disaster to Miss Harrogate!' ejaculated the poet, sitting up with some ferocity. 'Explain yourself; go on.'

'All my riddles, however, revolve round our bandit chief,' resumed the priest reflectively. 'And here is the second of them. Why did he put so prominently in his demand for ransom the fact that he had taken two thousand pounds from his victim on the spot? It had no faintest tendency to evoke the ransom. Quite the other way, in fact. Harrogate's friends would be far likelier to fear for his fate if they thought the thieves were poor and desperate. Yet the spoliation on the spot was emphasized and even put first in the demand. Why should Ezza Montano want so specially to tell all Europe that he had picked the pocket before he levied the blackmail?'

'I cannot imagine,' said Muscari, rubbing up his black hair for once with an unaffected gesture. 'You may think you enlighten me, but you are leading me deeper in the dark. What may be the third objection to the King of the Thieves?'

'The third objection,' said Father Brown, still in meditation, 'is this bank we are sitting on. Why does our brigand-courier call this his chief fortress and the Paradise of Thieves? It is certainly a soft spot to fall on and a sweet spot to look at. It is also quite true, as he says, that it is invisible from valley and peak, and is therefore a hiding-place. But it is not a fortress. It never could be a fortress. I think it would be the worst fortress in the world. For it is actually commanded from above by the common high-road across the mountains—the very place where the police would most probably pass. Why, five shabby short guns held us helpless here about half an hour ago. The quarter of a company of any kind of soldiers could have blown us over the precipice. Whatever is the meaning of this odd little nook of grass and flowers, it is not an entrenched position. It is something else; it has some other strange sort of importance: some value that I do not understand. It is more like an accidental theatre or a natural green-room; it is like the scene for some romantic comedy; it is like. . . .'

As the little priest's words lengthened and lost themselves in a dull and dreamy sincerity, Muscari, whose animal senses were alert and impatient, heard a new noise in the mountains. Even for him the sound was as yet very small and faint; but he could have sworn the evening breeze bore with it something like the pulsation of horses' hoofs and a distant hallooing.

At the same moment, and long before the vibration had touched the less-experienced English ears, Montano the brigand ran up the bank above them and stood in the broken hedge, steadying himself against a tree and peering down the road. He was a strange figure as he stood there, for he had assumed a flapped fantastic hat and swinging baldric and cutlass in his capacity of bandit king, but the bright prosaic tweed of the courier showed through in patches all over him.

The next moment he turned his olive, sneering face and made a movement with his hand. The brigands scattered at the signal, not in confusion, but in what was evidently a kind of guerilla discipline. Instead of occupying the road along the ridge, they sprinkled themselves along the side of it behind the trees and the hedge, as if watching unseen for an enemy. The noise beyond grew stronger, beginning to shake the mountain road, and a voice could be clearly heard calling out orders. The brigands swayed and huddled, cursing and whispering, and the evening air was full of little metallic noises as they cocked their pistols, or loosened their knives, or trailed their scabbards over the stones. Then the noises from both quarters seemed to meet on the road above; branches broke, horses neighed, men cried out.

'A rescue!' cried Muscari, springing to his feet and

waving his hat; 'the gendarmes are on them! Now for freedom and a blow for it! Now to be rebels against robbers! Come, don't let us leave everything to the police; that is so dreadfully modern. Fall on the rear of these ruffians. The gendarmes are rescuing us; come, friends, let us rescue the gendarmes!'

And throwing his hat over the trees, he drew his cutlass once more and began to escalade the slope up to the road. Frank Harrogate jumped up and ran across to help him, revolver in hand, but was astounded to hear himself imperatively recalled by the raucous voice of his father, who seemed to be in great agitation.

'I won't have it,' said the banker in a choking voice; 'I command you not to interfere.'

'But, father,' said Frank very warmly, 'an Italian gentleman has led the way. You wouldn't have it said that the English hung back.'

'It is useless,' said the older man, who was trembling violently, 'it is useless. We must submit to our lot.'

Father Brown looked at the banker; then he put his hand instinctively as if on his heart, but really on the little bottle of poison; and a great light came into his face like the light of the revelation of death.

Muscari meanwhile, without waiting for support, had crested the bank up to the road, and struck the brigand king heavily on the shoulder, causing him to stagger and swing round, Montano also had his cutlass unsheathed, and Muscari, without further speech, sent a slash at his head which he was compelled to catch and parry. But even as the two short blades crossed and clashed the King of Thieves deliberately dropped his point and laughed.

'What's the good, old man?' he said in spirited Italian slang; 'this damned farce will soon be over.'

'What do you mean, you shuffler?' panted the fire-eating poet. 'Is your courage a sham as well as your honesty?'

'Everything about me is a sham,' responded the ex-courier in complete good-humour. 'I am an actor; and if I ever had a private character, I have forgotten it. I am no more a genuine brigand than I am a genuine courier. I am only a bundle of masks, and you can't fight a duel with that.' And he laughed with boyish pleasure and fell into his old straddling attitude, with his back to the skirmish up the road.

Darkness was deepening under the mountain walls, and it was not easy to discern much of the progress of the struggle, save that tall men were pushing their horses' muzzles through a clinging crowd of brigands, who seemed more inclined to harass and hustle the invaders than to kill them. It was more like a town crowd pre-venting the passage of the police than anything the poet had ever pictured as the last stand of doomed and out-lawed men of blood. Just as he was rolling his eyes in bewilderment he felt a touch on his elbow, and found the odd little priest standing there like a small Noah with a large hat, and requesting the favour of a word or two.

'Signor Muscari,' said the cleric, 'in this queer crisis personalities may be pardoned. I may tell you without offence of a way in which you will do more good than by helping the gendarmes, who are bound to break through in any case. You will permit me the imperti-nent intimacy; but do you care about that girl? Care enough to marry her and make her a good husband, I mean?'

'Yes,' said the poet quite simply.

'Does she care about you?'

'I think so,' was the equally grave reply.

'Then go over there and offer yourself,' said the priest:

'offer her everything you can; offer her heaven and earth if you've got them. The time is short.'

'Why?' asked the astonished man of letters.

'Because,' said Father Brown, 'her Doom is coming up the road.'

'Nothing is coming up the road,' argued Muscari, 'except the rescue.'

'Well, you go over there,' said his adviser, 'and be ready to rescue her from the rescue.'

Almost as he spoke the hedges were broken all along the ridge by a rush of the escaping brigands. They dived into bushes and thick grass like defeated men pursued; and the great cocked hats of the mounted gendarmerie were seen passing along above the broken hedge. Another order was given; there was a noise of dismounting, and a tall officer with a cocked hat, a grey imperial, and a paper in his hand appeared in the gap that was the gate of the Paradise of Thieves. There was a momentary silence, broken in an extraordinary way by the banker, who cried out in a hoarse and strangled voice: 'Robbed! I've been robbed!'

'Why, that was hours ago,' cried his son in astonishment: 'when you were robbed of two thousand pounds.'

'Not of two thousand pounds,' said the financier, with an abrupt and terrible composure, 'only of a small bottle.'

The policeman with the grey imperial was striding across the green hollow. Encountering the King of the Thieves in his path, he clapped him on the shoulder with something between a caress and a buffet and gave him a push that sent him staggering away. 'You'll get into trouble, too,' he said, 'if you play these tricks.'

Again to Muscari's artistic eye it seemed scarcely like the capture of a great outlaw at bay. Passing on, the policeman halted before the Harrogate group and said:

'Samuel Harrogate, I arrest you in the name of the law for embezzlement of the funds of the Hull and Huddersfield Bank.'

The great banker nodded with an odd air of business assent, seemed to reflect a moment, and before they could interpose took a half turn and a step that brought him to the edge of the outer mountain wall. Then, flinging up his hands, he leapt exactly as he leapt out of the coach. But this time he did not fall into a little meadow just beneath; he fell a thousand feet below, to become a wreck of bones in the valley.

The anger of the Italian policeman, which he expressed volubly to Father Brown, was largely mixed with admiration. 'It was like him to escape us at last,' he said. '*He* was a great brigand if you like. This last trick of his I believe to be absolutely unprecedented. He fled with the company's money to Italy, and actually got himself captured by sham brigands in his own pay, so as to explain both the disappearance of the money and the disappearance of himself. That demand for ransom was really taken seriously by most of the police. But for years he's been doing things as good as that, quite as good as that. He will be a serious loss to his family.'

Muscari was leading away the unhappy daughter, who held hard to him, as she did for many a year after. But even in that tragic wreck he could not help having a smile and a hand of half-mocking friendship for the indefensible Ezza Montano. 'And where are you going next?' he asked him over his shoulder.

'Birmingham,' answered the actor, puffing a cigarette. 'Didn't I tell you I was a Futurist? I really do believe in those things if I believe in anything. Change, bustle, and new things every morning. I am going to Manchester, Liverpool, Leeds, Hull, Huddersfield,

Glasgow, Chicago—in short, to enlightened, energetic, civilized society!'

'In short,' said Muscari, 'to the real Paradise of Thieves.'

The Mistake of the Machine

FLAMBEAU and his friend the priest were sitting in the Temple Gardens about sunset; and their neighbourhood or some such accidental influence had turned their talk to matters of legal process. From the problem of the licence in cross-examination, their talk strayed to Roman and mediæval torture, to the examining magistrate in France and the Third Degree in America.

'I've been reading,' said Flambeau, 'of this new psychometric method they talk about so much, especially in America. You know what I mean; they put a pulsometer on a man's wrist and judge by how his heart goes at the pronunciation of certain words. What do you think of it?'

'I think it very interesting,' replied Father Brown; 'it reminds me of that interesting idea in the Dark Ages that blood would flow from a corpse if the murderer touched it.'

'Do you really mean,' demanded his friend, 'that you think the two methods equally valuable?'

'I think them equally valueless,' replied Brown. 'Blood flows, fast or slow, in dead folk or living, for so many more million reasons than we can ever know. Blood will have to flow very funnily; blood will have to flow up the Matterhorn, before I will take it as a sign that I am to shed it.'

'The method,' remarked the other, 'has been guaranteed by some of the greatest American men of science.'

'What sentimentalists men of science are!' exclaimed Father Brown, 'and how much more sentimental must American men of science be! Who but a Yankee would think of proving anything from heart-throbs? Why, they must be as sentimental as a man who thinks a woman is in love with him if she blushes. That's a test from the circulation of the blood, discovered by the immortal Harvey; and a jolly rotten test, too.'

'But surely,' insisted Flambeau, 'it might point pretty straight at something or other.'

'There's a disadvantage in a stick pointing straight,' answered the other. 'What is it? Why, the other end of the stick always points the opposite way. It depends whether you get hold of the stick by the right end. I saw the thing done once and I've never believed in it since.' And he proceeded to tell the story of his disillusionment.

It happened nearly twenty years before, when he was chaplain to his co-religionists in a prison in Chicago—where the Irish population displayed a capacity both for crime and penitence which kept him tolerably busy. The official second-in-command under the Governor was an ex-detective named Greywood Usher, a cadaverous, careful-spoken Yankee philosopher, occasionally varying a very rigid visage with an odd apologetic grimace. He liked Father Brown in a slightly patronizing way; and Father Brown liked him, though he heartily disliked his theories. His theories were extremely complicated and were held with extreme simplicity.

One evening he had sent for the priest, who, according to his custom, took a seat in silence at a table piled and littered with papers, and waited. The official selected from the papers a scrap of newspaper cutting, which he handed across to the cleric, who read it gravely. It appeared to be an extract from one of the pinkest of American Society papers, and ran as follows:

'Society's brightest widower is once more on the Freak Dinner stunt. All our exclusive citizens will recall the Perambulator Parade Dinner, in which Last-Trick Todd, at his palatial home at Pilgrim's Pond, caused so many of our prominent *débutantes* to look even younger than their years. Equally elegant and more miscellaneous and large-hearted in social outlook was Last-Trick's show the year previous, the popular Cannibal Crush Lunch, at which the confections handed round were sarcastically moulded in the forms of human arms and legs, and during which more than one of our gayest mental gymnasts was heard offering to eat his partner. The witticism which will inspire this evening is as yet in Mr. Todd's pretty reticent intellect, or locked in the jewelled bosoms of our city's gayest leaders; but there is talk of a pretty parody of the simple manners and customs at the other end of Society's scale. This would be all the more telling, as hospitable Todd is entertaining in Lord Falconroy, the famous traveller, a true-blooded aristocrat fresh from England's oak-groves. Lord Falconroy's travels began before his ancient feudal title was resurrected; he was in the Republic in his youth, and fashion murmurs a sly reason for his return. Miss Etta Todd is one of our deep-souled New Yorkers, and comes into an income of nearly twelve hundred million dollars.'

'Well,' asked Usher, 'does that interest you?'

'Why, words rather fail me,' answered Father Brown. 'I cannot think at this moment of anything in this world that would interest me less. And, unless the just anger of the Republic is at last going to electrocute journalists for writing like that, I don't quite see why it should interest you either.'

'Ah!' said Mr. Usher dryly, and handing across another scrap of newspaper. 'Well, does *that* interest you?'

The Paragraph was headed 'Savage Murder of a Warder. Convict Escapes,' and ran: 'Just before dawn this morning a shout for help was heard in the Convict Settlement at Sequah in this State. The authorities, hurrying in the direction of the cry, found the corpse of the warder who patrols the top of the north wall of the prison, the steepest and most difficult exit, for which one man has always been found sufficient. The unfortunate officer had, however, been hurled from the high wall, his brains beaten out as with a club, and his gun was missing. Further inquiries showed that one of the cells was empty; it had been occupied by a rather sullen ruffian giving his name as Oscar Rian. He was only temporarily detained for some comparatively trivial assault; but he gave everyone the impression of a man with a black past and a dangerous future. Finally, when daylight had fully revealed the scene of murder, it was found that he had written on the wall above the body a fragmentary sentence, apparently with a finger dipped in blood: "This was self-defence and he had the gun. I meant no harm to him or any man but one. I am keeping the bullet for Pilgrim's Pond—O.R." A man must have used most fiendish treachery or most savage and amazing bodily daring to have stormed such a wall in spite of an armed man.'

'Well, the literary style is somewhat improved,' admitted the priest cheerfully, 'but still I don't see what I can do for you. I should cut a poor figure, with my short legs, running about this State after an athletic assassin of that sort. I doubt whether anybody could find him. The convict settlement at Sequah is thirty miles from here; the country between is wild and tangled enough, and the country beyond, where he will surely have the sense to go, is a perfect no-man's land tumbling away to the prairies. He may be in any hole or up any tree.'

'He isn't in any hole,' said the governor; 'he isn't up any tree.'

'Why, how do you know?' asked Father Brown, blinking.

'Would you like to speak to him?' inquired Usher.

Father Brown opened his innocent eyes wide. 'He is here?' he exclaimed. 'Why, how did your men get hold of him?'

'I got hold of him myself,' drawled the American, rising and lazily stretching his lanky legs before the fire. 'I got hold of him with the crooked end of a walking-stick. Don't look so surprised. I really did. You know I sometimes take a turn in the country lanes outside this dismal place; well, I was walking early this evening up a steep lane with dark hedges and grey-looking ploughed fields on both sides; and a young moon was up and silvering the road. By the light of it I saw a man running across the field towards the road; running with his body bent and at a good mile-race trot. He appeared to be much exhausted; but when he came to the thick black hedge he went through it as if it were made of spiders' webs; or rather (for I heard the strong branches breaking and snapping like bayonets) as if he himself were made of stone. In the instant in which he appeared up against the moon, crossing the road, I slung my hooked cane at his legs, tripping him and bringing him down. Then I blew my whistle long and loud, and our fellows came running up to secure him.'

'It would have been rather awkward,' remarked Brown, 'if you had found he was a popular athlete practising a mile race.'

'He was not,' said Usher grimly. 'We soon found out who he was; but I had guessed it with the first glint of the moon on him.'

'You thought it was the runaway convict,' observed the priest simply, 'because you had read in the newspaper cutting that morning that a convict had run away.'

'I had somewhat better grounds,' replied the governor coolly. 'I pass over the first as too simple to be emphasized—I mean that fashionable athletes do not run across ploughed fields or scratch their eyes out in bramble hedges. Nor do they run all doubled up like a crouching dog. There were more decisive details to a fairly well-trained eye. The man was clad in coarse and ragged clothes, but they were something more than merely coarse and ragged. They were so ill-fitting as to be quite grotesque; even as he appeared in black outline against the moonrise, the coat-collar in which his head was buried made him look like a hunchback, and the long loose sleeves looked as if he had no hands. It at once occurred to me that he had somehow managed to change his convict clothes for some confederate's clothes which did not fit him. Second, there was a pretty stiff wind against which he was running; so that I must have seen the streaky look of blowing hair, if the hair had not been very short. Then I remembered that beyond these ploughed fields he was crossing lay Pilgrim's Pond, for which (you will remember) the convict was keeping his bullet; and I sent my walking-stick flying.'

'A brilliant piece of rapid deduction,' said Father Brown; 'but had he got a gun?'

As Usher stopped abruptly in his walk the priest added apologetically: 'I've been told a bullet is not half so useful without it.'

'He had no gun,' said the other gravely; 'but that was

doubtless due to some very natural mischance or change of plans. Probably the same policy that made him change the clothes made him drop the gun; he began to repent the coat he had left behind him in the blood of his victim.'

'Well, that is possible enough,' answered the priest.

'And it's hardly worth speculating on,' said Usher, turning to some other papers, 'for we know it's the man by this time.'

His clerical friend asked faintly: 'But how?' And Greywood Usher threw down the newspapers and took up the two press-cuttings again.

'Well, since you are so obstinate,' he said, 'let's begin at the beginning. You will notice that these two cuttings have only one thing in common, which is the mention of Pilgrim's Pond, the estate, as you know, of the millionaire Ireton Todd. You also know that he is a remarkable character; one of those that rose on stepping-stones ——'

'Of our dead selves to higher things,' assented his companion. 'Yes; I know that, Petroleum, I think.'

'Anyhow,' said Usher, 'Last-Trick Todd counts for a great deal in this rum affair.'

He stretched himself once more before the fire and continued talking in his expansive, radiantly explanatory style.

'To begin with, on the face of it, there is no mystery here at all. It is not mysterious, it is not even odd, that a jailbird should take his gun to Pilgrim's Pond. Our people aren't like the English, who will forgive a man for being rich if he throws away money on hospitals or horses. Last-Trick Todd has made himself big by his own considerable abilities; and there's no doubt that many of those on whom he has shown his abilities would like to show theirs on him with a shot-gun. Todd might easily get dropped by some man he'd never even heard of; some labourer he'd locked out, or some clerk in a business he'd busted. Last-Trick is a man of mental endowments and a high public character; but in this country the relations of employers and employed are considerably strained.

'That's how the whole thing looks supposing this Rian made for Pilgrim's Pond to kill Todd. So it looked to me, till another little discovery woke up what I have of the detective in me. When I had my prisoner safe, I picked up my cane again and strolled down the two or three turns of country road that brought me to one of the side entrances of Todd's grounds, the one nearest to the pool or lake after which the place is named. It was some two hours ago, about seven by this time; the moonlight was more luminous, and I could see the long white streaks of it lying on the mysterious mere with its grey, greasy, half-liquid shores in which they say our fathers used to make witches walk until they sank. I'd forgotten the exact tale; but you know the place I mean; it lies north of Todd's house towards the wilderness, and has two queer wrinkled trees, so dismal that they look more like huge fungoids than decent foliage. As I stood peering at this misty pool, I fancied I saw the faint figure of a man moving from the house towards it, but it was all too dim and distant for one to be certain of the fact, and still less of the details. Besides, my attention was very sharply arrested by something much closer. I crouched behind the fence which ran not more than two hundred yards from one wing of the great mansion, and which was fortunately split in places, as if specially for the application of a cautious eye. A door had opened in the dark bulk of the left wing, and a figure appeared black against the illuminated interior—a muffled figure bending forward, evidently peering out into the night.

It closed the door behind it, and I saw it was carrying a lantern, which threw a patch of imperfect light on the dress and figure of the wearer. It seemed to be the figure of a woman, wrapped up in a ragged cloak and evidently disguised to avoid notice; there was something very strange both about the rags and the furtiveness in a person coming out of those rooms lined with gold. She took cautiously the curved garden path which brought her within half a hundred yards of me; then she stood up for an instant on the terrace of turf that looks towards the slimy lake, and holding her flaming lantern above her head she deliberately swung it three times to and fro as for a signal. As she swung it the second time a flicker of its light fell for a moment on her own face, a face that I knew. She was unnaturally pale, and her head was bundled in her borrowed plebeian shawl; but I am certain it was Etta Todd, the millionaire's daughter.

'She retraced her steps in equal secrecy and the door closed behind her again. I was about to climb the fence and follow, when I realised that the detective fever that had lured me into the adventure was rather undignified; and that in a more authoritative capacity I already held all the cards in my hand. I was just turning away when a new noise broke on the night. A window was thrown up in one of the upper floors, but just round the corner of the house so that I could not see it; and a voice of terrible distinctness was heard shouting across the dark garden to know where Lord Falconroy was, for he was missing from every room in the house. There was no mistaking that voice. I have heard it on many a political platform or meeting of directors; it was Ireton Todd himself. Some of the others seemed to have gone to the lower windows or on to the steps, and were calling up to him that Falconroy had gone for a stroll down to the Pilgrim's Pond an hour before, and could not be traced since. Then Todd cried "Mighty Murder!" and shut down the window violently; and I could hear him plunging down the stairs inside. Repossessing myself of my former and wiser purpose, I whipped out of the way of the general search that must follow; and returned here not later than eight o'clock.

'I now ask you to recall that little Society paragraph which seemed to you so painfully lacking in interest. If the convict was not keeping the shot for Todd, as he evidently wasn't, it is most likely that he was keeping it for Lord Falconroy; and it looks as if he had delivered the goods. No more handy place to shoot a man than in the curious geological surroundings of that pool, where a body thrown down would sink through thick slime to a depth practically unknown. Let us suppose, then, that our friend with the cropped hair came to kill Falconroy and not Todd. But, as I have pointed out, there are many reasons why people in America might want to kill Todd. There is no reason why anybody in America should want to kill an English lord newly landed, except for the one reason mentioned in the pink paper—that the lord is paying his attentions to the millionaire's daughter. Our crop-haired friend, despite his ill-fitting clothes, must be an aspiring lover.

'I know the notion will seem to you jarring and even comic; but that's because you are English. It sounds to you like saying the Archbishop of Canterbury's daughter will be married in St. George's, Hanover Square, to a crossing-sweeper on ticket-of-leave. You don't do justice to the climbing and aspiring power of our more remarkable citizens. You see a good-looking grey-haired man in evening-dress with a sort of authority about him, you know he is a pillar of the State, and you fancy he had a father. You are in error. You do not realize that a comparatively few years ago he may have been in a tenement or (quite likely) in a jail. You don't allow for our national buoyancy and uplift. Many of our most influential citizens have not only risen recently, but risen comparatively late in life. Todd's daughter was fully eighteen when her father first made his pile; so there isn't really anything impossible in her having a hanger-on in low life; or even in her hanging on to him, as I think she must be doing, to judge by the lantern business. If so, the hand that held the lantern may not be unconnected with the hand that held the gun. This case, sir, will make a noise.'

'Well,' said the priest patiently, 'and what did you do next?'

'I reckon you'll be shocked,' replied Greywood Usher, 'as I know you don't cotton to the march of science in these matters. I am given a good deal of discretion here, and perhaps take a little more than I'm given; and I thought it was an excellent opportunity to test that Psychometric Machine I told you about. Now, in my opinion, that machine can't lie.'

'No machine can lie,' said Father Brown; 'nor can it tell the truth.'

'It did in this case, as I'll show you,' went on Usher positively. 'I sat the man in the ill-fitting clothes in a comfortable chair, and simply wrote words on a blackboard; and the machine simply recorded the variations of his pulse; and I simply observed his manner. The trick is to introduce some word connected with the supposed crime in a list of words connected with something quite different, yet a list in which it occurs quite naturally. Thus I wrote "heron" and "eagle" and "owl", and when I wrote "falcon" he was tremendously agitated; and when I began to make an "r" at the end of the word, that machine just bounded. Who else in this republic has any reason to jump at the name of a newly-arrived

Englishman like Falconroy except the man who's shot him? Isn't that better evidence than a lot of gabble from witnesses—the evidence of a reliable machine?'

'You always forget,' observed his companion, 'that the reliable machine always has to be worked by an unreliable machine.'

'Why, what do you mean?' asked the detective.

'I mean Man,' said Father Brown, 'the most unreliable machine I know of. I don't want to be rude; and I don't think you will consider Man to be an offensive or inaccurate description of yourself. You say you observed his manner; but how do you know you observed it right? You say the words have to come in a natural way; but how do you know that you did it naturally? How do you know, if you come to that, that he did not observe your manner? Who is to prove that you were not tremendously agitated? There was no machine tied on to your pulse.'

'I tell you,' cried the American in the utmost excitement, 'I was as cool as a cucumber.'

'Criminals also can be as cool as cucumbers,' said Brown with a smile. 'And almost as cool as you.'

'Well, this one wasn't,' said Usher, throwing the papers about. 'Oh, you make me tired!'

'I'm sorry,' said the other. 'I only point out what seems a reasonable possibility. If you could tell by his manner when the word that might hang him had come, why shouldn't he tell from your manner that the words that might hang him was coming? I should ask for more than words myself before I hanged anybody.'

Usher smote the table and rose in a sort of angry triumph.

'And that,' he cried, 'is just what I'm going to give you. I tried the machine first just in order to test the thing in other ways afterwards and the machine, sir, is right.'

He paused a moment and resumed with less excitement. 'I rather want to insist, if it comes to that, that so far I had very little to go on except the scientific experi-. ment. There was really nothing against the man at all. His clothes were ill-fitting, as I've said, but they were rather better, if anything, than those of the submerged class to which he evidently belonged. Moreover, under all the stains of his plunging through ploughed fields or bursting through dusty hedges, the man was comparatively clean. This might mean, of course, that he had only just broken prison; but it reminded me more of the desperate decency of the comparatively respectable poor. His demeanour was, I am bound to confess, quite in accordance with theirs. He was silent and dignified as they are; he seemed to have a big, but buried, grievance, as they do. He professed total ignorance of the crime and the whole question; and showed nothing but a sullen impatience for something sensible that might come to take him out of his meaningless scrape. He asked me more than once if he could telephone for a lawyer who had helped him a long time ago in a trade dispute, and in every sense acted as you would expect an innocent man to act. There was nothing against him in the world except that little finger on the dial that pointed to the change of his pulse.

'Then, sir, the machine was on its trial; and the machine was right. By the time I came with him out of the private room into the vestibule where all sorts of other people were awaiting examination, I think he had already more or less made up his mind to clear things up by something like a confession. He turned to me and began to say in a low voice: "Oh, I can't stick this any more. If you must know all about me——"

'At the same instant one of the poor women sitting on the long bench stood up, screaming aloud and pointing at him with her finger. I have never in my life heard anything more demoniacally distinct. Her lean finger seemed to pick him out as if it were a pea-shooter. Though the word was a mere howl, every syllable was as clear as a separate stroke on the clock.

'"Drugger Davis!" she shouted. "They've got Drugger Davis!"

'Among the wretched women, mostly thieves and street-walkers, twenty faces were turned, gaping with glee and hate. If I had never heard the words, I should have known by the very shock upon his features that the so-called Oscar Rian had heard his real name. But I'm not quite so ignorant, you may be surprised to hear. Drugger Davis was one of the most terrible and depraved criminals that ever baffled our police. It is certain he had done murder more than once long before his last exploit with the warder. But he was never entirely fixed for it, curiously enough because he did it in the same manner as those milder—or meaner—crimes for which he was fixed pretty often. He was a handsome, well-bred-looking brute, as he still is, to some extent; and he used mostly to go about with barmaids or shop-girls and do them out of their money. Very often, though, he went a good deal farther; and they were found drugged with cigarettes or chocolates and their whole property missing. Then came one case where the girl was found dead; but deliberation could not quite be proved, and, what was more practical still, the criminal could not be found. I heard a rumour of his having reappeared somewhere in the opposite character this time, lending money instead of borrowing it; but still to such poor widows as he might personally fascinate, and still with the same bad result for them. Well, there is your innocent man, and there is his innocent record. Even, since then, four criminals and three warders have identified him and confirmed the story. Now what have you got to say to my poor little machine after that? Hasn't the machine done for him? Or do you prefer to say that the woman and I have done for him?'

'As to what you've done for him,' replied Father Brown, rising and shaking himself in a floppy way, 'you've saved him from the electrical chair. I don't think they can kill Drugger Davis on that old vague story of the poison; and as for the convict who killed the warder, I suppose it's obvious that you haven't got him. Mr. Davis is innocent of that crime, at any rate.'

'What do you mean?' demanded the other. 'Why should he be innocent of that crime?'

'Why, bless us all!' cried the small man in one of his rare moments of animation, 'why, because he's guilty of the other crimes! I don't know what you people are made of. You seem to think that all sins are kept together in a bag. You talk as if a miser on Monday were always a spendthrift on Tuesday. You tell me this man you have here spent weeks and months wheedling needy women out of small sums of money; that he used a drug at the best, and a poison at the worst; that he turned up afterwards as the lowest kind of moneylender, and cheated most poor people in the same patient and pacific style. Let it be granted—let us admit, for the sake of argument, that he did all this. If that is so, I will tell you what he didn't do. He didn't storm a spiked wall against a man with a loaded gun. He didn't write on the wall with his own hand, to say he had done it. He didn't stop to state that his justification was self-defence. He didn't explain that he had no quarrel with the poor warder. He didn't name the house of the rich man to which he was going with the gun. He didn't write his own initials in a man's blood. Saints alive! Can't you see the whole character is different, in good and evil? Why, you don't seem to be like I am a bit. One would think you'd never had any vices of your own.'

The amazed American had already parted his lips in protest when the door of his private and official room was hammered and rattled in an unceremonious way to which he was totally unaccustomed.

The door flew open. The moment before Greywood Usher had been coming to the conclusion that Father Brown might possibly be mad. The moment after he began to think he was mad himself. There burst and fell into his private room a man in the filthiest rags, with a greasy squash hat still askew on his head, and a shabby green shade shoved up from one of his eyes, both of which were glaring like a tiger's. The rest of his face was almost undiscoverable, being masked with a matted beard and whiskers through which the nose could barely thrust itself, and further buried in a squalid red scarf or handkerchief. Mr. Usher prided himself on having seen most of the roughest specimens in the State, but he thought he had never seen such a baboon dressed as a scarecrow as this. But, above all, he had never in all his placid scientific existence heard a man like that speak to him first.

'See here, old man Usher,' shouted the being in the red handkerchief, 'I'm getting tired. Don't you try any of your hide-and-seek on me; I don't get fooled any. Leave go of my guests, and I'll let up on the fancy clockwork. Keep him here for a split instant and you'll feel pretty mean. I reckon I'm not a man with no pull.'

The eminent Usher was regarding the bellowing monster with an amazement which had dried up all other sentiments. The mere shock to his eyes had rendered his ears almost useless. At last he rang a bell with a hand of violence. While the bell was still strong and pealing, the voice of Father Brown fell soft but distinct.

'I have a suggestion to make,' he said, 'but it seems a little confusing. I don't know this gentleman—but—but I think I know him. Now, you know him—you know him quite well—but you don't know him—naturally. Sounds paradoxical, I know.'

'I reckon the Cosmos is cracked,' said Usher, and fell asprawl in his round office chair.

'Now, see here,' vociferated the stranger, striking the table, but speaking in a voice that was all the more mysterious because it was comparatively mild and rational though still resounding. 'I won't let you in. I want——'

'Who in hell are you?' yelled Usher, suddenly sitting up straight.

'I think the gentleman's name is Todd,' said the priest.

Then he picked up the pink slip of newspaper.

'I fear you don't read the Society papers properly,' he said, and began to read out in a monotonous voice, '"Or locked in the jewelled bosoms of our city's gayest leaders; but there is talk of a pretty parody of the manners and customs of the other end of Society's scale." There's been a big Slum Dinner up at Pilgrim's Pond to-night; and a man, one of the guests, disappeared. Mr. Ireton Todd is a good host, and has tracked him here, without even waiting to take off his fancy-dress.'

'What man do you mean?'

'I mean the man with the comically ill-fitting clothes you saw running across the ploughed field. Hadn't you better go and investigate him? He will be rather impatient to get back to his champagne, from which he ran away in such a hurry, when the convict with the gun hove in sight.'

'Do you seriously mean——' began the official.

'Why, look here, Mr. Usher,' said Father Brown quietly, 'you said the machine couldn't make a mistake; and in one sense it didn't. But the other machine did; the machine that worked it. You assumed that the man in rags jumped at the name of Lord Falconroy, because he was Lord Falconroy's murderer. He jumped at the name of Lord Falconroy because he *is* Lord Falconroy.'

'Then why the blazes didn't he say so?' demanded the staring Usher.

'He felt his plight and recent panic were hardly patrician,' replied the priest, 'so he tried to keep the name back at first. But he was just going to tell it you, when' —and Father Brown looked down at his boots—'when a woman found another name for him.'

'But you can't be so mad as to say,' said Greywood Usher, very white, 'that Lord Falconroy was Drugger Davis.'

The priest looked at him very earnestly, but with a baffling and undecipherable face.

'I am not saying anything about it,' he said. 'I leave all the rest to you. Your pink paper says that the title was recently revived for him; but those papers are very unreliable. It says he was in the States in youth; but the whole story seems very strange. Davis and Falconroy are both pretty considerable cowards, but so are lots of other men. I would not hang a dog on my own opinion about this. But I think,' he went on softly and reflectively, 'I think you Americans are too modest. I think you idealize the English aristocracy—even in assuming it to be so aristocratic. You see a good-looking Englishman in evening-dress; you know he's in the House of Lords; and you fancy he has a father. You don't allow for our national buoyancy and uplift. Many of our most influential noblemen have not only risen recently, but——'

'Oh, stop it!' cried Greywood Usher, wringing one lean hand in impatience against a shade of irony in the other's face.

'Don't stay talking to this lunatic!' cried Todd brutally. 'Take me to my friend.'

Next morning Father Brown appeared with the same demure expression, carrying yet another piece of pink newspaper.

'I'm afraid you neglect the fashionable press rather,' he said, 'but this cutting may interest you.'

Usher read the headlines, 'Last-Trick's Strayed Revellers: Mirthful Incident near Pilgrim's Pond.' The paragraph went on: 'A laughable occurrence took place outside Wilkinson's Motor Garage last night. A policeman on duty had his attention drawn by larrikins to a man in prison dress who was stepping with considerable coolness into the steering-seat of a pretty high-toned Panhard; he was accompanied by a girl wrapped in a ragged shawl. On the police interfering, the young woman threw back the shawl, and all recognized Millionaire Todd's daughter, who had just come from the Slum Freak Dinner at the Pond, where all the choicest guests were in a similar *déshabillé*. She and the gentleman who had donned prison uniform were going for the customary joy-ride.'

Under the pink slip Mr. Usher found a strip of a later paper, headed, 'Astounding Escape of Millionaire's Daughter with Convict. She had Arranged Freak Dinner. Now Safe in——'

Mr. Greenwood Usher lifted his eyes, but Father Brown was gone.

The Perishing of the Pendragons

FATHER BROWN was in no mood for adventures. He had lately fallen ill with over-work, and when he began to recover, his friend Flambeau had taken him on a cruise in a small yacht with Sir Cecil Fanshaw, a young Cornish squire and an enthusiast for Cornish coast scenery. But Brown was still rather weak; he was no very happy sailor; and though he was never of the sort that either grumbles or breaks down, his spirits did not rise above patience and civility. When the other two men praised the ragged violet sunset or the ragged volcanic crags, he agreed with them. When Flambeau pointed out a rock shaped like a dragon, he looked at it and thought it very like a dragon. When Fanshaw more excitedly indicated a rock that was like Merlin, he looked at it, and signified assent. When Flambeau asked whether this rocky gate of the twisted river was not the gate of Fairyland, he said 'Yes.' He heard the most important things and the most trivial with the same tasteless absorption. He heard that the coast was death to all but careful seamen; he also heard that the ship's cat was asleep. He heard that Fanshaw couldn't find his cigar-holder anywhere; he also heard the pilot deliver the oracle 'Both eyes bright, she's all right; one eye winks, down she sinks.' He heard Flambeau say to Fanshaw that no doubt this meant the pilot must keep both eyes open and be spry. And he heard Fanshaw say to Flambeau that, oddly enough, it didn't mean this: it meant that while they saw two of the coast-lights, one near and the other distant, exactly side by side, they were in the right river-channel; but that if one light was hidden behind the other, they were going on the rocks.

He heard Fanshaw add that his country was full of such quaint fables and idioms; it was the very home of romance; he even pitted this part of Cornwall against Devonshire, as a claimant to the laurels of Elizabethan seamanship. According to him there had been captains among these coves and islets compared with whom Drake was practically a landsman. He heard Flambeau laugh, and ask if, perhaps, the adventurous title of 'Westward Ho!' only meant that all Devonshire men wished they were living in Cornwall. He heard Fanshaw say there was no need to be silly; that not only had Cornish captains been heroes, but that they were heroes still: that near that very spot there was an old admiral, now retired, who was scarred by thrilling voyages full of adventures; and who had in his youth found the last group of eight Pacific Islands that was added to the chart of the world. This Cecil Fanshaw was, in person, of the kind that commonly urges such crude but pleasing enthusiasms; a very young man, light-haired, high-coloured, with an eager profile; with a boyish bravado of spirits, but an almost girlish delicacy of tint and type. The big shoulders, black brows and black mousquetaire swagger of Flambeau were a great contrast.

All these trivialities Brown heard and saw; but heard them as a tired man hears a tune in the railway wheels, or saw them as a sick man sees the pattern of his wallpaper. No one can calculate the turns of mood in convalescence: but Father Brown's depression must have had a great deal to do with his mere unfamiliarity with the sea. For as the river-mouth narrowed like the neck of a bottle, and the water grew calmer and the air warmer and more earthly, he seemed to wake up and take notice like a baby. They had reached that phase just after sunset when air and water both look bright, but earth and all its growing things look almost black by comparison. About this particular evening, however, there was something exceptional. It was one of those rare atmospheres in which a smoked-glass slide seems to have been slid away from between us and Nature; so that even dark colours on that day look more gorgeous than bright colours on cloudier days. The trampled earth of the river-banks and the peaty stain in the pools did not look drab but glowing umber, and the dark woods astir in the breeze did not look, as usual, dim blue with mere depth or distance, but more like wind-tumbled masses of some vivid violet blossom. This magic clearness and intensity in the colours was further forced on Brown's slowly reviving senses by something romantic and even secret in the very form of the landscape.

The river was still well wide and deep enough for a pleasure boat so small as theirs; but the curves of the country-side suggested that it was closing in on either hand; the woods seemed to be making broken and flying attempts at bridge-building—as if the boat were passing from the romance of a valley to the romance of a hollow and so to the supreme romance of a tunnel. Beyond this mere look of things there was little for Brown's freshening fancy to feed on; he saw no human beings, except some gipsies trailing along the river bank, with faggots and osiers cut in the forest; and one sight no longer unconventional, but in such remote parts still uncommon: a dark-haired lady, bare-headed, and paddling her own canoe. If Father Brown ever attached any importance to either of these, he certainly forgot them at the next turn of the river which brought in sight a singular object.

The water seemed to widen and split, being cloven by the dark wedge of a fish-shaped and wooded islet. With the rate at which they went, the islet seemed to swim towards them like a ship; a ship with a very high prow

—or, to speak more strictly, a very high funnel. For at the extreme point nearest them stood up an odd-looking building, unlike anything they could remember or connect with any purpose. It was not specially high, but it was too high for its breadth to be called anything but a tower. Yet it appeared to be built entirely of wood, and that in a most unequal and eccentric way. Some of the planks and beams were of good, seasoned oak; some of such wood cut raw and recent; some again of white pinewood, and a great deal more of the same sort of wood painted black with tar. These black beams were set crooked or criss-cross at all kinds of angles, giving the whole a most patchy and puzzling appearance. There were one or two windows, which appeared to be coloured and leaded in an old-fashioned but more elaborate style. The travellers looked at it with that paradoxical feeling we have when something reminds us of something, and yet we are certain it is something very different.

Father Brown, even when he was mystified, was clever in analysing his own mystification. And he found himself reflecting that the oddity seemed to consist in a particular shape cut out in an incongruous material; as if one saw a top-hat made of tin, or a frock-coat cut out of tartan. He was sure he had seen timbers of different tints arranged like that somewhere, but never in such architectural proportions. The next moment a glimpse through the dark trees told him all he wanted to know, and he laughed. Through a gap in the foliage there appeared for a moment one of those old wooden houses, faced with black beams, which are still to be found here and there in England, but which most of us see imitated in some show called 'Old London' or 'Shakespear's England.' It was in view only long enough for the priest to see that, however old-fashioned, it was a comfortable and well-kept country-house, with flower-beds in front of it. It had none of the piebald and crazy look of the tower that seemed made out of its refuse.

'What on earth's this?' said Flambeau, who was still staring at the tower.

Fanshaw's eyes were shining, and he spoke triumphantly. 'Aha! you've not seen a place quite like this before, I fancy; that's why I've brought you here, my friend. Now you shall see whether I exaggerate about the mariners of Cornwall. This place belongs to Old Pendragon, whom we call the Admiral; though he retired before getting the rank. The spirit of Raleigh and Hawkins is a memory with the Devon folk; it's a modern fact with the Pendragons. If Queen Elizabeth were to rise from the grave and come up this river in a gilded barge, she would be received by the Admiral in a house exactly such as she was accustomed to, in every corner and casement, in every panel on the wall or plate on the table. And she would find an English Captain still talking fiercely of fresh lands to be found in little ships, as much as if she had dined with Drake.'

'She'd find a rum sort of thing in the garden,' said Father Brown, 'which would not please her Renaissance eye. That Elizabethan domestic architecture is charming in its way; but it's against the very nature of it to break out into turrets.'

'And yet,' answered Fanshaw, 'that's the most romantic and Elizabethan part of the business. It was built by the Pendragons in the very days of the Spanish wars; and though it's needed patching and even rebuilding for another reason, it's always been rebuilt in the old way. The story goes that the lady of Sir Peter Pendragon built it in this place and to this height, because from the top you can just see the corner where vessels turn into the river mouth; and she wished to be the first to see her husband's ship, as he sailed home from the Spanish Main.'

'For what other reason,' asked Father Brown, 'do you mean that it has been rebuilt?'

'Oh, there's a strange story about that, too,' said the young squire with relish. 'You are really in a land of strange stories. King Arthur was here and Merlin and the fairies before him. The story goes that Sir Peter Pendragon, who (I fear) had some of the faults of the pirates as well as the virtues of the sailor, was bringing home three Spanish gentlemen in honourable captivity, intending to escort them to Elizabeth's court. But he was a man of flaming and tigerish temper, and coming to high words with one of them, he caught him by the throat and flung him, by accident or design, into the sea. A second Spaniard, who was the brother of the first, instantly drew his sword and flew at Pendragon, and after a short but furious combat in which both got three wounds in as many minutes, Pendragon drove his blade through the other's body and the second Spaniard was accounted for. As it happened the ship had already turned into the river mouth and was close to comparatively shallow water. The third Spaniard sprang over the side of the ship, struck out for the shore, and was soon near enough to it to stand up to his waist in water. And turning again to face the ship, and holding up both arms to Heaven—like a prophet calling plagues upon a wicked city—he called out to Pendragon in a piercing and terrible voice, that he at least was yet living, that he would go on living, that he would live for ever; and that generation after generation the house of Pendragon should never see him or his, but should know by very certain signs that he and his vengeance were alive. With that he dived under the wave, and was either drowned or swam so long under water that no hair of his head was seen afterwards.'

'There's that girl in the canoe again,' said Flambeau irrelevantly, for good-looking young women would call him off any topic. 'She seems bothered by the queer tower just as we were.'

Indeed, the black-haired young lady was letting her canoe float slowly and silently past the strange islet; and was looking intently up at the strange tower, with a strong glow of curiosity on her oval and olive face.

'Never mind girls,' said Fanshaw impatiently; 'there are plenty of them in the world, but not many things like the Pendragon Tower. As you may easily suppose, plenty of superstitions and scandals have followed in the track of the Spaniard's curse; and no doubt, as you would put it, any accident happening to this Cornish family would be connected with it by rural credulity. But it is perfectly true that this tower has been burnt down two or three times; and the family can't be called lucky, for more than two, I think, of the Admiral's near kin have perished by shipwreck; and one at least, to my own knowledge, on practically the same spot where Sir Peter threw the Spaniard overboard.'

'What a pity!' exclaimed Flambeau. 'She's going.'

'When did your friend the Admiral tell you this family history?' asked Father Brown, as the girl in the canoe paddled off, without showing the least intention of extending her interest from the tower to the yacht, which Fanshaw had already caused to lie alongside the island.

'Many years ago,' replied Fanshaw; 'he hasn't been to sea for some time now, though he is as keen on it as ever. I believe there's a family compact or something. Well, here's the landing-stage; let's come ashore and see the old boy.'

They followed him on to the island, just under the tower, and Father Brown, whether from the mere touch of dry land, or the interest of something on the other bank of the river (which he stared at very hard for some seconds), seemed singularly improved in briskness. They entered a wooded avenue between two fences of thin greyish wood, such as often enclose parks or gardens, and over the top of which the dark trees tossed to and fro like black and purple plumes upon the hearse of a giant. The tower, as they left it behind, looked all the quainter, because such entrances are usually flanked by two towers; and this one looked lopsided. But for this, the avenue had the usual appearance of the entrance to a gentleman's grounds; and, being so curved that the house was now out of sight, somehow looked a much larger park than any plantation on such an island could really be. Father Brown was, perhaps, a little fanciful in his fatigue, but he almost thought the whole place must be growing larger, as things do in a nightmare. Anyhow, a mystical monotony was the only character of their march, until Fanshaw suddenly stopped, and pointed to something sticking out through the grey fence—something that looked at first rather like the imprisoned horn of some beast. Closer observation showed that it was a slightly curved blade of metal that shone faintly in the fading light.

Flambeau, who like all Frenchmen had been a soldier, bent over it and said in a startled voice. 'Why, it's a sabre! I believe I know the sort, heavy and curved, but shorter than the cavalry; they used to have them in artillery and the——'

As he spoke the blade plucked itself out of the crack it had made and came down again with a more ponderous slash, splitting the fissiparous fence to the bottom with a rending noise. Then it was pulled out again, flashed above the fence some feet farther along, and again split it half-way down with the first stroke; and after waggling a little to extricate itself (accompanied with curses in the darkness) split it down to the ground with a second. Then a kick of devilish energy sent the whole loosened square of thin wood flying into the pathway, and a great gap of dark coppice gaped in the paling.

Fanshaw peered into the dark opening and uttered an exclamation of astonishment. 'My dear Admiral!' he exclaimed, 'do you—er—do you generally cut out a new front door whenever you want to go for a walk?'

The voice in the gloom swore again, and then broke into a jolly laugh. 'No,' it said; 'I've really got to cut down this fence somehow; it's spoiling all the plants, and no one else here can do it. But I'll only carve another bit off the front door, and then come out and welcome you.'

And sure enough, he heaved up his weapon once more, and, hacking twice, brought down another and similar strip of fence, making the opening about fourteen feet wide in all. Then through this larger forest gateway he came out into the evening light, with a chip of grey wood sticking to his sword-blade.

He momentarily fulfilled all Fanshaw's fable of an old piratical Admiral; though the details seemed afterwards to decompose into accidents. For instance, he wore a broad-brimmed hat as protection against the sun; but the front flap of it was turned up straight to the sky, and the two corners pulled down lower than the ears, so that it stood across his forehead in a crescent like the old cocked hat worn by Nelson. He wore an ordinary dark-blue jacket, with nothing special about the buttons, but the combination of it with white linen trousers somehow had a sailorish look. He was tall and loose, and walked with a sort of swagger, which was not a sailor's roll, and

yet somehow suggested it; and he held in his hand a
short sabre which was like a navy cutlass, but about
twice as big. Under the bridge of the hat his eagle face
looked eager, all the more because it was not only clean-
shaven, but without eyebrows. It seemed almost as if all
the hair had come off his face from his thrusting it
through a throng of elements. His eyes were prominent
and piercing. His colour was curiously attractive, while
partly tropical; it reminded one vaguely of a blood-
orange. That is, that while it was ruddy and sanguine,
there was a yellow in it that was in no way sickly, but
seemed rather to glow like gold apples of the Hesperides.
Father Brown thought he had never seen a figure so
expressive of all the romances about the countries of
the Sun.

When Fanshaw had presented his two friends to their
host he fell again into a tone of rallying the latter about
his wreckage of the fence and his apparent rage of pro-
fanity. The Admiral pooh-poohed it at first as a piece
of necessary but annoying garden work; but at length
the ring of real energy came back into his laughter, and
he cried with a mixture of impatience and good humour:

'Well, perhaps I do go at it a bit rabidly, and feel a
kind of pleasure in smashing anything. So would you if
your only pleasure was in cruising about to find some
new Cannibal Islands, and you had to stick on this
muddy little rockery in a sort of rustic pond. When I
remember how I've cut down a mile and a half of green
poisonous jungle with an old cutlass half as sharp as
this; and then remember I must stop here and chop this
matchwood, because of some confounded old bargain
scribbled in a family Bible, why, I——'

He swung up the heavy steel again; and this time
sundered the wall of wood from top to bottom at one
stroke.

'I feel like that,' he said laughing, but furiously flinging the sword some yards down the path, 'and now let's go up to the house; you must have some dinner.'

The semicircle of lawn in front of the house was varied by three circular garden beds, one of red tulips, a second of yellow tulips, and the third of some white, waxen-looking blossoms that the visitors did not know and presumed to be exotic. A heavy, hairy and rather sullen-looking gardener was hanging up a heavy coil of garden hose. The corners of the expiring sunset which seemed to cling about the corners of the house gave glimpses here and there of the colours of remoter flower-beds; and in a treeless space on one side of the house opening upon the river stood a tall brass tripod on which was tilted a big brass telescope. Just outside the steps of the porch stood a little painted green garden table, as if someone had just had tea there. The entrance was flanked with two of those half-featured lumps of stone with holes for eyes that are said to be South Sea idols; and on the brown oak beam across the doorway were some confused carvings that looked almost as barbaric.

As they passed indoors, the little cleric hopped suddenly on to the table, and standing on it peered unaffectedly through his spectacles at the mouldings in the oak. Admiral Pendragon looked very much astonished, though not particularly annoyed; while Fanshaw was so amused with what looked like a performing pigmy on his little stand, that he could not control his laughter. But Father Brown was not likely to notice either the laughter or the astonishment.

He was gazing at three carved symbols, which, though very worn and obscure, seemed still to convey some sense to him. The first seemed to be the outline of some tower or other building, crowned with what looked like

curly-pointed ribbons. The second was clearer: an old
Elizabethan galley with decorative waves beneath it, but
interrupted in the middle by a curious jagged rock,
which was either a fault in the wood or some conventional representation of the water coming in. The third
represented the upper half of a human figure, ending in
an escalloped line like the waves; the face was rubbed
and featureless, and both arms were held very stiffly up
in the air.

'Well,' muttered Father Brown, blinking, 'here is the
legend of the Spaniard plain enough. Here he is holding
up his arms and cursing in the sea; and here are the two
curses: the wrecked ship and the burning of Pendragon
Tower.'

Pendragon shook his head with a kind of venerable
amusement. 'And how many other things might it not
be?' he said. 'Don't you know that that sort of half-man,
like a half-lion or half-stag, is quite common in heraldry?
Might not that line through the ship be one of those
parti-per-pale lines, *indented*, I think they call it? And
though the third thing isn't so very heraldic, it would be
more heraldic to suppose it a tower crowned with laurel
than with fire; and it looks just as like it.'

'But it seems rather odd,' said Flambeau, 'that it
should exactly confirm the old legend.'

'Ah,' replied the sceptical traveller, 'but you don't know
how much of the old legend may have been made up
from the old figures. Besides, it isn't the only old legend.
Fanshaw, here, who is fond of such things, will tell you
there are other versions of the tale, and much more
horrible ones. One story credits my unfortunate ancestor
with having had the Spaniard cut in two; and that will
fit the pretty picture also. Another obligingly credits our
family with the possession of a tower full of snakes and
explains those little, wriggly things in that way. And a

third theory supposes the crooked line on the ship to be a conventionalized thunderbolt; but that alone, if seriously examined, would show what a very little way these unhappy coincidences really go.'

'Why, how do you mean?' asked Fanshaw.

'It so happens,' replied his host coolly, 'that there was no thunder and lightning at all in the two or three ship-wrecks I know of in our family.'

'Oh!' said Father Brown, and jumped down from the little table.

There was another silence in which they heard the continuous murmur of the river; then Fanshaw said, in a doubtful and perhaps disappointed tone: 'Then you don't think there is anything in the tales of the tower in flames?'

'There are the tales, of course,' said the Admiral, shrugging his shoulders; 'and some of them, I don't deny, on evidence as decent as one ever gets for such things. Someone saw a blaze hereabout, don't you know, as he walked home through a wood; someone keeping sheep on the uplands inland thought he saw a flame hovering over Pendragon Tower. Well, a damp dab of mud like this confounded island seems the last place where one would think of fires.'

'What is that fire over there?' asked Father Brown with a gentle suddenness, pointing to the woods on the left river-bank. They were all thrown a little off their balance, and the more fanciful Fanshaw had even some difficulty in recovering his, as they saw a long, thin stream of blue smoke ascending silently into the end of the evening light.

Then Pendragon broke into a scornful laugh again. 'Gipsies!' he said; 'they've been camping about here for a week. Gentlemen, you want your dinner,' and he turned as if to enter the house.

But the antiquarian superstition in Fanshaw was still quivering, and he said hastily: 'But, Admiral, what's that hissing noise quite near the island? It's very like fire.'

'It's more like what it is,' said the Admiral, laughing as he led the way; 'it's only some canoe going by.'

Almost as he spoke, the butler, a lean man in black, with very black hair and a very long, yellow face, appeared in the doorway and told him that dinner was served.

The dining-room was as nautical as the cabin of a ship; but its note was rather that of the modern than the Elizabethan captain. There were, indeed, three antiquated cutlasses in a trophy over the fireplace, and one brown sixteenth-century map with Tritons and little ships dotted about a curly sea. But such things were less prominent on the white panelling than some cases of quaint-coloured South American birds, very scientifically stuffed, fantastic shells from the Pacific, and several instruments so rude and queer in shape that savages might have used them either to kill their enemies or to cook them. But the alien colour culminated in the fact that, besides the butler, the Admiral's only servants were two negroes, somewhat quaintly clad in tight uniforms of yellow. The priest's instinctive trick of analysing his own impressions told him that the colour and the little neat coat-tails of these bipeds had suggested the word 'Canary,' and so by a mere pun connected them with southward travel. Towards the end of the dinner they took their yellow clothes and black faces out of the room, leaving only the black clothes and yellow face of the butler.

'I'm rather sorry you take this so lightly,' said Fanshaw to the host; 'for the truth is, I've brought these friends of mine with the idea of their helping you, as they know a good deal of these things. Don't you really believe in the family story at all?'

'I don't believe in anything,' answered Pendragon very briskly, with a bright eye cocked at a red tropical bird. 'I'm a man of science.'

Rather to Flambeau's surprise, his clerical friend, who seemed to have entirely woken up, took up the digression and talked natural history with his host with a flow of words and much unexpected information, until the dessert and decanters were set down and the last of the servants vanished. Then he said, without altering his tone:

'Please don't think me impertinent, Admiral Pendragon. I don't ask for curiosity, but really for my guidance and your convenience. Have I made a bad shot if I guess you don't want these old things talked of before your butler?'

The Admiral lifted the hairless arches over his eyes and exclaimed. 'Well, I don't know where you got it, but the truth is I can't stand the fellow, though I've no excuse for discharging a family servant. Fanshaw, with his fairy tales, would say my blood moved against men with that black, Spanish-looking hair.'

Flambeau struck the table with his heavy fist. 'By Jove!' he cried; 'and so had that girl!'

'I hope it'll all end to-night,' continued the Admiral, 'when my nephew comes back safe from his ship. You looked surprised. You won't understand, I suppose, unless I tell you the story. You see, my father had two sons; I remained a bachelor, but my elder brother married, and had a son who became a sailor like all the rest of us, and will inherit the proper estate. Well, my father was a strange man; he somehow combined Fanshaw's superstition with a good deal of my scepticism; they were always fighting in him; and after my first voyages, he

developed a notion which he thought somehow would
settle finally whether the curse was truth or trash. If all
the Pendragons sailed about anyhow, he thought there
would be too much chance of natural catastrophes to
prove anything. But if we went to sea one at a time in
strict order of succession to the property, he thought it
might show whether any connected fate followed the
family as a family. It was a silly notion, I think, and I
quarrelled with my father pretty heartily; for I was an
ambitious man and was left to the last, coming, by succession, after my own nephew.'

'And your father and brother,' said the priest, very
gently, 'died at sea, I fear.'

'Yes,' groaned the Admiral; 'by one of those brutal
accidents on which are built all the lying mythologies
of mankind, they were both shipwrecked. My father,
coming up this coast out of the Atlantic, was washed up
on these Cornish rocks. My brother's ship was sunk, no
one knows where, on the voyage home from Tasmania.
His body was never found. I tell you it was from perfectly
natural mishap; lots of other people besides Pendragons
were drowned; and both disasters are discussed in a
normal way by navigators. But, of course, it set this
forest of superstition on fire; and men saw the flaming
tower everywhere. That's why I say it will be all right
when Walter returns. The girl he's engaged to was
coming to-day; but I was so afraid of some chance delay
frightening her that I wired her not to come till she
heard from me. But he's practically sure to be here
some time to-night, and then it'll all end in smoke—
tobacco smoke. We'll crack that old lie when we crack
a bottle of this wine.'

'Very good wine,' said Father Brown, gravely lifting
his glass, 'but, as you see, a very bad wine-bibber. I most
sincerely beg your pardon': for he had spilt a small spot

of wine on the table-cloth. He drank and put down the glass with a composed face; but his hand had started at the exact moment when he became conscious of a face looking in through the garden window just behind the Admiral—the face of a woman, swarthy, with southern hair and eyes, and young, but like a mask of tragedy.

After a pause the priest spoke again in his mild manner. 'Admiral,' he said, 'will you do me a favour? Let me, and my friends if they like, stop in that tower of yours just for to-night? Do you know that in my business you're an exorcist almost before anything else?'

Pendragon sprang to his feet and paced swiftly to and fro across the window, from which the face had instantly vanished. 'I tell you there is nothing in it,' he cried, with ringing violence. 'There is one thing I know about this matter. You may call me an atheist. I am an atheist.' Here he swung round and fixed Father Brown with a face of frightful concentration. 'This business is perfectly natural. There is no curse in it at all.'

Father Brown smiled. 'In that case,' he said, 'there can't be any objection to my sleeping in your delightful summer-house.'

'The idea is utterly ridiculous,' replied the Admiral, beating a tattoo on the back of his chair.

'Please forgive me for everything,' said Brown in his most sympathetic tone, 'including spilling the wine. But it seems to me you are not quite so easy about the flaming tower as you try to be.'

Admiral Pendragon sat down again as abruptly as he had risen; but he sat quite still, and when he spoke again it was in a lower voice. 'You do it at your own peril,' he said; 'but wouldn't *you* be an atheist to keep sane in all this devilry?'

Some three hours afterwards Fanshaw, Flambeau and

the priest were still dawdling about the garden in the dark; and it began to dawn on the other two that Father Brown had no intention of going to bed either in the tower or the house.

'I think the lawn wants weeding,' said he dreamily. 'If I could find a spud or something I'd do it myself.'

They followed him, laughing and half remonstrating; but he replied with the utmost solemnity, explaining to them, in a maddening little sermon, that one can always find some small occupation that is helpful to others. He did not find a spud; but he found an old broom made of twigs, with which he began energetically to brush the fallen leaves off the grass.

'Always some little thing to be done,' he said with idiotic cheerfulness; 'as George Herbert says: "Who sweeps an Admiral's garden in Cornwall as for Thy laws makes that and the action fine." And now,' he added, suddenly slinging the broom away, 'let's go and water the flowers.'

With the same mixed emotions they watched him uncoil some considerable lengths of the large garden hose, saying with an air of wistful discrimination: 'The red tulips before the yellow, I think. Look a bit dry, don't you think?'

He turned the little tap on the instrument, and the water shot out straight and solid as a long rod of steel.

'Look out, Samson,' cried Flambeau; 'why, you've cut off the tulip's head.'

Father Brown stood ruefully contemplating the decapitated plant.

'Mine does seem to be a rather kill or cure sort of watering,' he admitted, scratching his head. 'I suppose it's a pity I didn't find the spud. You should have seen me with the spud! Talking of tools, you've got that swordstick, Flambeau, you always carry? That's right; and Sir Cecil could have that sword the Admiral threw away by the fence here. How grey everything looks!'

'The mist's rising from the river,' said the staring Flambeau.

Almost as he spoke the huge figure of the hairy gardener appeared on a higher ridge of the trenched and terraced lawn, hailing them with a brandished rake and a horribly bellowing voice. 'Put down that hose,' he shouted; 'put down that hose and go to your——'

'I am fearfully clumsy,' replied the reverend gentleman weakly; 'do you know, I upset some wine at dinner.' He made a wavering half-turn of apology towards the gardener, with the hose still spouting in his hand. The gardener caught the cold crash of the water full in his face like the crash of a cannon-ball; staggered, slipped and went sprawling with his boots in the air.

'How very dreadful!' said Father Brown, looking round in a sort of wonder. 'Why, I've hit a man!'

He stood with his head forward for a moment as if looking or listening; and then set off at a trot towards the tower, still trailing the hose behind him. The tower was quite close, but its outline was curiously dim.

'Your river mist,' he said, 'has a rum smell.'

'By the Lord it has,' cried Fanshaw, who was very white. 'But you can't mean——'

'I mean,' said Father Brown, 'that one of the Admiral's scientific predictions is coming true to-night. This story is going to end in smoke.'

As he spoke a most beautiful rose-red light seemed to burst into blossom like a gigantic rose; but accompanied with a crackling and rattling noise that was like the laughter of devils.

'My God! what is this?' cried Sir Cecil Fanshaw.

'The sign of the flaming tower,' said Father Brown,

and sent the driving water from his hose into the heart of the red patch.

'Lucky we hadn't gone to bed!' ejaculated Fanshaw. 'I suppose it can't spread to the house.'

'You may remember,' said the priest quietly, 'that the wooden fence that might have carried it was cut away.'

Flambeau turned electrified eyes upon his friend, but Fanshaw only said rather absently: 'Well, nobody can be killed, anyhow.'

'This is rather a curious kind of tower,' observed Father Brown; 'when it takes to killing people, it always kills people who are somewhere else.'

At the same instant the monstrous figure of the gardener with the streaming beard stood again on the green ridge against the sky, waving others to come on; but now waving not a rake but a cutlass. Behind him came the two negroes, also with the old crooked cutlasses out of the trophy. But in the blood-red glare, with their black faces and yellow figures, they looked like devils carrying instruments of torture. In the dim garden behind them a distant voice was heard calling out brief directions. When the priest heard the voice, a terrible change came over his countenance.

But he remained composed; and never took his eye off the patch of flame which had begun by spreading, but now seemed to shrink a little as it hissed under the torch of the long silver spear of water. He kept his finger along the nozzle of the pipe to ensure the aim, and attended to no other business, knowing only by the noise and that semi-conscious corner of the eye, the exciting incidents that began to tumble themselves about the island garden. He gave two brief directions to his friends. One was: 'Knock these fellows down somehow and tie them up, whoever they are; there's some rope down by those faggots. They want to take away my nice hose.' The other was: 'As soon as you get a chance, call out to that canoeing girl; she's over on the bank with the gipsies. Ask her if they could get some buckets across and fill them from the river.' Then he closed his mouth and continued to water the new red flower as ruthlessly as he had watered the red tulip.

He never turned his head to look at the strange fight that followed between the foes and friends of the mysterious fire. He almost felt the island shake when Flambeau collided with the huge gardener; he merely imagined how it would whirl round them as they wrestled. He heard the crashing fall; and his friend's gasp of triumph as he dashed on to the first negro; and the cries of both the blacks as Flambeau and Fanshaw bound them. Flambeau's enormous strength more than redressed the odds in the fight, especially as the fourth man still hovered near the house, only a shadow and a voice. He heard also the water broken by the paddles of a canoe; the girl's voice giving orders, the voices of gipsies answering and coming nearer, the plumping and sucking noise of empty buckets plunged into a full stream; and finally the sound of many feet around the fire. But all this was less to him than the fact that the red rent, which had lately once more increased, had once more slightly diminished.

Then came a cry that very nearly made him turn his head. Flambeau and Fanshaw, now reinforced by some of the gipsies, had rushed after the mysterious man by the house; and he heard from the other end of the garden the Frenchman's cry of horror and astonishment. It was echoed by a howl not to be called human, as the being broke from their hold and ran along the garden. Three times at least it raced round the whole island, in a way that was as horrible as the chase of a lunatic, both in the cries of the pursued and the ropes carried by the pursuers; but was more horrible still, because it some-how suggested one of the chasing games of children in a garden. Then, finding them closing in on every side, the figure sprang upon one of the higher river banks and disappeared with a splash into the dark and driving river.

'You can do no more, I fear,' said Brown in a voice cold with pain. 'He has been washed down to the rocks by now, where he has sent so many others. He knew the use of a family legend.'

'Oh, don't talk in these parables,' cried Flambeau impatiently. 'Can't you put it simply in words of one syllable?'

'Yes,' answered Brown, with his eye on the hose. '"Both eyes bright, she's all right; one eye blinks, down she sinks."'

The fire hissed and shrieked more and more, like a strangled thing, as it grew narrower and narrower under the flood from the pipe and buckets, but Father Brown still kept his eye on it as he went on speaking:

'I thought of asking this young lady, if it were morn-ing yet, to look through that telescope at the river mouth and the river. She might have seen something to interest her: the sign of the ship, or Mr. Walter Pendragon coming home, and perhaps even the sign of the half-man, for though he is certainly safe by now, he may very well have waded ashore. He has been within a shave of another shipwreck; and would never have escaped it, if the lady hadn't had the sense to suspect the old Admiral's telegram and come down to watch him. Don't let's talk about the old Admiral. Don't let's talk about anything. It's enough to say that whenever this tower, with its pitch and resin-wood, really caught fire, the spark on the horizon always looked like the twin light to the coast lighthouse.'

'And that,' said Flambeau, 'is how the father and brother died. The wicked uncle of the legends very nearly got his estate after all.'

Father Brown did not answer; indeed, he did not speak again, save for civilities, till they were all safe round a cigar-box in the cabin of the yacht. He saw that the frustrated fire was extinguished; and then refused to linger, though he actually heard young Pendragon, escorted by an enthusiastic crowd, come tramping up the river bank; and might (had he been moved by romantic curiosities) have received the combined thanks of the man from the ship and the girl from the canoe. But his fatigue had fallen on him once more, and he only started once, when Flambeau abruptly told him he had dropped cigar-ash on his trousers.

'That's no cigar-ash,' he said rather wearily. 'That's from the fire, but you don't think so because you're all smoking cigars. That's just the way I got my first faint suspicion about the chart.'

'Do you mean Pendragon's chart of his Pacific Islands?' asked Fanshaw.

'You thought it was a chart of the Pacific Islands,' answered Brown. 'Put a feather with a fossil and a bit of coral and everyone will think it's a specimen. Put the same feather with a ribbon and an artificial flower and everyone will think it's for a lady's hat. Put the same feather with an ink-bottle, a book, and a stack of writing-paper, and most men will swear they've seen a quill pen. So you saw that map among tropic birds and shells and thought it was a map of Pacific Islands. It was the map of this river.'

'But how do you know?' asked Fanshaw.

'I saw the rock you thought was like a dragon, and the one like Merlin, and——'

'You seem to have noticed a lot as we came in,'

cried Fanshaw. 'We thought you were rather abstracted.'

'I was sea-sick,' said Father Brown simply. 'I felt
simply horrible. But feeling horrible has nothing to do
with not seeing things.' And he closed his eyes.

'Do you think most men would have seen that?' asked
Flambeau. He received no answer: Father Brown was
asleep.

The Strange Crime of John Boulnois

MR. CALHOUN KIDD was a very young gentleman with
a very old face, a face dried up with its own eagerness,
framed in blue-black hair and a black butterfly tie. He
was the emissary in England of the colossal American
daily called the *Western Sun*—also humorously described as the 'Rising Sunset.' This was in allusion to
a great journalistic declaration (attributed to Mr. Kidd
himself) that 'he guessed the sun would rise in the west
yet, if American citizens did a bit more hustling.' Those,
however, who mock American journalism from the
standpoint of somewhat mellower traditions forget a
certain paradox which partly redeems it. For while the
journalism of the States permits a pantomimic vulgarity
long past anything English, it also shows a real excitement about the most earnest mental problems, of which
English papers are innocent, or rather incapable. The
Sun was full of the most solemn matters treated in the
most farcical way. William James figured there as well
as 'Weary Willie,' and pragmatists alternated with pugi-
lists in the long procession of its portraits.

Thus, when a very unobtrusive Oxford man named
John Boulnois wrote in a very unreadable review called

the *Natural Philosophy Quarterly* a series of articles on alleged weak points in Darwinian evolution, it fluttered no corner of the English papers; though Boulnois's theory (which was that of a comparatively stationary universe visited occasionally by convulsions of change) had some rather faddy fashionableness at Oxford, and got so far as to be named 'Catastrophism.' But many American papers seized on the challenge as a great event; and the *Sun* threw the shadow of Mr. Boulnois quite gigantically across its pages. By the paradox already noted, articles of valuable intelligence and enthusiasm were presented with headlines apparently written by an illiterate maniac; headlines such as 'Darwin Chews Dirt; Critic Boulnois says He Jumps the Shocks'—or 'Keep Catastrophic, says Thinker Boulnois.' And Mr. Calhoun Kidd, of the *Western Sun*, was bidden to take his butterfly tie and lugubrious visage down to the little house outside Oxford where Thinker Boulnois lived in happy ignorance of such a title.

That fated philosopher had consented, in a somewhat dazed manner, to receive the interviewer, and had named the hour of nine that evening. The last of a summer sunset clung about Cumnor and the low wooded hills; the romantic Yankee was both doubtful of his road and inquisitive about his surroundings; and seeing the door of a genuine feudal old-country inn, The Champion Arms, standing open, he went in to make inquiries.

In the bar parlour he rang the bell, and had to wait some little time for a reply to it. The only other person present was a lean man with close red hair and loose, horsey-looking clothes, who was drinking very bad whisky, but smoking a very good cigar. The whisky, of course, was the choice brand of The Champion Arms; the cigar he had probably brought with him from London. Nothing could be more different than his cynical *négligé* from the dapper dryness of the young American; but something in his pencil and open notebook, and perhaps in the expression of his alert blue eye, caused Kidd to guess, correctly, that he was a brother journalist.

'Could you do me the favour,' asked Kidd, with the courtesy of his nation, 'of directing me to the Grey Cottage, where Mr. Boulnois lives as I understand?'

'It's a few yards down the road,' said the red-haired man, removing his cigar; 'I shall be passing it myself in a minute, but I'm going on to Pendragon Park to try and see the fun.'

'What is Pendragon Park?' asked Calhoun Kidd.

'Sir Claude Champion's place—haven't you come down for that, too?' asked the other pressman, looking up. 'You're a journalist, aren't you?'

'I have come to see Mr. Boulnois,' said Kidd.

'I've come to see Mrs. Boulnois,' replied the other. 'But I shan't catch her at home.' And he laughed rather unpleasantly.

'Are you interested in Catastrophism?' asked the wondering Yankee.

'I'm interested in catastrophies; and there are going to be some,' replied his companion gloomily. 'Mine's a filthy trade, and I never pretend it isn't.'

With that he spat on the floor; yet somehow in the very act and instant one could realize that the man had been brought up as a gentleman.

The American pressman considered him with more attention. His face was pale and dissipated, with the promise of formidable passions yet to be loosed; but it was a clever and sensitive face; his clothes were coarse and careless, but he had a good seal ring on one of his long, thin fingers. His name, which came out in the course of talk, was James Dalroy; he was the son of a bankrupt Irish landlord, and attached to a pink paper which he heartily despised, called *Smart Society*, in the capacity of reporter and something painfully like a spy.

Smart Society, I regret to say, felt none of that interest in Boulnois on Darwin which was such a credit to the head and hearts of the *Western Sun*. Dalroy had come down, it seemed, to snuff up the scent of a scandal which might very well end in the Divorce Court, but which was at present hovering between Grey Cottage and Pendragon Park.

Sir Claude Champion was known to the readers of the *Western Sun* as well as Mr. Boulnois. So were the Pope and the Derby Winner; but the idea of their intimate acquaintanceship would have struck Kidd as equally incongruous. He had heard of (and written about. nay, falsely pretended to know) Sir Claude Champion, as 'one of the brightest and wealthiest of England's Upper Ten'; as the great sportsman who raced yachts round the world; as the great traveller who wrote books about the Himalayas, as the politician who swept constituencies with a startling sort of Tory Democracy, and as the great dabbler in art, music, literature, and, above all, acting. Sir Claude was really rather magnificent in other than American eyes. There was something of the Renascence Prince about his omnivorous culture and restless publicity; he was not only a great amateur, but an ardent one. There was in him none of that antiquarian frivolity that we convey by the word 'dilettante.'

That faultless falcon profile with purple-black Italian eye, which had been snap-shotted so often both for *Smart Society* and the *Western Sun*, gave everyone the impression of a man eaten by ambition as by a fire, or even a disease. But though Kidd knew a great deal about Sir Claude—a great deal more, in fact, than there was to know—it would never have crossed his wildest dreams to connect so showy an aristocrat with the newly-un-earthed founder of Catastrophism, or to guess that Sir Claude Champion and John Boulnois could be intimate friends. Such, according to Dalroy's account, was never-theless the fact. The two had hunted in couples at school and college, and, though their social destinies had been very different (for Champion was a great landlord and almost a millionaire, while Boulnois was a poor scholar and, until just lately, an unknown one), they still kept in very close touch with each other. Indeed, Boulnois's cottage stood just outside the gates of Pendragon Park.

But whether the two men could be friends much longer was becoming a dark and ugly question. A year or two before, Boulnois had married a beautiful and not unsuccessful actress, to whom he was devoted in his own shy and ponderous style; and the proximity of the household to Champion's had given that flighty cele-brity opportunities for behaving in a way that could not but cause painful and rather base excitement. Sir Claude had carried the arts of publicity to perfection; and he seemed to take a crazy pleasure in being equally osten-tatious in an intrigue that could do him no sort of honour. Footmen from Pendragon were perpetually leaving bouquets for Mrs. Boulnois; carriages and motor-cars were perpetually calling at the cottage for Mrs. Boulnois; balls and masquerades perpetually filled the grounds in which the baronet paraded Mrs. Boul-nois, like the Queen of Love and Beauty at a tourna-ment. That very evening, marked by Mr. Kidd for the exposition of Catastrophism, had been marked by Sir Claude Champion for an open-air rendering of *Romeo and Juliet*, in which he was to play Romeo to a Juliet it was needless to name.

'I don't think it can go on without a smash,' said the young man with red hair, getting up and shaking himself. 'Old Boulnois may be squared—or he may be square. But if he's square he's thick—what you might call cubic. But I don't believe it's possible.'

'He is a man of grand intellectual powers,' said Calhoun Kidd in a deep voice.

'Yes,' answered Dalroy; 'but even a man of grand intellectual powers can't be such a blighted fool as all that. Must you be going on? I shall be following myself in a minute or two.'

But Calhoun Kidd, having finished a milk and soda, betook himself smartly up the road towards the Grey Cottage, leaving his cynical informant to his whisky and tobacco. The last of the daylight had faded; the skies were of a dark, green-grey, like slate, studded here and there with a star, but lighter on the left side of the sky, with the promise of a rising moon.

The Grey Cottage, which stood entrenched, as it were, in a square of stiff, high thorn-hedges, was so close under the pines and palisades of the Park that Kidd at first mistook it for the Park Lodge. Finding the name on the narrow wooden gate, however, and seeing by his watch that the hour of the 'Thinker's' appointment had just struck, he went in and knocked at the front door. Inside the garden hedge, he could see that the house, though unpretentious enough, was larger and more luxurious than it looked at first, and was quite a different kind of place from a porter's lodge. A dog-kennel and a beehive stood outside, like symbols of old English country-life; the moon was rising behind a plantation of prosperous pear trees; the dog that came out of the kennel was reverend-looking and reluctant to bark; and the plain, elderly manservant who opened the door was brief but dignified.

'Mr. Boulnois asked me to offer his apologies, sir,' he said, 'but he has been obliged to go out suddenly.'

'But see here, I had an appointment,' said the interviewer, with a rising voice. 'Do you know where he went to?'

'To Pendragon Park, sir,' said the servant, rather sombrely, and began to close the door.

Kidd started a little.

'Did he go with Mrs. —— with the rest of the party?' he asked rather vaguely.

'No, sir,' said the man shortly; 'he stayed behind, and then went out alone.' And he shut the door, brutally, but with an air of duty not done.

The American, that curious compound of impudence and sensitiveness, was annoyed. He felt a strong desire to hustle them all along a bit and teach them business habits; the hoary old dog and the grizzled, heavy-faced old butler with his prehistoric shirt-front, and the drowsy old moon, and above all the scatter-brained old philosopher who couldn't keep an appointment.

'If that's the way he goes on he deserves to lose his wife's purest devotion,' said Mr. Calhoun Kidd. 'But perhaps he's gone over to make a row. In that case I reckon a man from the *Western Sun* will be on the spot.'

And turning the corner by the open lodge-gates, he set off, stumping up the long avenue of black pine-woods that pointed in abrupt perspective towards the inner gardens of Pendragon Park. The trees were as black and orderly as plumes upon a hearse; there were still a few stars. He was a man with more literary than direct natural associations; the word 'Ravenswood' came into his head repeatedly. It was partly the raven colour of the pine-woods; but partly also an indescribable atmosphere almost described in Scott's great tragedy; the smell of something that died in the eighteenth century; the smell of dank gardens and broken urns, of wrongs that will never now be righted; of something that is none the less incurably sad because it is strangely unreal.

More than once, as he went up that trim, black road of tragic artifice, he stopped startled, thinking he heard steps in front of him. He could see nothing in front but the twin sombre walls of pine and the wedge of starlit sky above them. At first he thought he must have fancied it or been mocked by a mere echo of his own tramp. But as he went on he was more and more inclined to conclude, with the remains of his reason, that there really were other feet upon the road. He thought hazily of ghosts; and was surprised how swiftly he could see the image of an appropriate and local ghost, one with a face as white as Pierrot's, but patched with black. The apex of the triangle of dark-blue sky was growing brighter and bluer, but he did not realize as yet that this was because he was coming nearer to the lights of the great house and garden. He only felt that the atmosphere was growing more intense; there was in the sadness more violence and secrecy—more—he hesitated for the word, and then said it with a jerk of laughter—Catastrophism.

More pines, more pathway slid past him, and then he stood rooted as by a blast of magic. It is vain to say that he felt as if he had got into a dream; but this time he felt quite certain that he had got into a book. For we human beings are used to inappropriate things; we are accustomed to the clatter of the incongruous; it is a tune to which we can go to sleep. If one appropriate thing happens, it wakes us up like the pang of a perfect chord. Something happened such as would have happened in such a place in a forgotten tale.

Over the black pinewood came flying and flashing in the moon a naked sword—such a slender and sparkling rapier as may have fought many an unjust duel in that ancient park. It fell on the pathway far in front of him and lay there glistening like a large needle. He ran like a hare and bent to look at it. Seen at close quarters it had rather a showy look: the big red jewels in the hilt and guard were a little dubious. But there were other red drops upon the blade which were not dubious.

He looked round wildly in the direction from which the dazzling missile had come, and saw that at this point the sable façade of fir and pine was interrupted by a smaller road at right angles; which, when he turned it, brought him in full view of the long, lighted house, with a lake and fountains in front of it. Nevertheless, he did not look at this, having something more interesting to look at.

Above him, at the angle of the steep green bank of the terraced garden, was one of those small picturesque surprises common in the old landscape gardening; a kind of small round hill or dome of grass, like a giant mole-hill, ringed and crowned with three concentric fences of roses, and having a sundial in the highest point in the centre. Kidd could see the finger of the dial stand up dark against the sky like the dorsal fin of a shark, and the vain moonlight clinging to that idle clock. But he saw something else clinging to it also, for one wild moment—the figure of a man.

Though he saw it there only for a moment, though it was outlandish and incredible in costume, being clad from neck to heel in tight crimson, with glints of gold, yet he knew in one flash of moonlight who it was. That white face flung up to heaven, clean-shaven and so unnaturally young, like Byron with a Roman nose, those black curls already grizzled—he had seen the thousand public portraits of Sir Claude Champion. The wild red figure reeled an instant against the sundial; the next it had rolled down the steep bank and lay at the American's feet, faintly moving one arm. A gaudy, unnatural gold ornament on the arm suddenly reminded Kidd of *Romeo and Juliet*; of course the tight crimson suit was part of the play. But there was a long red stain down the bank from which the man had rolled—that was no part of the play. He had been run through the body.

Mr. Calhoun Kidd shouted and shouted again. Once more he seemed to hear phantasmal footsteps, and started to find another figure already near him. He knew the figure, and yet it terrified him. The dissipated youth who had called himself Dalroy had a horribly quiet way with him; if Boulnois failed to keep appointments that had been made, Dalroy had a sinister air of keeping appointments that hadn't. The moonlight discoloured everything; against Dalroy's red hair his wan face looked not so much white as pale green.

All this morbid impressionism must be Kidd's excuse for having cried out, brutally and beyond all reason: 'Did you do this, you devil?'

James Dalroy smiled his unpleasing smile; but before he could speak, the fallen figure made another movement of the arm, waving vaguely towards the place where the sword fell; then came a moan, and then it managed to speak.

'Boulnois . . . Boulnois, I say . . . Boulnois did it . . . jealous of me . . . he was jealous, he was, he was. . . .'

Kidd bent his head down to hear more, and just managed to catch the words:

'Boulnois . . . with my own sword . . . he threw it. . . .'

Again the failing hand waved towards the sword, and then fell rigid with a thud. In Kidd rose from its depth all that acrid humour that is the strange salt of the seriousness of his race.

'See here,' he said sharply and with command, 'you must fetch a doctor. This man's dead.'

'And a priest, too, I suppose,' said Dalroy in an undecipherable manner. 'All these Champions are papists.'

The American knelt down by the body, felt the heart, propped up the head and used some last efforts at restoration: but before the other journalist reappeared, followed by a doctor and a priest, he was already prepared to assert they were too late.

'Were you too late also?' asked the doctor, a solid prosperous-looking man, with conventional moustache and whiskers, but a lively eye, which darted over Kidd dubiously.

'In one sense,' drawled the representative of the *Sun*. 'I was too late to save the man, but I guess I was in time to hear something of importance. I heard the dead man denounce his assassin.'

'And who was the assassin?' asked the doctor, drawing his eyebrows together.

'Boulnois,' said Calhoun Kidd, and whistled softly.

The doctor stared at him gloomily with a reddening brow; but he did not contradict. Then the priest, a shorter figure in the background, said mildly: 'I understood that Mr. Boulnois was not coming to Pendragon Park this evening.'

'There again,' said the Yankee grimly, 'I may be in a position to give the old country a fact or two. Yes, *sir*, John Boulnois was going to stay in all this evening; he fixed up a real good appointment there with me. But John Boulnois changed his mind; John Boulnois left his home abruptly and all alone, and came over to this derned Park an hour or so ago. His butler told me so. I think we hold what the all-wise police call a clue—have you sent for them?'

'Yes,' said the doctor; 'but we haven't alarmed anyone else yet.'

'Does Mrs. Boulnois know?' asked James Dalroy; and

again Kidd was conscious of an irrational desire to hit him on his curling mouth.

'I have not told her,' said the doctor gruffly; 'but here come the police.'

The little priest had stepped out into the main avenue, and now returned with the fallen sword, which looked ludicrously large and theatrical when attached to his dumpy figure, at once clerical and commonplace. 'Just before the police come,' he said apologetically, 'has anyone got a light?'

The Yankee journalist took an electric torch from his pocket, and the priest held it close to the middle part of the blade, which he examined with blinking care. Then, without glancing at the point or pommel, he handed the long weapon to the doctor.

'I fear I'm no use here,' he said, with a brief sigh. 'I'll say good night to you, gentlemen.' And he walked away up the dark avenue towards the house, his hands clasped behind him and his big head bent in cogitation.

The rest of the group made increased haste towards the lodge-gates, where an inspector and two constables could already be seen in consultation with the lodge-keeper. But the little priest only walked slower and slower in the dim cloister of pine, and at last stopped dead, on the steps of the house. It was his silent way of acknowledging an equally silent approach; for there came towards him a presence that might have satisfied even Calhoun Kidd's demands for a lovely and aristocratic ghost. It was a young woman in silvery satins of a Renascence design; she had golden hair in two long shining ropes, and a face so startlingly pale between them that she might have been chryselephantine— made, that is, like some old Greek statues, out of ivory and gold. But her eyes were very bright, and her voice, though low, was confident.

'Father Brown?' she said.

'Mrs. Boulnois?' he replied gravely. Then he looked at her and immediately said: 'I see you know about Sir Claude.'

'How do you know I know?' she asked steadily.

He did not answer the question, but asked another: 'Have you seen your husband?'

'My husband is at home,' she said. 'He has nothing to do with this.'

Again he did not answer; and the woman drew nearer to him, with a curiously intense expression on her face.

'Shall I tell you something more?' she said, with a rather fearful smile. 'I don't think he did it, and *you* don't either.'

Father Brown returned her gaze with a long, grave stare, and then nodded, yet more gravely.

'Father Brown,' said the lady, 'I am going to tell you all I know, but I want you to do me a favour first. Will you tell me *why* you haven't jumped to the conclusion of poor John's guilt, as all the rest have done? Don't mind what you say: I—I know about the gossip and the appearances that are against him.'

Father Brown looked honestly embarrassed, and passed his hand across his forehead. 'Two very little things,' he said. 'At least, one's very trivial and the other very vague. But such as they are, they don't fit in with Mr. Boulnois being the murderer.'

He turned his blank, round face up to the stars and continued absent-mindedly: 'To take the vague idea first. I attach a good deal of importance to vague ideas. All those things that "aren't evidence" are what convince me. I think a moral impossibility the biggest of all impossibilities. I know your husband only slightly, but I think this crime of his, as generally conceived, something very like a moral impossibility. Please do not think I mean that Boulnois could not be so wicked. Anybody can be wicked—as wicked as he chooses. We can direct our moral wills; but we can't generally change our instinctive tastes and ways of doing things. Boulnois might commit a murder, but not this murder. He would not snatch Romeo's sword from its romantic scabbard; or slay his foe on the sundial as on a kind of altar; or leave his body among the roses; or fling the sword away among the pines. If Boulnois killed anyone he'd do it quietly and heavily, as he'd do any other doubtful thing —take a tenth glass of port, or read a loose Greek poet. No, the romantic setting is not like Boulnois. It's more like Champion.'

'Ah!' she said, and looked at him with eyes like diamonds.

'And the trivial thing was this,' said Brown. 'There were finger-prints on that sword; finger-prints can be detected quite a time after they are made if they're on some polished surface like glass or steel. These were on a polished surface. They were half-way down the blade of the sword. Whose prints they were I have no earthly clue; but why should anybody hold a sword halfway down? It was a long sword, but length is an advantage in lunging at an enemy. At least, at most enemies. At all enemies except one.'

'Except one!' she repeated.

'There is only one enemy,' said Father Brown, 'whom it is easier to kill with a dagger than a sword.'

'I know,' said the woman. 'Oneself.'

There was a long silence, and then the priest said quietly but abruptly: 'Am I right, then? Did Sir Claude kill himself?'

'Yes,' she said, with a face like marble. 'I saw him do it.'

'He died,' said Father Brown, 'for love of you?'

233

An extraordinary expression flashed across her face, very different from pity, modesty, remorse, or anything her companion had expected: her voice became suddenly strong and full. 'I don't believe,' she said, 'he ever cared about me a rap. He hated my husband.'

'Why?' asked the other, and turned his round face from the sky to the lady.

'He hated my husband because . . . it is so strange I hardly know how to say it . . . because. . . .'

'Yes?' said Brown patiently.

'Because my husband wouldn't hate him.'

Father Brown only nodded, and seemed still to be listening; he differed from most detectives in fact and fiction in a small point—he never pretended not to understand when he understood perfectly well.

Mrs. Boulnois drew near once more with the same contained glow of certainty. 'My husband,' she said, 'is a great man. Sir Claude Champion was not a great man: he was a celebrated and successful man. My husband has never been celebrated or successful; and it is the solemn truth that he has never dreamed of being so. He no more expects to be famous for thinking than for smoking cigars. On all that side he has a sort of splendid stupidity. He has never grown up. He still liked Champion exactly as he liked him at school; he admired him as he would admire a conjuring trick done at the dinner-table. But he couldn't be got to conceive the notion of *envying* Champion. *And Champion wanted to be envied*. He went mad and killed himself for that.'

'Yes,' said Father Brown; 'I think I begin to understand.'

'Oh, don't you see?' she cried; 'the whole picture is made for that—the place is planned for it. Champion put John in a little house at his very door, like a dependant—to make him *feel* a failure. He never felt it. He thinks no more about such things than—than an absent-minded lion. Champion would burst in on John's shabbiest hours or homeliest meals with some dazzling present or announcement or expedition that made it like the visit of Haroun Alraschid, and John would accept or refuse amiably with one eye off, so to speak, like one lazy schoolboy agreeing or disagreeing with another. After five years of it John had not turned a hair; and Sir Claude Champion was a monomaniac.'

'And Haman began to tell them,' said Father Brown, 'of all the things wherein the king had honoured him; and he said: "All these things profit me nothing while I see Mordecai the Jew sitting in the gate."'

'The crisis came,' Mrs. Boulnois continued, 'when I persuaded John to let me take down some of his speculations and send them to a magazine. They began to attract attention, especially in America, and one paper wanted to interview him. When Champion (who was interviewed nearly every day) heard of this late little crumb of success falling to his unconscious rival, the last link snapped that held back his devilish hatred. Then he began to lay that insane siege to my own love and honour which has been the talk of the shire. You will ask me why I allowed such atrocious attentions. I answer that I could not have declined them except by explaining to my husband, and there are some things the soul cannot do, as the body cannot fly. Nobody could have explained to my husband. Nobody could do it now. If you said to him in so many words, "Champion is stealing your wife," he would think the joke a little vulgar: that it could be anything but a joke—that notion could find no crack in his great skull to get in by. Well, John was to come and see us act this evening, but just as we were starting he said he wouldn't; he had got an interesting book and a cigar. I told this to Sir Claude, and it was his death-blow. The monomaniac suddenly saw despair. He stabbed himself, crying out like a devil that Boulnois was slaying him; he lies there in the garden dead of his own jealousy to produce jealousy; and John is sitting in the dining-room reading a book.'

There was another silence, and then the little priest said: 'There is only one weak point, Mrs. Boulnois, in all your very vivid account. Your husband is not sitting in the dining-room reading a book. That American reporter told me he had been to your house, and your butler told him Mr. Boulnois had gone to Pendragon Park after all.'

Her bright eyes widened to an almost electric glare; and yet it seemed rather bewilderment than confusion or fear. 'Why, what *can* you mean?' she cried. 'All the servants were out of the house, seeing the theatricals. And we don't keep a butler, thank goodness!'

Father Brown started and spun half round like an absurd teetotum. 'What, what?' he cried seeming galvanized into sudden life. 'Look here—I say—can I make your husband hear if I go to the house?'

'Oh, the servants will be back by now,' she said, wondering.

'Right, right!' rejoined the cleric energetically, and set off scuttling up the path towards the Park gates. He turned once to say: 'Better get hold of that Yankee, or "Crime of John Boulnois" will be all over the Republic in large letters.'

'You don't understand,' said Mrs. Boulnois. 'He wouldn't mind. I don't think he imagines that America really is a place.'

When Father Brown reached the house with the beehive and the drowsy dog, a small and neat maid-servant showed him into the dining-room, where Boulnois sat reading by a shaded lamp, exactly as his wife described him. A decanter of port and a wineglass were at his elbow; and the instant the priest entered he noted the long ash stand out unbroken on his cigar.

'He has been here for half an hour at least,' thought Father Brown. In fact, he had the air of sitting where he had sat when his dinner was cleared away.

'Don't get up, Mr. Boulnois,' said the priest in his pleasant, prosaic way. 'I shan't interrupt you a moment. I fear I break in on some of your scientific studies.'

'No,' said Boulnois; 'I was reading "The Bloody Thumb."' He said it with neither frown nor smile, and his visitor was conscious of a certain deep and virile indifference in the man which his wife had called greatness. He laid down a gory yellow 'shocker' without even feeling its incongruity enough to comment on it humorously. John Boulnois was a big, slow-moving man with a massive head, partly grey and partly bald, and blunt, burly features. He was in shabby and very old-fashioned evening-dress, with a narrow triangular opening of shirt-front: he had assumed it that evening in his original purpose of going to see his wife act Juliet.

'I won't keep you long from "The Bloody Thumb" or any other catastrophic affairs,' said Father Brown, smiling. 'I only came to ask you about the crime you committed this evening.'

Boulnois looked at him steadily, but a red bar began to show across his broad brow; and he seemed like one discovering embarrassment for the first time.

'I know it was a strange crime,' assented Brown in a low voice. 'Stranger than murder perhaps—to you. The little sins are sometimes harder to confess than the big ones—but that's why it's so important to confess them. Your crime is committed by every fashionable hostess six times a week: and yet you find it stick to your tongue like a nameless atrocity.'

'It makes one feel,' said the philosopher slowly, 'such a damned fool.'

'I know,' assented the other, 'but one often has to choose between feeling a damned fool and being one.'

'I can't analyse myself well,' went on Boulnois; 'but sitting in that chair with that story I was as happy as a schoolboy on a half-holiday. It was security, eternity—I can't convey it . . . the cigars were within reach . . . the matches were within reach . . . the *Thumb* had four more appearances to . . . it was not only a peace, but a plenitude. Then that bell rang, and I thought for one long, mortal minute that I couldn't get out of that chair—literally, physically, muscularly couldn't. Then I did it like a man lifting the world, because I knew all the servants were out. I opened the front door, and there was a little man with his mouth open to speak and his notebook open to write in. I remembered the Yankee interviewer I had forgotten. His hair was parted in the middle, and I tell you that murder——'

'I understand,' said Father Brown. 'I've seen him.'

'I didn't commit murder,' continued the Catastrophist mildly, 'but only perjury. I said I had gone across to Pendragon Park and shut the door in his face. That is my crime, Father Brown, and I don't know what penance you would inflict for it.'

'I shan't inflict any penance,' said the clerical gentleman, collecting his heavy hat and umbrella with an air of some amusement; 'quite the contrary. I came here specially to let you off the little penance which would otherwise have followed your little offence.'

'And what,' asked Boulnois, smiling, 'is the little penance I have so luckily been let off?'

'Being hanged,' said Father Brown.

PENGUIN POPULAR CLASSICS

Published or forthcoming

Aesop	Aesop's Fables
Hans Andersen	Fairy Tales
Louisa May Alcott	Good Wives
	Little Women
Eleanor Atkinson	Greyfriars Bobby
Jane Austen	Emma
	Mansfield Park
	Northanger Abbey
	Persuasion
	Pride and Prejudice
	Sense and Sensibility
R. M. Ballantyne	The Coral Island
J. M. Barrie	Peter Pan
Frank L. Baum	The Wonderful Wizard of Oz
Anne Brontë	Agnes Grey
	The Tenant of Wildfell Hall
Charlotte Brontë	Jane Eyre
	The Professor
	Shirley
	Villette
Emily Brontë	Wuthering Heights
John Buchan	Greenmantle
	The Thirty-Nine Steps
Frances Hodgson Burnett	A Little Princess
	Little Lord Fauntleroy
	The Secret Garden
Samuel Butler	The Way of All Flesh
Lewis Carroll	Alice's Adventures in Wonderland
	Through the Looking Glass
Geoffrey Chaucer	The Canterbury Tales
G. K. Chesterton	Father Brown Stories
Erskine Childers	The Riddle of the Sands
John Cleland	Fanny Hill
Wilkie Collins	The Moonstone
	The Woman in White
Sir Arthur Conan Doyle	The Adventures of Sherlock Holmes
	His Last Bow
	The Hound of the Baskervilles

PENGUIN POPULAR CLASSICS

Published or forthcoming

Joseph Conrad	Heart of Darkness
	Lord Jim
	Nostromo
	The Secret Agent
	Victory
James Fenimore Cooper	The Last of the Mohicans
Stephen Crane	The Red Badge of Courage
Daniel Defoe	Moll Flanders
	Robinson Crusoe
Charles Dickens	Bleak House
	The Christmas Books
	David Copperfield
	Great Expectations
	Hard Times
	Little Dorrit
	Martin Chuzzlewit
	Nicholas Nickleby
	The Old Curiosity Shop
	Oliver Twist
	The Pickwick Papers
	A Tale of Two Cities
Fyodor Dostoyevsky	Crime and Punishment
George Eliot	Adam Bede
	Middlemarch
	The Mill on the Floss
	Silas Marner
John Meade Falkner	Moonfleet
Henry Fielding	Tom Jones
F. Scott Fitzgerald	The Diamond as Big as the Ritz
	The Great Gatsby
	Tender is the Night
Gustave Flaubert	Madame Bovary
Elizabeth Gaskell	Cousin Phillis
	Cranford
	Mary Barton
	North and South
Kenneth Grahame	The Wind in the Willows

PENGUIN POPULAR CLASSICS

PENGUIN POPULAR CLASSICS

Published or forthcoming

PENGUIN POPULAR CLASSICS

Published or forthcoming

PENGUIN POPULAR POETRY

Published or forthcoming

The Selected Poems *of:*

Matthew Arnold
William Blake
Robert Browning
Robert Burns
Lord Byron
John Donne
Thomas Hardy
John Keats
Rudyard Kipling
Alexander Pope
Alfred Tennyson
William Wordsworth
William Yeats

and collections of:

Seventeenth-Century Poetry
Eighteenth-Century Poetry
Poetry of the Romantics
Victorian Poetry
Twentieth-Century Poetry
Scottish Folk and Fairy Tales